For my five siblings,
Growing up with you all was the best!
I am so thankful for our adult friendships.

A special thank you goes to
my eleven-year-old niece Allee
who helped inspire this story.
Like me, Allee loves to write,
and when I release a new novel,
she always buys the first copy
with her own money.

The Date Night Jar

Kris,

I appreciate your support! I hope you have a Merry Christmas!!!

Joey Jones

A Novel by
JOEY JONES

ISBN: 978-1-948978-07-1 (PRINT)

ISBN: 978-1-948978-08-8 (EPUB)

ISBN: 978-1-948978-09-5 (MOBI)

Also by Joey Jones
A Bridge Apart

A Bridge Apart, the debut novel by Joey Jones, is a remarkable love story that tests the limits of trust and forgiveness . . .

In the quaint river town of New Bern, North Carolina, at 28 years of age, the pieces of Andrew Callaway's life are all falling into place. His real estate firm is flourishing, and he's engaged to be married in less than two weeks to a beautiful banker named Meredith Hastings. But when Meredith heads to Tampa, Florida—the wedding location—with her mother, fate, or maybe some human intervention, has it that Andrew happens upon Cooper McKay, the only other woman he's ever loved.

A string of shocking emails lead Andrew to question whether he can trust his fiancée, and in the midst of trying to unravel the mystery, he finds himself spending time with Cooper. When Meredith catches wind of what's going on back at home, she's forced to consider calling off the wedding, which ultimately draws Andrew closer to Cooper. Andrew soon discovers he's making choices he might not be able, or even want, to untangle. As the story unfolds, the decisions that are made will drastically change the lives of everyone involved and bind them closer together than they could have ever imagined.

Also by Joey Jones
Losing London

Losing London is an epic love story filled with nail-biting suspense, forbidden passion, and unexpected heartbreak.

When cancer took the life of Mitch Quinn's soulmate, London Adams, he never imagined that one year later her sister, Harper, whom he had never met before, would show up in Emerald Isle, NC. Until this point, his only reason to live, a five-year-old cancer survivor named Hannah, was his closest tie to London.

Harper, recently divorced, never imagined that work—a research project on recent shark attacks—and an unexpected package from London would take her back to the island town where her family had vacationed in her youth. Upon her arrival, she meets and is instantly swept off her feet by a local with a hidden connection that eventually causes her to question the boundaries of love.

As Mitch's and Harper's lives intertwine, they discover secrets that should have never happened. If either had known that losing London would have connected their lives in the way that it did, they might have chosen different paths.

Also by Joey Jones
A Field of Fireflies

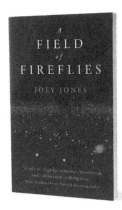

Growing up, Nolan Lynch's family was unconventional by society's standards, but it was filled with love, and his parents taught him everything he needed to know about life, equality, and family. A baseball player with a bright future, Nolan's on his way to the major leagues when tragedy occurs. Six years later, he's starting over as the newest instructor at the community college in Washington, North Carolina, where he meets Emma Pate, who seems to be everything he's ever dreamed of—beautiful, assertive, and a baseball fan to boot.

Emma Pate's dreams are put on hold after her father dies, leaving her struggling to keep her family's farm. When a chance encounter with a cute new guy in town turns into an impromptu date, Emma finds herself falling for him. But she soon realizes Nolan Lynch isn't who she thinks he is.

Drawn together by a visceral connection that defies their common sense, Emma's and Nolan's blossoming love is as romantic as it is forbidden, until secrets—both past and present—threaten to tear them apart. Now, Nolan must confront his past and make peace with his demons or risk losing everything he loves . . . again.

Emotionally complex and charged with suspense, *A Field of Fireflies* is the unforgettable story of family, love, loss, and an old baseball field where magic occurs, including the grace of forgiveness and second chances.

Acknowledgments

The Date Night Jar, my fourth novel, exposes the power of love. There is an abundance of amazing people who helped make this book become a reality. First and foremost, I would like to thank God for giving me the ability to write and planting that passion within my soul. Branden, my oldest son, just graduated high school, and I am excited to watch him become a young man. Parker, my little guy, is always by my side. I love hearing him call me Daddy and watching the smile grow on his face as he runs to my arms.

I would also like to thank my wonderful family. My parents, Joe and Patsy Jones, taught me about the essential aspects of life, and I hope I leave a legacy that makes them proud. My dad now lives in Heaven, and I miss him dearly. My mom, who is my breakfast partner and one of my best friends, is the most humble person I know. My brothers and sisters, DeAnn, Judy, Lee, Penny, and Richard, are some of my closest friends. In many ways, their support is my foundation.

My editors, Erin Haywood, Donna Matthews, and Krisann Blackwell, are incredibly talented at polishing my writing. My graphics designer, Meredith Walsh, has done a fantastic job with all of my novel covers and supporting pieces. Bob Peele (Sozo Fine Art Photography) is responsible for the cover photo of this book as well as my author photo. Our photo shoots are always memorable. Polgarus Studio made the intricate process of formatting the interior of this novel a breeze.

Lastly, I would like to thank some people who have been influential throughout my life. Some for a season, but each for a reason. Thank you to Amber Gray, Andrew Haywood, BJ Horne, Billy Nobles, Cathy Errick, Diane Tyndall, Jan Raynor, Jeanette Towne, Josh Haywood, Josh Towne, Kenny Ford, Kim Jones, Mitch Fortescue, Nicholas Sparks, Ray White, Rebekah Jones, Richard Banks, Steve Cobb, Steven Harrell, and Steve Haywood. It is a privilege to call each of you my friend.

The Date Night Jar

1

Listening to Cleve Fields tell The Date Night Jar stories always caused Ansley Stone, M.D. to inch toward the edge of the vinyl seat beneath her overworked body. Before plopping into the dark-colored hospital chair nestled at his bedside and feeling the tension of another long day give way to the first true moment of relaxation, she folded her white lab coat and carefully placed it across the high back of the seat. On this particular night in early-April, the pants covering her long legs were a deep blue color which almost perfectly accented her eyes. Her blonde hair traveled in a straight line nearly to the halfway point of the matching top as she held her chin in the palms of her hands, her elbows resting atop her achy knees. Even though Ansley didn't recognize it, she wedged her fingernails between her teeth again, and her entire body was as tense as a tightrope at the circus.

Cleve, a wrinkly man old enough to be her grandfather, had recently begun sharing these tales with Ansley in the confines of his lonely hospital room in Raleigh, North Carolina. At the end of her nightly rounds, she would wander back here to his bedside and sit as close as possible, hanging on to his every word like they were rocks attached to a cliff from which she was dangling.

Resting on a small square table next to Ansley, an aged mason jar held yellowed slivers of paper, each one rolled neatly and tied with a fine piece of brown twine. On the inside of the scroll-like notes, simple instructions were handwritten in cursive. The thick glass had become hazy over the years, and the rusted lid wasn't as easy to unscrew as it might have been when Cleve used to twist it with youthful fingers. Later on, whenever Ansley decided it was time to head home, she would make sure to slide the cherished jar back into her bag and keep it safe for her friend until the next time they met.

In many ways, Ansley and Cleve were the unlikeliest of friends. At least that's what many of the other doctors and nurses whispered after she punched the time clock. Instead of heading home or out for cocktails, it baffled her coworkers when Ansley would visit with the man in Room 112. Some warned her not to get close to a patient, but it was too late for that.

Ansley understood why the people she worked with gave the advice they did. In fact, some of her male patients on Cleve's hall seemed to make it a point to stare uneasily into her eyes with mischievous grins on their faces the moment she would push through one of the heavy doors that led into the rooms. However, Ansley never felt uneasy about overseeing their medical needs. On the way out, though, she had a hunch that some of them were undressing her with their eyes although she never turned around to find out for sure. Earlier today, a patient had literally told her that he could spend the whole day staring at her from behind but that she needed to invest a portion of her ridiculous doctor's salary on breast implants. The comments she heard from the peanut gallery never ceased to amaze her although she was surprised that she let any of them prick her pale skin anymore.

For some reason, Ansley felt more comfortable telling Cleve about that jerk's remark rather than sharing it with one of her girlfriends. She figured the thought slipped out in Cleve's presence because he never treated her like anything less than a lady. He sometimes asked why she wasn't out for dinner with some good-looking fellow rather than chatting with him and eating hospital food, but he never made comments about her body or looked at her in the way that creepy old men sometimes glare at attractive younger women.

"Did you slap the snot out of him?" Cleve asked in his usual thick southern drawl. He wore a sideways smirk on a face filled with more lines than a crusty leaf. The head of his bed was lifted, and his stringy gray hair was strewn across the pillow where he was resting.

Ansley laughed out loud. "You know I can't do that, not in here anyway," she reminded him.

The sky outside the window at Ansley's back had been dark for some time now, and her tight muscles reminded her that she needed to make an appointment at the spa for a deep tissue massage. Her overwhelming schedule often made such a thought merely a good idea in theory. It had been way too long since her skin had been lathered with a layer of oil and rubbed until she dozed off to the sensual sounds of a cello or a flute. It would be nice if she had a sweet, handsome gentleman to go home to who would pamper her in such a way.

"True, but next time you hook up an IV in his arm maybe you should jab it in a little harder and deeper than normal," Cleve suggested with a sly grin.

Ansley smiled again. "Fortunately for him, the nurses are the ones who handle patient IVs." The mere mention of an IV prompted her to glance at the monitors connected to Cleve's body. It was a habit, and for now, everything read normally.

"Well, accidentally spill hot coffee on him, then," Cleve said.

Ansley's eyes darted to the tall stainless steel coffee mug in her left hand—the same one she'd used to sign stacks of paperwork this morning. A steady dose of caffeine seemed to help her get through each day without choking patients. "Are you trying to get me sued for medical malpractice, Cleve Fields?"

"Just trying to help you teach that pervert a lesson," he uttered grizzly.

"You're a sweet man," Ansley reminded Cleve. "I bet your wife used to tell you that all the time."

Ansley often wondered how Cleve's wife Violet had died since he had never shared that part of their story. If he wanted her to know though, she assumed he would reveal such information in his own time. In her mind, she tried to pretend that everyone who passed away did so peacefully in their sleep, but her profession often had a way of reminding her of reality.

"She spoke such nonsense a time or two, I guess," the old man said as if remembering a specific occasion as the words trickled off his tongue.

Ansley purposefully let the air between them remain silent as Cleve's glazed eyes seemed to wander inside his mind. In college at the University of Chapel Hill and Duke University where she obtained her undergrad and medical doctorate degrees, respectfully, she had studied human anatomy and the functions of the brain in-depth. She knew that scientifically speaking, people didn't have an extra set of pupils on the backside of their eyeballs. But it kind of made sense to imagine that we did, as well as a small television-like display in there where those inner eyes could watch memories play out on command. It had always intrigued her how a human could visualize past events and other created scenes—whether in the form of daydreams or unconscious dreams—inside the mind. Which meant that vision, at least to some degree, was not merely limited to what we could see outwardly with our eyeballs.

Looking down, Ansley noticed Cleve's hands steady on the bed next to his hips, like always, and she could see the tips of his toes poking through the thin white sheet covering his frail body. Based on the stories he'd told her, Ansley imagined Cleve had once been as strong as a mule, and she assumed the family farm had probably had a few such animals to pull the plow back in the day.

The only life Cleve had ever known revolved around farming. He often talked about working from sunup to sundown for as long as he could remember which is why being trapped inside this room was more painful for him than many of Ansley's other patients. She found herself wishing she could tell Cleve that he would be able to leave the hospital soon and go home, but the truth of the matter was that this option wasn't on the table in his situation, and being cognizant of that often forced her to fight back the tears when she visited this room. It also bothered her that no one else visited her friend, not even his own son who had taken over the family farm in Oriental, North Carolina, when Cleve had been sent here. Over time, as Ansley had grown closer to Cleve, she had found herself wanting to help reunite the two of them. She felt that an inch had been gained when she reached out to Mason Fields asking him to mail her The Date Night Jar so that his father could have it again. Technically, Cleve hadn't asked for it, and she hadn't mentioned to him that she was attempting to contact his son whom he often talked about with tremendous love as well as a great deal of underlying sadness. She wanted it to be a surprise for the man who had once explained to her how he'd left home with nothing more than the clothes on his back.

Her first attempts to reach Mason had been unsuccessful. She'd made several phone calls to a number she'd been able to locate for him, but no one ever answered and there wasn't an option to leave a voicemail. Her best friend Betty, who also happened to be the longest tenured nurse in the hospital, had warned her that maybe the unanswered calls were a sign to leave well enough alone. During the ensuing weeks, they'd had several in-depth discussions about the potential risks of Ansley meddling in her patient's family affairs, but Ansley couldn't seem to let it go. She felt sure Cleve wanted his son to visit him, but the stubborn man just wouldn't admit it. She also believed that

Mason, even though she didn't know him from Adam, needed to spend some time with his dad before this disease got the best of him. She knew of way too many people who lived in regret for not patching up things with a family member before it was too late. Eventually, Ansley handwrote a letter to Mason explaining who she was and asked if he would please consider sending The Date Night Jar.

"Now you leavin' evidence out there lettin' it be known you steppin' outside your bounds, Dr. Stone," Betty warned. When they were on shift at the hospital together, Betty had always been insistent upon calling Ansley by her proper title. "It's a sign of respect," she would say, "and heaven knows these young know-it-all nurses in this hospital need a little more of that in their life. If they hear me callin' you Ansley, they gonna think they can get away with it, too. No ma'am, ain't happenin' on my watch." Betty always had a way of making Ansley smile. She was one of those rare people who could even make a man on death row laugh.

It had taken quite some time for Ansley to receive a response from her letter, but one day out of the blue a package showed up at her doorstep. Inside, she discovered the requested item wrapped in old newspapers on which the headings read: *The Pamlico News*. Nothing more was in the tattered box, not even a note. Ansley recollected from a class on North Carolina history and geography—which she'd taken back in high school—that Oriental was located in Pamlico County. She hadn't visited the place, although that would soon change due to some secret plans she'd been scheming with Cleve. She'd heard the town was quite a treasure in its own regard and definitely off the beaten path.

When Ansley first presented The Date Night Jar to Cleve, he had broken into tears immediately. He wanted to touch it. Smell it. Hold onto it for as long as possible and remember all the good times it brought to him and his wife so many years ago. Having the jar in his presence also caused him to wonder out loud about

Mason. Initially, he was very inquisitive about how Ansley had gone about getting the jar, and he wanted to know everything she had found out about Mason. "Is he married?" Cleve wondered with excitement lining his voice. "Does he have kids?" he asked, pausing when he noticed the tears building in Ansley's eyes. She could remember wishing she had the answers, and it broke her heart at how disheartened Cleve appeared when he discovered that she'd had relatively no communication with Mason. "I just hope he is happy," her friend finally uttered. "I wish someone could tell me if my son is happy," he cried.

That specific evening in Cleve's room is when Ansley decided she had to do something regardless of the risks. A few days later, she made up a story about wanting to visit Oriental on her upcoming vacation and Cleve's eyes lit up like a kid at Christmas. "Would you check in on my boy?" he asked. "I even know somewhere you can stay and it won't cost you a dime," he offered.

Ansley's mind wandered back to the present time as Cleve's voice sputtered to life again. "How was your date with the guy you met through your phone?" he asked.

Unable to hold in her laughter, Ansley buried her head in her hands, letting her long hair spill toward the black specks on the floor. When she collected herself, she combed her hair back with her thin fingers and began giving Cleve an update on modern technology. "I met him through an online dating website," she reminded him.

"Yeah, on your phone," he reminded her.

"Yes, I access the site through my cell phone," she acknowledged.

"What's a cell phone?" Cleve queried, purposefully furrowing his brow for nothing more than dramatic purposes. "A phone inside a prison cell?" he asked before making the sound of a drumroll with his mouth, but his hands remained by his sides rather than emulating the motion of a drummer.

Ansley often wondered how much it bothered Cleve that he

could barely move his limbs. In her present state, she couldn't imagine being confined in such a manner, but seeing the restrictions that Cleve and her other patients faced reminded her to thank God for her own capabilities and freedoms that so many people take for granted until they somehow lose one or more of them.

"Very clever," Ansley replied. "You know what a cell phone is, Old Timer."

Cleve glanced at the phone that had been resting atop Ansley's thigh since the moment she'd taken a seat.

"You don't look at yours as much as the other doctors and nurses."

"I prefer to live in the present."

"Sometimes it feels like those little computers keep the others alive, like the machines attached to my body are doing for me now."

Ansley chuckled. "Sadly enough, some people would lose all sense of purpose without their phones."

"Back in my day we had phones mounted on the walls, you know," he recollected.

"I've heard about those," Ansley replied teasing him in return. "The ones where you poke your finger into the little round holes and spin the contraption around like you're playing *Wheel of Fortune* with one finger." When she finished the comparison, Ansley couldn't help but portray amusement at her own joke.

"You're far prettier than that Vanna White, you know," Cleve said out of the blue.

Ansley blushed. "And you're much funnier than that Pat Sajak," she shot back.

"You know what, I think I was about your age when the first episode of *Wheel of Fortune* hit the airwaves on the tube."

At the mention of age, Ansley wondered if Cleve even knew how old she was; she didn't recall sharing that bit of information with him. Some days it was hard to believe that she was thirty-two and still single. She often felt the pressure from her parents and other prestigious people within their social circle to be married by now. There seemed to be an unwritten plan by which children from her upbringing were meant to follow: complete undergraduate studies at a well-known university, continue said education with at least a master's degree, finish law school or a preferred doctoral program, then marry an upstanding gentleman of a high social class who has accomplished the same academic protocols and have two or three children. Oh, and add in a multi-story home with a white picket fence in the suburbs, a nanny who keeps the kids fed and the inside of the house meticulously clean, and a gardener and pool boy who handle the outward appearance.

"Wow, I bet it first aired on one of those black and white televisions, huh?" Ansley quizzed.

"Color television sets actually became popular in the mid-1960s, I believe, which would have made me a little over twenty years old. But I grew up on black and white television, and back then we didn't know anything different." Like an instant Polaroid picture, the memory of the first television set Cleve recalled his family owning popped into his mind. Some of his friends' families acquired televisions before his parents were able to save up cash for the one that sat in the corner of their living room until it bit the dust many years later. He could remember all of the neighborhood children gathering in the evenings every once in a while to watch a show. There was very little time to watch television during his rearing days, though. Kids of all ages spent most of their time outside of school helping their families either on the farm, at the lumberyard, in the town market, or at the boatyard when the shrimp and fishing boats arrived in the evenings to prepare their catch for the market. Back then it was all hands on deck in order to survive.

Cleve and Ansley carried on this conversation about the good ole' days versus the days of modern technology as the hands on the clock circled like they always did. No faster, no slower than at any other time in history yet it was ironic how life seemed to move more briskly as a person aged.

Cleve convinced Ansley that the longer a person lives, the quicker time seems to move because of the amount of time that person has experienced. To a five-year-old, five years seems like forever, he explained, but to a seventy-five-year-old like himself, five years seems to fly by like a stealth bomber.

Ansley had to admit that she hadn't grown up doing manual labor like Cleve although she also hadn't enjoyed the freedom that many children in the modern era take for granted. During the school year, she attended a prestigious private school and was expected to make straight A's and stay out of trouble. Each night she was required to tackle homework promptly, read whether or not a reading assignment had been given at school, and practice piano or tennis depending on the night of the week. She rarely ever helped prepare family meals, wash the dishes, do the laundry, or clean the house. Those were tasks for which the family hired the services of a professional who was responsible for taking care of the home as well as helping with the children. Ansley didn't have a single memory of helping her mother with any chores. However, she loved to help her nanny Wanda when her parents weren't around—usually, the opportunity only arose when they traveled out of town for business or a vacation. Ansley being a hard-working little helper was one of her and Wanda's secrets back then, and the few times her mother or father caught Ansley elbows deep in dirty dishwater, she had been scolded for something for which many children would have been praised.

A full hour had somehow passed when Ansley finally asked Cleve if he would share one of his date night stories with her before she left the hospital for the evening.

Cleve grinned from ear to ear like he always did when given the opportunity to talk about his and Violet's date nights. The memories were good, and they were real. As he sat up in his bed as much as possible, breathing a little heavier than the moment before Ansley had asked, he closed his eyes and traveled back in time to the evening when he held Violet's hand for the very first time.

Ansley, nestled at the edge of the chair beneath her, waited eagerly for the story to begin. Like every other time when Cleve would share a story, she knew he would keep his eyes closed as he reminisced. It was like he was visiting another world, and he took her there with him. As he began to talk, she did not dare speak a word in fear of interrupting the magic. Ansley only listened and dreamed about the possibility of a day when a man would talk about her in the way Cleve Fields talked about his Violet.

I knocked on her parent's front door with a frog in my throat and the hair on my arms standing like morning grass blades chasing the sunrise. Just like every other visit before that evening, Violet's father answered and immediately inspected me like a drill instructor checking a new recruit for flaws. I kept expecting him to show up with a double barrel shotgun in his hands.

Even though Violet was eighteen, her father made it known to me that I better take good care of his little girl.

"Whatever you do to her," that big husky man swore as serious as a judge sentencing a criminal, "I'll do to you."

His choice of words both terrified me and grossed me out. I was like any other eighteen-year-old male, I had urges, but they were definitely tempered by the thought of that man taking me out behind the woodshed and having his way with me. I never entirely convinced myself that he meant what he said in a sexual manner, but I couldn't help but imagine him kissing me if I kissed Violet or heaven forbid doing something more intimate. So, at that point in our courting, I wasn't willing to take any chances.

Needless to say, I minded my P's and Q's even though I had no idea what those letters stood for when mother used to mention them as she gave me the instructions to behave.

"Yes, sir," was how I responded to Violet's father almost every time it was my turn to talk. I figured the less I said, the better, so if he or Violet's mother didn't directly address me, I kept my lips zipped as tightly as my jeans.

When Violet, wearing that pollen-yellow dress her mamma handmade for her, showed up in that doorframe and stood next to her daddy, I nearly fainted onto the tattered boards beneath my two left feet. Violet Horne was more beautiful than any flower I'd ever seen any bee pollinating. To be honest, she was out of my league in the looks department.

When we walked down the make-shift concrete steps together, I made sure to leave two foot of space between her body and mine because I knew her daddy was glaring at my every move. It wouldn't have surprised me if he had walked right down those three steps and followed us up the dirt road in front of her house.

A walk was our date that night.

You see, the scroll I'd plucked from The Date Night Jar earlier that week read: Take The Lady Out For An Evening Stroll *in the neatest handwriting you'd ever seen.*

2

Mason Fields slipped out of bed before giving the sunrise a chance to force its way through the windows of the farmhouse where he'd woken up nearly every morning of his life. His ancestors had built this log cabin a century prior to his birth which on most days was hard to believe had taken place thirty-five years ago. Other days, he could feel the toll that the physical demands of farming had taken on his relatively young body.

After making a pit stop in the only bathroom in the house, Mason touched his pointer finger on a little round hole in the living room wall that led straight through to the kitchen. Touching that spot as he walked through the area was a habit and so was hearing the sound of dry dog food jingle in the round tin bowl next to the back door as he poured breakfast for Callie.

Mason's best friend in the world was an aging purebred collie he'd found as a puppy on the side of the road near his house on the evening of his eighteenth birthday. He reached down to pet her while waiting for the coffee to brew. A few moments later, Callie followed him outside and nestled in at the base of the rocking chair where Mason sat facing east every morning on the wraparound porch. When stepped on, some of the boards below his tattered boots creaked but most of them were as sturdy as the house itself.

As for Mason, his frame was nearly as solid as the concrete he'd poured for a new mailbox post last week. He didn't live in one of those neighborhoods where all the mailboxes were matching; in fact, he didn't live in a neighborhood at all. He lived out in the country, and the only reason he'd gotten a new box was because the other one had been demolished by either a car that had veered off the road at the wrong time or some aggravating teenagers out bashing mailboxes for giggles.

He rarely purchased anything that didn't serve a practical purpose, which is why he didn't own a scale or know his own weight, but he knew how he felt, somewhere between skinny and overweight. Average, maybe. He couldn't remember the last time he visited a doctor's office, but the stack of old blue jeans in his dresser drawer fit just right, and so did the long-sleeved flannel shirt he'd buttoned up this morning.

The curve of the coffee mug handle in his right hand felt as natural as the wind blowing across the dark fields that surrounded the home. Soon a glow would begin to creep onto the horizon, and hundreds of acres of dew-covered strawberry plants would become visible this morning—the second Monday in April according to the Old Farmer's Almanac.

Waiting patiently for one of the best views on the planet, Mason's lips met the rim of the mug for one slow sip after another. His family had owned this farm for ages, and almost everyone within a hundred-mile radius of Oriental knew of the place. Most had handpicked strawberries from the plants or at least eaten from a crop harvested on these grounds.

Although Mason followed his routines on this particular morning just like every other day of the year—whether the outdoor thermometer read thirty degrees or ninety degrees—today was a bit different. Hired pickers would soon begin flocking to the fields for the first harvest of the season. Mason knew each picker by name, but even when they were off in the distance too far to recognize, he could easily tell the difference between a worker and a customer who was at the farm picking their own berries.

Pickers were paid an hourly rate plus a piece-rate based on the number of flats or buckets filled, so they were always moving at a quicker pace than customers. The goal of an employee was to pick as many strawberries as possible during their time in the fields. The seasoned veterans knew precisely which berries to snag and they didn't have to think about whether one was ripe enough for market. The newbies often second-guessed themselves, and in turn, it took a bit more time for them to make it to the weighing station with each filled basket.

When posted in the local newspaper, the job description for a strawberry picker sounded simple, but new pickers quickly discovered the physical demands of the responsibility. Many of them quit within the first week. The position required a lot of bending and squatting as well as enduring the elements, and the job was by no means for the average person looking to make a quick buck.

Mason himself rarely picked crops these days since he spent most of his time managing the fields and the market out by the road where customers parked and paid, as well as overseeing retail distribution of the harvest. He still made sure to grab a bucket from time to time and join his employees in the trenches. Of course, Callie always tagged along for old times sake, and Mason's presence in the fields let the workers see firsthand that he was willing to perform every task asked of them. It also allowed him the opportunity to provide helpful tips that he'd picked up on over time as well as spot potential issues with both crops and employees. This decision had proven to save the farm thousands of dollars over the years. Mason didn't mind his pickers sampling a strawberry every once in a while, but when one of them attempted to eat a recognizable bite out of his profits, they were sent along on their merry way.

Many independent grocery stores across the Carolinas carried the farm's strawberries in their produce sections, and the farm also had a presence at local farmers markets across the region. Although Mason had noticed that fewer and fewer people seemed to understand the importance of locally grown crops these days, there were still regulars who supported local farmers through thick and thin. At the markets, the same faces would show up week after week without fail.

Rocking slowly on this front porch just like he was today was where Mason first imagined the idea of rebranding the farm's packaging which had, in turn, made him busier than ever before. *Mr. Fields' Berries* had been the name of the farm since its inception, and the red-painted wooden sign that hovered above the entrance to the dusty driveway wore the name proudly. From time to time a customer would ask why the parking lot had yet to be paved. Also, when it rained, certain people would complain about the puddles that formed in the craters that were created over time by cars driving in and out of the area. Mason, just like family members who'd come before him, would typically say to them, in a somewhat teasing manner, "It hasn't been paved because the strawberry fields aren't paved." Most people would then cock their head sideways while wearing a confused expression until Mason added something to the tune of, "This is a farm. We do things the old-fashioned way around here." He tried to be polite about such things even though some of the customers' concerns didn't initially come across with the same respect. It almost always appeased the customers when he promised to hop on the tractor right away and bring around rock or dirt depending on which part of the lot needed attention.

Some mornings, Mason used to find himself wishing there was a second rocking chair on the porch next to the one where he chose to watch the day begin. As time moved along and he grew older—actually, wiser is how he preferred to think of it—he'd started to wonder if having a person sitting next to him and Callie would ruin the ambiance. He'd dabbled in the dating world in his twenties, and his expectations had been proven right. One of the women he'd dated for a while always talked his ear off the entire time they sat out here. Even when he would only respond with a nod, she would just keep babbling. He could remember trying not to laugh when Callie would glance up at the woman with a cocked head as if she didn't understand why the lady was talking during what Callie had come to realize as their quiet time.

Another woman who'd spent some time with him wouldn't even get out of bed to sit with him on the porch. When Mason's alarm clock sounded the first morning they woke up together, she merely grunted and rolled back over. Hesitantly, he asked if she wanted to join him for coffee on the porch, and she said, "Are you serious? It's still dark outside, plus it's cold." He never asked again, and their romance faded just like every other relationship he'd ever known.

People in Mason's life always seemed to leave in some form or fashion, giving him yet another reason not to get close to a woman or anyone for that matter. He didn't have any relatives, at least not the kind that he saw regularly. The only friends he'd ever known moved out of Oriental after high school graduation. A lot of people who grew up here in his generation would head off to college, and many would decide they were too good to come home to a little country bumpkin county in the middle of nowhere. For the most part, that didn't bother Mason because those were the type of people he didn't care much for back then anyway. For some reason, they thought they were better than the locals. Some would return to visit family for the holidays, and during those times when he'd spot a somewhat familiar face at the grocery store or the little white church he attended until he turned eighteen, he'd often pretend not to recognize the person. Nowadays, he only went to service on special occasions like Easter and

Christmas. Being a part of those events felt right for some reason, but he always made sure to wander in after the choir began to sing. Then, from one of the uncomfortable wooden pews at the back of the sanctuary, he would mouth the words to the hymns, take in the sermon, and eventually sneak out while the preacher was saying that final prayer when everyone's eyes were closed and their stomachs were grumbling. He still believed in God and even read his bible, but he didn't see the need to be a part of a group of people who met a few times every week. Plus, on Sundays—the only day he took off—he preferred to lounge around and watch NASCAR or football.

When the glow of the sun began to filter light on the fields, Mason hopped onto the four-wheeler that he kept sheltered behind the house. His messy black hair blew in the wind as he followed the dirt drive toward the market out by the main road. Callie trotted behind him just like she did every morning.

When the two of them walked toward the back entrance of the market, Mason pulled a dull bronze key from his pocket and used his free hand to brush his thick hair back into place. It was a little oily because he hadn't showered since yesterday evening, but as a farmer, it made sense to shower before dinner since he'd been working up a sweat all day long. There didn't seem to be any need to shower again in the morning just to jump back into the daily grind all over again. However, the chatty woman he'd dated had informed him on several occasions that not taking a shower after a night of sleep was gross.

Inside the building that featured a log exterior similar to the main farmhouse, Mason flipped on the lights and straightened up a bit before unlocking the front door from the inside. Although the farm was famous for its strawberries, a variety of fruits and vegetables grown on the land were haphazardly arranged in containers atop wooden tables that lined the walls. Some of the crops were in old milk crates of various colors while others were in wooden boxes as aged as the market itself. A few shelves of local honey and canned jellies climbed each of the far corners of the market. Mason had been offered good money by antique dealers for several of the displays in the roadside market, but selling memories had never been an option.

Callie wandered briskly around the bins and the barrels in the middle of the floor as if inspecting the place, and with each step her toenails made a tap-dancing sound on the concrete. Mason made his way over to the small counter near the front door that housed a cash register and other items needed for running the market. When pickers began to trickle in, he greeted each of them with a hello and a firm handshake, and most of them stopped to pet Callie's thick fur coat.

Memories of standing in this spot with his father on the first day of strawberry harvest year after year flooded into Mason's mind once again. He could remember being a little boy clinging to his father's leg as employees made their way into the market. At first, little Mason was shy because he hadn't seen some of the pickers in quite some time and other faces were new, but eventually, he would warm up. At the beginning of the season, he'd always end up letting Mr. Hatcher—his dad's chief farmhand—carry him on his shoulders out into the fields where eventually Mason would climb down and help pick with the rest of the crew. Back then, Mason's mom handmade special kid-sized buckets for Mason and all of the other children who came to the farm to pick with their families. As the years went by, Mason actually became quite the picker. From about age two to five, he was short enough to have to barely bend down to pick the berries, and he'd learned precisely which ones to snatch. He became strong enough to carry the basket in one hand and pluck with the other.

Back then, Mr. Hatcher lived in a tiny cabin on the farm a little way down the dirt road from the main house. Mason's mother often warned Mason to stay away from Mr. Hatcher because he was a no good drunk, she'd say, but Mason's father always said the man was harmless. Mason could remember overhearing arguments between his parents about Mr. Hatcher, usually at night when they assumed Mason was sound asleep. His mom would tell his dad that the man needed to be fired, but his dad always stood his ground saying that Mr. Hatcher was the best employee he'd ever hired. He said the man could run circles around his next best employee and any employee at any of the other farms in all of Pamlico County.

"What if he does something to harm Mason?" his mom would argue.

"The man drinks alcohol on his own time, Violet," his father would combat. "He doesn't show up to work drunk or drink on the job, and he looks after Mason like he's his own child."

That's usually when Mason would hear the emphatic stomping of his mother's two feet, and a few moments later the slamming of his parent's bedroom door would rattle the walls. From what Mason could remember, his parents didn't argue much, but like any other child, he didn't know everything that went on behind closed doors.

3

Ansley woke up entwined in the softest set of organic cotton sheets her mother had been able to order when she moved into this townhouse. Personally, it didn't matter all that much to Ansley what type of sheets on which she slept, but thread count and the varieties of cotton had been a part of her education while growing up in the Stone family. She had to admit that she could feel the difference between Egyptian cotton and Prima cotton and quickly spot whether fabric was single-ply or double-ply. She also knew that high thread count could be misleading and that one side of a quality bed sheet was smoother than the other. On several occasions, she recalled her mother snatching sheets off the beds in her childhood home and demanding that Wanda place them back on the proper way.

Along with the bedding and furniture, much of the décor in Ansley's townhome in one of the more upscale neighborhoods in the Raleigh area had been curated by none other than Eleanor Stone, the mother hen in her life. Her mother was the intrusive type when it came to making sure Ansley had the finest things available, and by now Ansley was accustomed to the posh lifestyle. She didn't, however, feel the need to live up to the same country club standards as her parents, but at the same time she found it best not to debate specific topics with her mother. For instance, when her mom wanted to buy her a painting, that cost nearly as much as a new vehicle, to display above the fireplace when she first moved into this place, Ansley suggested that it would be ridiculous to spend so much money on a piece of art that meant nothing to her. After that conversation, a week went by before her mother would answer her phone calls.

When Ansley rolled over onto her back, her mind immediately traveled to the date night story Cleve shared with her at the hospital last night. Relaxing on her form-fitting foam pillow, she found herself thinking about how terrified Cleve had been of Violet's father, which made her laugh on the inside both then and now. She could visualize Cleve and Violet walking down the driveway and turning onto the dusty road eventually losing sight of the house where their walk had begun . . .

When me and Violet made it out of her father's sight, I felt my shoulders relax just a bit. I was still nervous, though. Her mere presence had that effect on me, causing my words to slur and my body to tremble at times. At that moment, both of our arms dangled like pendulums in the empty space between us, and I found myself wishing for the courage to reach over and take hold of her hand.

"How was your day?" I eventually asked. The question seemed generic, but I really wanted to know. I desired to hear about every little thing she'd done from the moment she woke up to the moment I spotted her beyond that doorframe when the sight of her took my breath away.

She smiled and twisted her body slightly in my direction as we walked. Her dress, floating to the motion of her torso as if she were dancing, caught my eye. Immediately, her movement reminded me of the latest dance craze, The Twist.

"I had a rather fine day, thank you," she answered in a polite

tone that assured me of her appreciation of my asking about her day. "This morning, I gathered fresh eggs from the chickens and then helped Mamma cook breakfast."

"What did you make for breakfast?"

"We had scrambled eggs, grits, bacon, and biscuits with homemade jellies."

I found myself imagining the table in their kitchen lined with these scrumptious foods. Truth be told, I'd been so nervous about our date that I'd only nibbled on snacks all day long rather than actually eating meals, so listening to Violet talk about food made my stomach rumble.

An instant later, I found myself tightening my abs, hoping she wouldn't hear my belly talking. I'm not sure why I was so embarrassed by the thought of her hearing the noise, it wasn't like I had passed gas.

It's funny how in the beginning stage of a relationship people are so concerned about such things. Later in life, when I would belch, Violet would just shake her head in silence. If we were at the dinner table at home, which is the only table at which I would burp, I'd say, "Not bad manners, just good food."

Mason always thought bodily noises were hilarious. I can remember him sitting in his highchair at the kitchen table with his little hand holding a small fork like it was a candle. When I would belch, he would giggle uncontrollably and eventually try to imitate the sound. Surprisingly, Violet thought it was cute at that point in his life, but as he grew older, she would ask me not to teach him my bad habits. Of course, by then the damage had been done.

When Violet and I were growing up, relationships between men and women were much different. Rarely ever would a wife disagree with her husband in front of the children and definitely not in the presence of friends or out in public. If a woman had something to say, she knew it would be best to hold onto her thoughts for a private conversation. Violet carried similar values into our marriage, and I think it made life easier for both of us because in return I respected her enough to know not to embarrass her in front of others as well.

As tiny dust clouds kicked up beneath my noticeably tattered boots, I hoped Violet wouldn't notice the sounds my stomach was churning out. If she did hear them, she didn't let on one bit.

"Breakfast was delicious," Violet shared. "Mamma has been teaching me how to cook for as long as I can remember. She's much better in the kitchen than me, but I am learning."

"I bet you are a good cook," I said knowing I would eat a clump of dirt if she put it on the table in front of me.

"Maybe one day I'll make supper for you," she mentioned.

"I'd like that very much," I admitted, glancing at the toe of one of my boots as I spoke the words. I'd had those boots for years, and at the end of each day in the fields, they looked as worn out as I felt.

"Me too," she uttered.

On our left, a cornfield flanked the road. Stalks were higher than our heads with rows as straight as wooden church pews.

"Want to walk through the field?" I suddenly asked.

Violet turned her head and seemed to be contemplating the idea for a short moment before answering. "Daddy would kill you if he came looking for us and couldn't find us on this road."

At this point, we had walked around a couple of bends in the road and were a reasonable distance from Violet's house. If anyone came looking for us, they'd either have to run or drive a car to catch up with us. I knew no one was following us because on the straightaways I'd been glancing back to make sure.

Thinking about her comment, the image of her father with a double barrel shotgun suddenly reentered my mind. "You are probably right," I responded. "I do need to remain in his good graces."

"I would if I were you," she suggested.

"He scares me a little," I admitted. If I were completely honest, I would have said he scares me a lot.

Truth be told, Violet Horne's daddy scared everybody or at least every teenage boy who'd had his eyes on his daughter since grade school. I was smart enough to realize that the fear this beast of a man put in all of us boys was the only reason I had a chance with Violet. All the other, more suitable boys were too scared to ask her father if they could court her. When a boy at school would ask Violet out on a date, she'd tell him, "Daddy says I can't date until I'm eighteen, and you would have to ask his permission then."

Violet chuckled. "Daddy's a big teddy bear."

"I agree with the words big *and* bear*," I announced causing her to snicker again. I liked it when she laughed, and I found myself hoping I could always make her smile. You see, I'd already made up my mind that I wanted to marry Violet Horne. She was as beautiful as God had made any girl and as sweet as chocolate syrup.*

We passed under a row of large oak trees, their limbs dangling above the road like palm branches covering royalty. I sure felt like someone special walking with Violet, but in reality, I knew I wasn't worthy of her. I wasn't anywhere close. I was a poor country boy whose family didn't even have an indoor john. We used the outhouse by the tobacco field. "That works just fine," Daddy would remind me when I would tell him how much I liked the indoor toilets at the schoolhouse. We only owned one vehicle, a rusted pick-up truck that we used on the farm and for trips to town. The passenger side door wouldn't open, so mother and I had to climb out the driver's side door after father got out. He always drove. I don't remember mother driving the truck anywhere.

Suddenly, a snake slithered out of the tall grass on the side of the road on which Violet was walking. As soon as she spotted it, she screeched like a little school girl on the playground and jumped into my arms like we were newlyweds about to enter our first home together. An instant later, I followed her eyes and then her pointer finger to the ground near my feet, and that's when I first spotted the copperhead. Granted, I'd never been afraid of snakes but this situation felt different. Although I wasn't the type of kid who would pick them up and play with them, I liked to study them close up and didn't have any problem being within an arm's reach of any of them, venomous or not. Out in the fields, we saw corn snakes all the time. But this particular snake wasn't harmless, and it was displaying signs of aggression.

If Violet hadn't been wrapped around my chest at the moment, I have to admit that I probably would have danced with this creature. I would have picked up a nearby stick and poked at him just to see how he would react. But with her in my arms, I needed to make a move, and I needed to make it fast. Not just because of the snake, but because I suddenly realized if her daddy's truck came around that bend behind us and he saw us like this, I would be toast. Burnt toast. The snake would surely slither away, and in her father's eyes, we'd be caught red-handed.

Speaking of hands, my hand was somewhere it wasn't supposed to be. Not only somewhere Violet's daddy wouldn't approve of, but somewhere I most certainly would not have put it on my own accord—a place where people in the Bible Belt were taught it didn't belong until a couple walked through the front door of that house I mentioned earlier.

Somehow, when Violet had popped into my arms like a kernel of corn in a kettle, her yellow dress had wafted into the air, and one of my hands ended up wedged between her legs.

My hands had been a lot of places they weren't supposed to be in my eighteen years of life, but they had never been up a girl's dress.

I was almost sure that the location of my hand had yet to register in Violet's mind. If it had, I figured she would have either jumped down as quickly as she'd jumped up or slapped the snot out of me, but at that moment I had no idea how terrified she was of snakes. She was holding onto me as tightly as a python, and the copperhead was rearing its head to strike when I took two giant steps to our left and cleared the drainage ditch between the road and the cornfield.

Before I knew it, we were thirty yards into the corn, and as I slowed my trot, my hand was still tucked beneath her dress. When my feet came to a stop in the soft soil, Violet looked me square in the eyes, and I swear life seemed to stand still as if that moment had been designed for the two of us. I felt an intense desire to kiss her lips as I gazed into her eyes. If there ever was a perfect opportunity to kiss a girl, this was it. Both of our hearts were racing. I could literally feel hers beating against my chest. To be honest, I hadn't imagined in a million years that I might kiss Violet that day.

In the days before our walk, as I'd thought about the time I would spend with her on that old dirt road, I often found myself wondering if I might be able to build up the courage to hold her hand, but that had been the height of my expectations.

An unexpected knock came at Ansley's door, abruptly yanking her out of the trance she had been under while living inside Cleve's memory of the date night. The way he told the story made it so real, and she could see him and Violet just as clearly as she could see her mother's face after twisting the knob.

"Hello, Mom." *I didn't expect you* was the greeting she wanted to share, but she knew her mother would take the comment the wrong way. Ansley had made that mistake once or twice in her adult life.

For a moment, Eleanor Stone stood in the doorway, her eyes traveling up and down her daughter's body as if in a state of shock. "Ansley, why in God's sake do you look like that?" she asked pointing with her eyes rather than her finger.

Ansley glanced down at the baggy t-shirt dangling low enough to cover her comfy cotton shorts. Her feet were bare, and when she grabbed the sides of her head to feel her hair, she realized it was an absolute mess. Her appearance in the confines of her own home wasn't a big deal to her, but she knew her mother would never even consider stepping foot out of her bedroom looking unkempt.

As this thought crossed Ansley's mind, she realized she couldn't recall a single time when she'd seen her mother in a nightgown or any type of clothing that wasn't put together.

"I just got out of bed," Ansley yawned.

"Cover your mouth, dear," her mother instructed, the strap of her purse dangling from her arm positioned at a perfect ninety-degree angle. "And are you planning to work today?"

Instead of answering the question, Ansley asked, "Would you like to come inside?"

"I'm not sure," her mother responded as if the place might be crawling with roaches. "You have a man in there, don't you?" she suddenly probed.

A crow's foot formed between Ansley's eyebrows. "What?" she countered. "Why would you ask such a thing?"

Eleanor stepped inside, just far enough for Ansley to be able to close the door behind her without it hitting her in the back.

"You have an aura of romance in your eyes, and you look like you just had morning sex."

Ansley's eyebrows climbed her forehead. "Mother!" she exclaimed wishing morning sex *was* the reason for her current appearance. If she'd had a man in her bed, she definitely wouldn't have come to the door. At the sound of the knock, she would have rolled over and wrapped her arms around him instead.

"Well, what is his name and why did you not introduce him to your father and me before you invited him into your bedroom?"

"Mother, there is no one else here," she assured in a disgruntled tone. "I am home alone."

"Then let's go out for breakfast. My treat."

Searching for the proper response, Ansley was somewhat relieved that her mother had changed the topic. "I wish I could," she conveyed.

"Why can't you? I thought today was your day off?"

"It is," she revealed. Actually, she had much more than just one day off, but she had purposefully neglected to share this news with her mother.

"Do you have an appointment scheduled?"

Knowing she had never been good at lying to her mother, Ansley turned and walked toward the kitchen so her mom couldn't see her face as she spoke. "Yes, I have somewhere to be." Looking in the cabinets for nothing in particular, she waited for her mother to ask where, but after an unusual length of silence, she turned, and her mother was nowhere to be seen.

"Mom?" she called out before walking toward the hallway that led to her bedroom in which she found her mother wandering around like a detective searching for clues.

"What are you doing?" Ansley snarled.

"Looking for him—"

"*He's* not here."

"Oh, so *he* was here?"

"No, there is no he. I am not dating anyone."

"That's good because I want to introduce you to a new gentleman who recently joined the country club."

Oh, no, Ansley immediately thought, not another man hand selected by her mom.

Eleanor continued, "He's a lawyer, a man of intelligence and wisdom."

Figures, Ansley imagined. Wisdom probably meant this man was fifteen or twenty years her elder. The last man her mother had set her up with from the club was bald and not because he chose to shave his head for the sleek look.

"Thanks, Mom, but—"

Eleanor interrupted, "He is free tomorrow evening."

"Why do you know that?"

"I asked him if he would like to go on a date with my daughter, that's how I know."

"What? Why?"

"Because you need a good man in your life."

"What did he say?" Ansley asked then immediately wished she hadn't. "Nevermind, I don't care what he said, I'm not—"

Before Ansley could finish her sentence, her mother chimed in with the answer to her question. "He said yes."

"What? He doesn't even know what I look like."

"Yes, he most certainly does. I showed him pictures on my phone," she shared, holding up the device as if it was evidence.

"Mom!"

"So, let's venture out for breakfast, then we can shop at the downtown boutiques, and I'll buy you a new outfit that will be sure to impress him," she offered, glaring again at Ansley's current attire. "But first you need to freshen up," she added with a scowl on her face.

Ansley wasn't sure how she was going to wiggle her way out of this one, but the one thing she wasn't going to do was tell her mother the truth. As soon as she could get her out of the house, she was planning to shower—the part of the plan her mother would approve of—and then drive several hours toward the coast to enjoy a relaxing vacation. This trip was something completely out of character for her, and for some reason, she found the idea absolutely thrilling.

4

The first official day of strawberry season at the farm went about as well as Mason could have hoped. Every single picker had shown up for work, and no one was late. A few of them asked as many questions as a first grader at the zoo, but that was to be expected. The only animal running around the farm these days, though, was Callie, following Mason everywhere he ventured.

With his companion by his side, Mason had spent most of the day wandering around the strawberry fields providing answers and inspecting everything from the berries to the soil to the clouds above his head. When he'd scrolled through the forecast on his phone last night—an evening ritual—the chance of rain was minimal, but in Eastern North Carolina a rain shower or thunderstorm could pop up out of nowhere at any time without warning. Thankfully, today the rain had held off to allow for a perfect day for picking.

Once back at the farmhouse, Mason filled Callie's bowls with dog food and water. "There you go, girl," he said to his best friend, petting her as she lowered her long, pointy snout into the bowl and began chomping. "While you're eating, I'm going to go shower off and then it will be my turn to eat."

Callie glanced up as if she understood precisely what Mason was telling her. Actually, he knew she did because this was their routine after a long day's work on the farm.

After Mason toweled off and brushed his hair, he pulled a fresh pair of boxers and blue jeans up his hairy legs then headed back to the kitchen in a different colored flannel shirt. He touched the hole in the wall then noticed that Callie's bowl was already empty as he wandered to the refrigerator in search of an idea for dinner. He'd never been good at planning meals.

"I've been so busy getting ready for strawberry season that I forgot to go grocery shopping, girl," he said to Callie who was now sprawled across the wide plank hardwood floor as if she was done for the night.

Every piece of flooring and the walls of this home—inside and out—had been handmade from trees chopped down on the family farm. Anytime Mason stopped to think about how much work his ancestors had put into building this house, he found himself mesmerized. He couldn't even imagine waking up for days on end, cranking the chainsaw he kept in the barn out back, dropping trees like dominoes, then hauling pieces of them back to the barn where the old log splitter now sat as more of a reminder of how things once were than a functional piece of equipment. He had no idea how much time it would take to produce each flat board like the ones beneath his feet, but he sure was thankful that his family had known what they were doing when it came to building a house.

Of course, the home had been updated gradually as years went by, but structurally most everything was still original. The refrigerator was newish in relation to the age of the house but probably outdated by conventional standards. The dishwasher was an early 1980s model named Mason Fields. Past girlfriends had encouraged him to buy a real dishwasher, but he always shrugged off their suggestions. He found washing dishes by hand to be therapeutic, and depending on how much time he had on any given evening, he would dry each one by hand or set them into a dish drainer to dry overnight.

At the end of an evening, Mason had about as many friends as he had dishes to wash, probably less depending on the definition of friends. Acquaintances might be a better word. For as long as he could remember, he had felt awkward around people. He didn't know why, but he just did. It wasn't that he didn't like people or didn't know how to carry on a conversation, he'd just rather be alone, especially after the tragedy involving his parents that caused people in town to look at him differently. Since then, he had become accustomed to enjoying quiet time whether he was fishing, hunting, camping, or simply relaxing in the confines of his own home. He found these activities much more interesting than being out and about in town or at social gatherings.

He would venture into town when in need of items from the local home and garden shop, the grocery store, or the gas station to refill the gas containers for the tractor and four-wheeler and other machinery used on the farm. Rarely ever did he eat out although he enjoyed the food at M&M's Café, The Silos, and Brantley's Village Restaurant. When he did have dinner at one of these places, he made sure to go at off-peak hours. Some of the restaurants in Oriental had been around for ages, and others had opened to attract tourists.

The locals had mixed feelings about tourists visiting their quaint town. These outsiders consisted of a large number of snowbirds, many of whom would dock their sailboats for a stay as they headed south for the winter and back north for the summer. Following such trips, people from all over the country would often end up choosing to retire here. Most retirees arrived with good intentions, typically because they'd visited this little piece of paradise and instantly fell in love with the ambiance and the soul of this place that was impossible to overlook.

Mason didn't much mind new residents although he avoided

them just like he did most of the locals. He did wish transplants wouldn't get overly involved in the town's politics and economic development. Oh, how quickly many of these folks could forget why they moved here in the first place. It was like once the new wore off, their eyes became hazy with dollar signs. Instead of appreciating the slow pace of an area rich in history and heritage, they wanted to build condos and neighborhoods with matching mailboxes where people lived on top of each other. Those weren't the roots on which Oriental had grown to become one of the nation's best-kept secrets. Instead of letting the town grow like an oak tree on the dirt God provided, they wanted to plant new trees and douse them with dump truck loads of fertilizer.

Many businessmen had offered to purchase the hundreds of acres of Mason's family farm over the years, and he'd literally laughed at every single one of them. The thought of his home being bulldozed and the crops being paved over with streets or shopping mall parking lots irked him.

"Callie, let's go for a ride," Mason announced as he grabbed his keys from an old hook that had adorned the wall next to the back door for as long as he could remember. Surprised, Callie did a doggie pushup and met him at the door with a smile wrapped around her narrow face. She absolutely loved going for rides in the pickup truck especially with the windows rolled down.

The instant Mason's fingers twisted the doorknob on the back door, he could have sworn he heard a knock at the front door. Standing still for a moment as if he'd been touched in a game of freeze tag, he found himself questioning whether he or Callie might have come into contact with something that created the knocking sound. He glanced around, but upon noticing Callie's perked ears just before she turned to trot toward the front door, he realized he hadn't been imagining things.

He wasn't expecting anyone, and all of the workers had left for the day long before Mason himself had closed down the roadside market and driven the four-wheeler back to the house with the headlight shining.

Callie stood anxiously in front of the closed door while Mason peeked through the curtains that almost always remained pulled together. Other than a dim lamp in the corner, not a single light in the house was on which is what Mason preferred when it was dark outside. During the daytime hours, he rarely kept on any lights at all.

The porch light had recently burned out, and Mason had forgotten to replace it, so he could barely make out the silhouette of the person standing on the other side of the door. It looked like the individual was holding something in his or her hand and turning from side to side as if they were nervous or watching for something or someone.

"Callie, why didn't you tell me someone was here?" Mason whispered as she stood at the door with her furry tail wagging.

Callie's demeanor made Mason aware of several things. First, since she wasn't barking or growling, he knew that she didn't sense danger. Secondly, he had a hunch that the car which he could barely make out must be a relatively new vehicle, which meant it was quieter than most of the ones locals were willing to drive down driveways like his that were filled with potholes and bugs and dust that loved to cover metal. Every now and then, someone who didn't understand boundaries would knock on his door a little after dark and ask if they could buy something from the market. Usually, when a car drove up, Callie would be at the window or door by the time it came to a halt. Her ears were as keen as a hawk's eyes, but Mason figured that tonight she must have been so tuckered out from the demands of the first day of strawberry season that while napping she hadn't heard the vehicle.

"Who is it, Callie?" Mason whispered, wandering toward the window on the other side of the doorframe to see if he could get a better view.

Callie just cocked her head sideways and seemed to ask the same question of him.

"I don't know who it is," Mason revealed in a hushed tone. "I didn't invite anybody."

Mason thought about pretending no one was home—which he'd done before—and waiting it out to see how long it would take the person to leave if no one answered the knock. Callie then stretched her paw toward the door and scratched on the wood, not hard enough to leave a mark but with enough force that Mason figured the visitor standing on the other side probably heard the sound. He threw up his hands at Callie and bulged his eyes.

"What are you doing?" he whispered in a heavier tone than before, throwing up his hands with a grin covering his face. He felt like Callie's gesture might be a sign that he should answer the door.

As he stood there in limbo, a second knock echoed throughout the room. For some reason, the sound nearly caused him to let out a screech which would have been embarrassing since he should have been expecting the visitor to knock again.

Mason took a deep breath and reached for the doorknob. There was no need to hold onto Callie's collar because it was apparent that she was calm and would probably greet this person with a friendly lick. When the door squeaked open, Mason discovered a woman standing on the porch holding an object in her hand, and she appeared as lost as Callie had been the day Mason found her. It was a day Mason had tried to forget every day for the last seventeen years of his life, but he had come to realize it was one he would vividly remember for as long as he lived.

5

nsley had ended up departing Raleigh later than planned, mainly because it took her nearly two hours to convince her mother that they couldn't spend the entire day together. Begrudgingly, she'd allowed her mom to talk her into going out for breakfast just so that she could get her out of the house. However, leaving with her mother meant that Ansley had to shower, blow dry her hair, and apply makeup. After dressing to her mother's liking—dressy chinos, a lightweight cashmere sweater, and a pair of slingbacks—for breakfast at a restaurant where most of the women held their pinky fingers in the air sipping on coffee or tea, it had taken Ansley almost ten minutes to explain why they needed to drive separate vehicles. The real reason was that she knew if they rode together, her mother would have wanted to drive and then Ansley would have been at her mercy all day, which meant the two of them would have ended up shopping, receiving manicures, and who knows what else. Or even worse, her mother might have dragged her to the lawyer's office and demanded that Ansley let her introduce her to her future husband.

Once Ansley arrived home after breakfast, she was able to pack nearly a week's worth of clothes and necessities into a three-piece set of matching luggage. She made sure any bills that were due soon were paid, ate a sandwich at the house, grabbed some cash at the bank, and ran a few other errands around town.

Initially, she had hoped to reach her destination by five o'clock, but that plan had been blown way out of the water. Once she realized that wasn't going to happen, she'd hoped to arrive before sundown which would have come to fruition if one of the tires on her vehicle hadn't decided to blow out near Kinston.

Angels must have been flying above her because the flat tire occurred less than a football field away from where a man was selling produce out of the bed of a pickup truck. Ansley steered the vehicle onto the side of the road, and before she could think about walking toward the stranger to ask for help, she noticed him heading in her direction.

He was a husky fellow wearing a tight tank top, a pair of worn-out jeans, and a red bandana on his head.

"You lucky that nice car o' yours didn't end up in that ditch over there," the man called out. "Or wrapped 'round one of those-there pine trees."

Ansley's eyebrows rose. She hadn't even thought about the possibility of wrecking. She'd heard the tire blow, steadied the wheel, and before she knew it, the vehicle came to a halt as she was inching it off the road.

"I guess I am," she realized.

"You got a jack?"

Ansley shrugged. "I'm not sure." She didn't know much about cars, but she knew enough to understand that the jack in question wasn't a person.

"Let's have a look in your boot," he mentioned.

Ansley furrowed her brow as she glanced down at the brown leather boots covering her dark blue jeans up to her knees. As soon as she'd parted ways with her mother, she'd changed into a more comfortable outfit. *My boot?* Ansley contemplated saying. *Why do you want to have a look in my boot?*

Recognizing her puzzled expression, the man made a motion toward the trunk. "Your trunk," he clarified. "'round here, some of us call it a boot."

"Oh," Ansley gasped suddenly feeling uneducated in an unfamiliar sort of way.

Upon the revelation, she pressed the button on her key fob to release the trunk's lid, then the two of them peered inside. It wasn't until that moment that Ansley remembered that her paisley-patterned luggage was taking up the entire space.

"Okay if I move these to your backseat, ma'am?" the man asked politely. "They look like high-dollar bags, so I don't want to put 'em on the dirt."

"Of course, and let me help you," she offered.

The stranger held up one of his large hands, and that's when Ansley realized he was much more than a man, he was a gentleman. "Ma'am, 'round here a lady don't tote heavy items lessen she has to. I'll handle these, no problem."

She watched as he snatched up the two larger pieces like they were merely grocery bags. Back at the townhouse, she'd had to roll them out one at a time, and even then she struggled to lift them into the trunk.

"I'll let you open that-there door for me," the gentleman said, gesturing to the back door with a nod.

In a matter of moments, he had the suitcases situated, the back wheel off the vehicle, and the spare tire spinning.

"There you go, ma'am," he said, greasy hands and all.

"You sure I don't owe you anything," Ansley asked for about the fifth time.

"Just pay it frorward, Miss."

Thankful, Ansley grinned. Due to his broken language, she wasn't sure if he'd said *pay* or *pray*, but she knew for sure he'd said frorward. She didn't dare ask for clarification in fear of embarrassing the fellow, so instead, Ansley decided she would both pay *and* pray it forward, which reminded her that she would miss her bible study group this week. The church her family attended was rather large; in fact, it had been labeled a mega-church. So it was comforting to have a small group of ladies to meet with on a regular basis. It gave them the opportunity to get to know each other on a personal level and be there for one another when needs arose. This week, their meeting was scheduled to be held at her mother's house, and she knew she'd hear an earful about missing that.

She cringed a little when she realized she'd also miss book club. The wrath of her mother would definitely be felt in full effect in the days to come.

A little over an hour later a dark sky hovered above as Ansley was nearing her destination on a donut tire that the gentleman suggested being replaced with a new regular sized one as soon as possible. Slowly, she turned down a dirt driveway with no end in sight, and the scene in front of her high beams reminded her of some of Cleve's date night jar stories. He had been on her mind just about the entire trip.

Cleve was the only person who knew she had changed her vacation plans. Ansley's friends thought she was going to Myrtle Beach for a week alone to enjoy walks on the beach and reading novels while lounging by the Atlantic Ocean. That was her initial plan, but her heart had led her elsewhere. She hadn't told her mom she was leaving town because she knew she'd want to tag along.

As the wheels on her car kicked up a cloud of dust behind its red taillights, her mind wandered back to the dusty road where Cleve and Violet had been walking and the cornfield where they'd ended up.

Instead of kissing Violet Horne like I wanted to so badly, I let her down gently, removing my hand from between her legs in the same motion.

As she straightened her dress, my eyes dropped to the soil beneath us. That's when I noticed that her feet were as bare as a baby's bottom which meant her shoes must have fallen off as we'd plowed into the cornfield.

I'd plowed many a cornfield in my day but never before with a woman in my arms. "I'm sorry about where my hand ended up," I felt the need to say before we went searching for her shoes.

Violet's face turned a shade of red I hadn't seen before, and for a moment I wondered if she would run off in shock, bare feet and all.

She stood still for a moment, glaring at her dirty toes. "It's okay," she finally uttered. "I was the one who jumped into your arms like a damsel in distress." She paused and glanced back up at me. "It's just that I am terrified of snakes. Always have been. I have nightmares about them, and I wake up sweating and kicking, and I end up jumping out of my bed just as fast as I jumped into your arms. It just happens." She looked down the row searching with her eyes for her shoes. "I should be the one apologizing," she said.

"No," I insisted. "You don't have to apologize for being afraid of snakes," I declared, adding a smile.

She snickered, then her face turned real serious looking again. "Please promise you won't tell all the boys from school that you had your hand up my dress."

I furrowed my brow. "I would never do such a thing," I guaranteed. "It can be our secret."

Violet later told me that this was the moment she fell in love with me. She said she saw something in my eyes that said I wouldn't even think of going around to all my friends bragging about being the first and only boy to ever have his hand up Violet Stone's dress.

"Will you help me find my shoes?" she asked, reaching for my hand as naturally as if she'd done so a thousand times.

My fingers slid gradually into the spaces between hers, and when our palms touched, I wrapped the ends of my fingers around her knuckles. It felt so nice to hold her hand in mine, even better than holding her beneath her dress.

Ansley held the images of Cleve and Violet in her mind as she walked toward the front door of a stranger's house—a home where a love story as thick as the sky is high had somehow come to an end. She didn't know how, but what she did know was that Cleve's and Violet's life together had ultimately produced a son. Part of her suddenly wished she knew more about the Fields, especially about what had torn Cleve and Mason apart. She also wished she knew how Cleve's and Violet's story had ended although she realized that their love story would never truly end because she held it in her hand at this very moment—The Date Night Jar.

When the man on the other side of the log cabin door finally opened it and stared at her, she held up the jar even though she realized that through the darkness he probably couldn't make out the color of her eyes.

The man whom she assumed to be Mason Fields peered at the jar, and as soon as he realized what she was holding, he began to gasp for air. The dog sitting steadily at his side instantaneously let out a whimper and nuzzled the man's leg with the tip of her nose.

"I brought this for you," were the only words Ansley was able to get out of her mouth before the grown man in front of her fell to his knees and began wailing like a child who'd been thrown from his bike on that dusty road that had led her to this farmhouse.

6

Standing above the man whom Ansley figured must be Mason Fields, she found herself at a loss for words. As a medical doctor, knowing how to think on her feet and respond instantly to a plethora of emotions usually came naturally. This particular reaction from this man whom she expected to be a tough-skinned farmer, Ansley hadn't seen coming in the least. Since she didn't know Mason, she honestly hadn't had a clue how he would respond to a stranger showing up at his home unannounced especially after dark. Surprised, maybe? A little irritated, possibly? But this . . . this wasn't one of the options that had played out in her mind as she had taken in the scenic drive across Eastern North Carolina that led to Oriental.

She'd absolutely fallen in love with the views as she passed by hundreds of acres of wide open fields where farmhouses were nestled at the end of winding gravel driveways. There were similar places on the outskirts of Raleigh, but as she'd traveled east such scenery seemed to become the norm. Many of the houses featured wraparound porches like the one on which she was standing at this very moment. She couldn't see the structure all that well right now, but when her headlights had illuminated the quaint log cabin, she could tell that the porch stretched around either side of the home, and she assumed it connected around the backside.

Eventually, Ansley took a small step back to give the emotional man some space. His head was tucked between his legs as if he were practicing yoga, and his dog had nestled up next to him and poked her snout through a small open space near her owner's face.

Ansley didn't know what to say now, and in hindsight, she realized she should have chosen a more subtle introduction. Inwardly, she scolded herself for not starting with a greeting like, "Hey, are you Mason Fields?" or "Hello, my name is Ansley Stone. I am your father's physician."

She had no idea why the mere sight of The Date Night Jar caused such an emotional reaction for Mason, but for whatever reason, it had. She decided she should have left it in her bag like she'd planned and given the jar to him following an opportunity to explain why she'd come here in the first place.

After letting him sob a bit longer, Ansley knelt down slowly, close enough that she could stretch out her hand and reach the shoulder of his red flannel shirt. Unsure of how the dog might react to a stranger encroaching on his owner's personal space, she did so with caution. The gorgeous collie didn't appear as though it would be aggressive although she remembered hearing somewhere that this particular breed could be snappy at times. At the moment, though, the dog seemed somber and completely focused on emotionally supporting his owner.

The loyalty a dog is capable of showing a person brushed through Ansley's mind, and she couldn't help but be reminded of how much humans could learn from animals. In her particular case, she had never felt like having a pet was a feasible option even though she lived alone; not because she wouldn't enjoy the companionship but because she couldn't give a dog the amount of time and attention it would need to be happy.

There were two types of dog owners who drove Ansley crazy. The ones that chained their dogs to a stake in the ground and pretty much abandoned the animal leaving only a bowl of water and a dish of food, and then the ones who crated their pet indoors while they worked all day. It just didn't seem humane. She believed that animals were created to be free, to roam the land, and to enjoy nature.

When Ansley cupped her hand around Mason's left shoulder, she took note that the dog's right eye, the only one visible from her perspective, rose in her direction observing her movements carefully. She kept her hand steady, realizing the animal seemed to be okay with it being there.

"Mason," Ansley finally whispered, hoping the man she was touching was indeed Mason Fields. "My name is Ansley Stone. I'm a physician."

The moment she finished the introduction of herself, she felt dumb once again. The way she had spoken the words made it sound like he was lying on the ground due to an injury and she was letting him know that she was qualified to help. Since she wasn't a psychiatrist, psychologist, or some other type of certified counselor, she wasn't technically qualified to help a person in this state of mind although in the hospital she often consoled emotionally unstable patients, family members, and friends.

At the sound of the woman's voice, Mason forced himself to pick up his head, and with the sleeve of his button up shirt, he wiped the tears from his face. "I'm sorry," he uttered as the realization that he was sobbing in front of a stranger suddenly sunk in. "I just didn't expect it to happen like this," he added sniffing deeply.

Ansley suddenly wore a look of confusion although she was certain that Mason, through his blurred vision in the dark of night, couldn't see the thoughts present on her face. She recalled thinking it was odd that he hadn't turned on the porch light before twisting the knob. She'd heard a scratch on the door, which must have been the dog, and then all of a sudden the silhouette of a burly man became visible. She hadn't even noticed the dog at first, not until the man had begun to drop to his knees.

Moments ago as his torso had risen, Ansley's hand fell from his shoulder, and she let it slip to her side. Now, sitting knee to knee as if they were praying at an altar, she waited for him to speak again rather than respond to his comment.

"My dad was a good man," Mason expressed, feeling the need to convince Ansley. "I promise he was, I just couldn't force myself to visit him and see him like that. I wanted to remember him the way I knew him." He paused for a moment as his mind was replaying specific memories with his dad. All the while, Callie was gazing up at him as if holding onto every word. "I should have gone to see him. I owed him that. He loved me and provided for me, and he was the best dad he could be under the circumstances."

Ansley suddenly realized what Mason was thinking, why he had broken down the moment he saw The Date Night Jar which was now resting on the porch next to some type of wood-carved animal. "Mason, your dad—" Before going on, Ansley searched for the best way to put this. She wanted to be honest with him, relieve the man of his unexpected grief, but at the same time, not give him false hope.

Mason jumped to a conclusion before Ansley could speak again. "I know," he said. "I know why you're here. My dad is dead."

"Your dad isn't in good health," Ansley quickly clarified, "but he's not dead."

A look of confusion clouded Mason's face. "He's not?"

"No, he's alive."

"Then why are you bringing me The Date Night Jar?" Mason asked, his demeanor suddenly changing as he glanced at the object out of the corner of his eye.

"Your dad asked me to," she said simply.

"Why?" Mason queried. "Aren't you the doctor that wrote me

the letter asking if I would mail the jar to you so that my dad could have access to it?"

"Yes, that was me," she clarified.

"So if he's not dead, why is he sending it back to me?"

Ansley was utterly confused, noticing how suddenly Mason's emotions shifted from a grief-stricken state to being seemingly irritated that his dad had decided to return The Date Night Jar. At the moment, she didn't feel like she could tell him the exact reason why his father wanted him to have the jar. Cleve had said, "Please take The Date Night Jar back to my son, and if he doesn't have someone as special as Violet in his life, tell him to let it help guide him to true love." But, the way Mason was responding, she didn't think he would want to hear this news especially not right now. Plus, there was more to it—she had intentions of her own. At the least, she wanted to figure out why Mason chose not to visit his father.

"This jar is very special to your dad, and he wanted you to have it," Ansley shared, holding it up like they were at show-and-tell in elementary school. What she'd said was the truth, she realized, just not the whole truth and nothing but the truth. Her hand wasn't on a Bible, she reminded herself.

"I don't understand," Mason responded. "Why did he want the jar so badly that he asked you to write me a letter to request it and then a few weeks later turn around and have you bring it back to me?" Mason was trying to put the pieces of this puzzle together, but it just didn't make sense to him. "And why didn't you just mail it back?" he investigated, wondering why this woman had decided to show up on his doorstep in the dark.

Ansley felt discouragement overtaking her. It was suddenly clear that she had gone about all of this the wrong way. She should have planned out this trip better instead of showing up in Oriental on a whim. Everything had sounded so simple when she and Cleve had talked about her coming here. *Silly me*, she thought to herself, *I should have known better.*

"I should probably just leave," Ansley uttered as she rose to her feet, fully expecting to hear Mason say, *that would be a good idea,* as he stood as well. She hated to jump to conclusions, especially about Cleve's son, but upon this first impression, he didn't come across as a friendly guy.

"Why did you come here?" he asked.

If she told Mason the truth now, she felt like he would probably laugh in her face. "Listen, I obviously didn't think this through, and now I realize that you think I'm a moron for driving all the way here to bring you The Date Night Jar." She paused for a moment to collect her thoughts. "Cleve," she said, "I mean, your dad—"

Mason cut her off. "You can call him Cleve," he snapped as the crickets chirped in the background, "that's fine." He leaned against the doorframe with the left side of his body turned toward her. "Sometimes I call him Cleve too, but usually I don't talk about him at all."

Ansley furrowed her brow although trying her best to hide the confusion dancing around in her brain. This situation was growing weirder by the moment, and she found herself wishing she *was* a therapist, maybe then she would know how to respond to Mason and be able to help him sort through all the conflicting emotions he was battling. It was evident that he had a lot of pent-up anger toward his father, but she didn't know exactly why. She knew enough from the stories Cleve had told her to understand that there was tension between the two of them, but the vibe coming from Mason seemed to rise to another level. Cleve always talked highly of his son even though she had come to realize that there must be a reason why Mason didn't come to visit. She didn't have to be a psychologist to figure that out.

"I have some time off from work, and initially I had a trip to Myrtle Beach planned." This was going to sound so ridiculous,

Ansley realized as she quickly formulated the thought in her mind just before speaking it aloud. "But then at the last minute, Cleve told me about the guest cabin here on his property." Realizing how that sounded, she paused momentarily to reorganize her wording. "I mean *your* property, I guess, since you live here—"

Mason butted in again. "You're right; technically, it is Cleve's property," he conveyed reaching down to pet Callie whose tail was slapping against his ankle.

Ansley recognized that for the first time since her arrival, Mason called his dad Cleve, and she found herself wishing she could pause life to ask Cleve fifty questions right now and then press play again once she'd absorbed the answers.

Instead, she accepted reality and finished her thought. "He asked if I'd bring you The Date Night Jar, and he said I could stay in the guest cabin for a few days and enjoy some quiet time out here." Ansley paused for a moment, suddenly feeling as dumb as the doorknob on the open door as she spoke her next thought. "He told me where the key was hidden for the guest cabin—under the porch steps, but he said I should probably stop in to let you know I'd be there this week."

This time it was Mason who was furrowing his brow. Thanks to the moonlight, Ansley could see his face better now that her eyes had adjusted to the darkness surrounding the log cabin. At some point while standing on his front porch, she had noticed there was very little light coming from inside the house.

"That's not possible," Mason responded without hesitation.

"I was afraid you might say that," Ansley admitted. This particular outcome had been floating in and out of her mind ever since last night when Cleve made the whole scenario sound so transparent: "Just knock on the door, tell Mason who you are and that I said it's okay for you to stay in the cabin, and he'll be fine with it," he'd insisted. Now that Ansley knew things weren't that simple, she realized Mason probably didn't like the idea of some strange woman spending time on his property or maybe someone else was occupying the cabin. Why hadn't she thought of that? "Based on how your dad put it, I made the mistake of assuming that staying in the cabin wouldn't be a problem, but I think maybe I have done way too much assuming with this situation."

Ansley's mind flashed back to the many evenings she'd spent at Cleve's bedside, and suddenly she wondered about his intentions behind convincing her to stay on the family property. Over time she had begun to trust him, but now she suddenly began to second-guess letting down her guard with a man in his position. She found herself contemplating this thought as she started to back away from Mason and the dog that had been standing nearly as still as a statue by his side.

When she reached the packed dirt at the bottom of the steps, she turned around to ask Mason one last question. "Is there a hotel in town that you recommend?" She knew she should have just made a reservation in the first place.

"Won't be any need for that," Mason declared, "unless you feel more comfortable staying in a hotel than out here at the farm."

Following his comment, Ansley found herself puzzled once again. "Don't take this the wrong way," she suggested, "but based on what you said a minute ago, I got the feeling you didn't like the idea of me staying in your guest cabin."

Mason remained quiet for a moment as his eyes peered toward the dirt drive before shifting back to Ansley. In the distance an owl let out a hoot, and critters of all types had been chattering in the background ever since he'd opened the door.

"There is no guest cabin," he finally revealed.

She took a deep, concentrated breath and exhaled slowly. Had Cleve lied about the other cabin? Ansley began to wonder. At this moment, she felt more vulnerable than she had all evening. Her mind began to wander down trails that led to scary places. Why had Cleve really sent her here? Suddenly, she could hear her

THE DATE NIGHT JAR

mother's voice echoing inside her head, *Ansley, how could you be so stupid? Leave. Just leave.*

Cleve was the only patient under her care whom she believed to be trustworthy, but had she made a big mistake by trusting him? Management had always advised the doctors and nurses for the sake of their own safety not to get too close to the patients. Of course, that statement had many meanings behind it based on the unit in which she worked, but she had chosen the placement because she wanted to make a difference in the lives of those who many people in society had already cast off. For heaven's sake, it seemed as though the man standing in the doorway next to his dog had even shunned his own father. Why would Cleve have told her there was a guest log cabin on the family farm where she could stay if there really wasn't? Her mind kept traveling back to that thought, and just when she was about to tell Mason *thanks, but no thanks*, he added a bit of interesting information about the cabin.

"Dad doesn't know this, but the cabin burned down."

At least he didn't call him Cleve again, Ansley thought for some reason.

"Oh," she responded simply, not sure what else to say, but relieved nonetheless to find out that at some point there had been a second cabin.

"I would like to keep it that way if you don't mind," he expressed sternly.

"Okay," Ansley agreed, surprised that he would trust her with that bit of information when he didn't even know her. She guessed it was none of her business anyway, which led to her next thought. "So, if there is no guest cabin, where on the farm would I be able to stay?"

"Well, you could stay in the barn if you'd like, but there's no bathroom out there," Mason mentioned. "There is an outhouse nearby that is still in working order, but I can't imagine a doctor using an outdoor john," he added with a hint of a laugh.

Ansley wasn't sure whether to chuckle along with Mason or to take his comment as an insult. Hesitantly, she let out a snicker because even though she wouldn't admit it out loud at this moment, he was right. There was no way on God's green earth that she was going to use an outhouse unless she had absolutely no other option. Like he said, she was a doctor, and thankfully that meant she had the means to afford a hotel where there would be indoor plumbing, electricity, and many other amenities that his barn wouldn't offer.

Mason continued. "But when I mentioned staying on the farm, I was referring to the main house where Callie and I live. We have an extra room, so it's not like you'd have to sleep on the couch or anything."

Ansley glanced at Callie—she liked that name for a dog, especially this dog, Callie the collie—then she made a point to stare straight into Mason's eyes as if she could read him like a book. Even though this was one of the most awkward situations she'd been in at any point in her life, for some reason she felt comfortable around Mason Fields in the same way that she felt at ease in the presence of Cleve Fields. It was like they were both old souls, the type of people you rarely if ever come into contact with when living in a populated city.

"Okay," she said without entirely thinking through what she was agreeing to as she peered into the darkness beyond Mason and his dog. At that moment, she had a hunch that she might not ever make mention of the days and nights that lie ahead, not to her mother or to anyone else for that matter.

7

"I would invite you inside," Mason said to Ansley, "but we're about to leave."

For a moment, Ansley felt like her mind and body became frozen as she tried to process Mason's comment. Before he'd spoken, she was just about to make mention of walking back to her car to grab her bags, but now she wasn't sure how to respond. Once again, this man had managed to throw her for a loop.

"O—kay," Ansley eventually replied, letting the word draw out. Either Mason was having an off night, or he was one of the oddest human beings she had ever met. Just moments ago, he invited her to stay, and now she was being informed that he was leaving. *Wait*, Ansley thought as her mind caught up with Mason's choice of words—he'd said *we're* about to leave. Who was *we*?

"Would you like to ride into town for dinner with us?" Mason asked. Remembering that he and Callie had been on their way out the door when Ansley arrived, he figured he might as well carry on with those plans even though the pang of hunger seemed to have dissipated.

Us? He'd used a plural word again, Ansley noticed, and she wondered who he meant by *us*. Was there someone else here? A woman maybe? There didn't seem to be another person in the house unless maybe that individual was in the shower or in another room getting ready. If there had been another person in the living area of the house, Ansley assumed that with all of the commotion happening at the front door he or she would have appeared by now. Maybe Mason was meeting someone for dinner—enough assuming, she finally told herself.

"Who is *us*?" Ansley asked directly, hoping that the answer would allow her to report back to Cleve that Mason did indeed have someone special in his life.

Mason glanced down. "Me and Callie," he explained as if she should have known exactly who he was talking about in the first place.

"Oh," Ansley responded with a sigh. No report needed, unfortunately, but honestly, she wasn't sure if she would have found comfort in having another woman around or if it would have made things even more awkward. "You take your dog out to dinner with you?" she asked without thinking that it might offend him.

"Yeah, is that a problem?" he quizzed. "Do you not like dogs?"

Ansley found it ironic that his mind instantly wandered to whether she liked dogs rather than to her finding it odd that a person would take his dog to dinner with him. The animal didn't seem to be a service dog, but she could be wrong.

"I like dogs just fine," Ansley clarified, but a few moments later when she found herself climbing into Mason's pickup truck, she realized that at least one of her mother's pet peeves had rubbed off onto her.

The truck's cabin smelled like a mixture of sweat, dog, and the strawberry air freshener dangling from the rearview mirror that looked as though it had been there since the vehicle was purchased decades ago.

Callie was perched on the part cloth, part vinyl seat between her and Mason and seemed to be excited about going for a ride. The dog herself didn't appear to smell bad at the moment, but Ansley realized the odor must have sunk in over the years.

As the tires crunched the gravel below the vehicle, Ansley wished she had offered to drive her car instead. It wasn't that she thought her new BMW was better than this old truck, but she was positive that it smelled better. She'd had it detailed over the weekend, inside and out. Although, on second thought, she had to admit that the temporary tire might pose an issue especially on these less than pristine country roads. During the last leg of her drive, she'd noticed that the small tire didn't seem to respond well to the uneven asphalt, and the onslaught of dust and bugs had already done a number on the exterior of the vehicle.

As the truck's high beams illuminated the way down the driveway that Ansley had traveled up less than twenty minutes ago, she wondered why Mason was driving just as slowly as she had when heading toward the house. Her reason for driving cautiously had to do with the unfamiliarity of the surroundings, but he'd probably navigated this dirt path thousands of times.

Reminding herself that she was on vacation with no need to rush around like she always did at home and at work, Ansley made an attempt to push the thought to the back of her mind. Although when the truck's wheels turned onto the first paved road that led toward the town of Oriental, she found herself expecting Mason to push the gas pedal a little further toward the rubber floorboard. She soon realized that he didn't seem to be in any hurry whatsoever even though it was well past an average person's dinnertime. She was actually quite hungry herself since the only food she'd eaten this evening was fruit given to her by the man who'd changed the tire. As they passed a driveway here and there and a deer crossing road sign, she shared her flat tire story with Mason, and the only response she received in return was, "That was mighty kind of him."

It didn't take long for Ansley to determine that Mason was the quiet type, or maybe he just didn't want to talk to her, she also considered.

As she carried on the bulk of the conversation, he would glance at her briefly before shifting his eyes back to the road where bugs were diving into the windshield like steady drops of rain. Every now and then, he would nod his head in agreement with something she said or respond with a short sentence, but he didn't start a single conversation during the entire trip.

When Mason turned the steering wheel to lead the truck into the restaurant parking lot, he wondered if he would have been better off giving Ansley directions to the Oriental Marina and Inn. However, she came across as more of the bed and breakfast type, and there was a handful of those in town from which to choose. The woman had nearly talked his ear off already, and they'd only known each other for thirty or so minutes. She had gone on and on about the mosquitoes hitting the windshield, the man who'd changed her tire, and given more details about the fruit she'd eaten than what he usually shared with customers about the fruit they bought at his market.

Upon arrival at the restaurant, Ansley, for some reason, expected Callie to waltz right in next to Mason. But as soon as he opened the driver's side door, Callie hopped out behind him and headed straight for the tailgate where she leaped into the bed and sat at attention as if in charge of guarding the truck while they ate at Brantley's Village Restaurant.

Out front, the green wooden sign with white lettering which displayed the name of the establishment was illuminated by a lone floodlight and supported by tattered pylons that looked like they might have once held together an old dock.

"You're not afraid Callie will run away?" Ansley inquired as they walked toward the entrance.

"She hasn't run away in the past seventeen years, so I don't expect her to start now," Mason shared as he knocked on the glass door.

As they stood at what appeared to be a locked entrance, Ansley found herself surveying the area. There were only a few other vehicles in the lot and minimal lighting. She had never been to a restaurant where customers had to knock on the door, and even though Oriental was a small town, she couldn't imagine that such would be a standard business practice.

"I think they're closed," Ansley mentioned after discovering the hours posted on the building.

Before Mason could respond, a woman, probably in her fifties, appeared and unlocked the door with a smile on her round face and an apron tied around her rather plump waist.

"Hey, Mason," the lady said in a welcoming tone. "Come on in," she added, waving her hand as though she was directing traffic.

Ansley smiled, but as the waitress held the door for them, she couldn't help but notice that the woman was giving her the once-over. She didn't feel as though this person was judging her, but more so that she was surprised to see her here with Mason.

Before leading them to a high-back booth in the corner of the restaurant, the woman turned the lock on the door behind them, and Ansley tried her best not to show the confusion she was feeling about the whole scenario playing out around her.

Once the waitress took their beverage order and disappeared behind the counter, Ansley figured Mason would say something about the deal with the door and the nearly empty restaurant with low lighting. The seating area was relatively large for a small-town eatery, and thank God they weren't the only customers in the place, she thought, as she spotted people sitting at several of the other tables.

By the time the lady returned with their drinks, Mason hadn't spoken a word about the door. He'd only made mention that Oriental was recognized as the sailing capital of North Carolina and that there were over three thousand boats here, which made sense based on the town—which she recalled Cleve calling a village—being surrounded by so much water. When Ansley asked questions about the bodies of water in the area, Mason gave her a brief geography lesson on the Pamlico Sound, the Neuse River, and the Intracoastal Waterway as well as the creeks and coves that provided sailors shelter from storms.

"I'll give you a moment to glance over the menu," the waitress suggested, leaving one in front of Ansley but not Mason.

When she walked away, Ansley spoke up. "So, I don't find it odd that she didn't give you a menu since you probably eat here often, but what's the deal with knocking on the door?"

"Oh, they're closed for regular business," Mason explained nonchalantly.

Ansley furrowed her brow and spoke slowly. "Yet they let us in, brought us drinks, and gave me a menu," she pointed out.

"Yeah, there's kind of an unwritten rule that farmers and fishermen can show up within an hour or so after sunset, which happens to be after this place turns the sign in the window."

"Why is that?" Ansley probed.

As the questions spilled out, Mason began to wonder if he should have brought Ansley here. For him, it was just the usual place to come after a long day in the fields even though he didn't come here as regularly as Ansley probably assumed based on the menu situation. It might have been best if he had taken her somewhere else where the food and the crowd would be more diverse. About the only thing she had in common with anyone in this place at the present moment was that she was wearing blue jeans. Of course, hers were much cleaner and tighter than anyone else's, and her fancy sweater and knee-high boots had drawn a few looks.

"They know we work until dark, and for the ones of us that don't have a spouse at home who has dinner waiting on the table, they realize we appreciate a home-cooked meal every once in a while."

As his response sank in, Ansley suddenly realized that she and the waitress were the only women in the restaurant. It also explained why everyone else, at this point in their respective days, looked like they could pass for the homeless people she often met when volunteering at the Raleigh Rescue Mission. These people's clothing were worn, stained, and dirty which made sense because they had been working outdoors all day. Some wore caps and others' hair looked about as unkempt as Mason's, but at least he had taken a shower, Ansley could ascertain.

"Well, that's very kind of them to serve you all after hours," she noted.

Mason simply nodded his head in agreement.

"The whole menu might not be available," he warned, "but Celia will let you know."

Celia, the waitress, had introduced herself when she first seated the two of them, and Ansley thought her country accent was to die for. It was much thicker than Mason's although she could tell without a shadow of a doubt that he was raised in the South, too.

A few moments later, Celia showed up and rested her hand atop Ansley's shoulder. "Baby, I had a talk with the cook, and since this is your first time eating here with us, you can order anything your heart desires off that-there menu," she offered with a friendly wink.

Ansley grinned, and she was relieved she'd had the conversation with Mason about the menu because otherwise, she would have thought this woman might be a bit crazy. When she'd asked Mason which dishes were the best, he'd said that she couldn't go wrong but that the seafood was fresh and local, and his personal favorite.

"Thank you," Ansley replied to Celia. "Then, I think I'll have the flounder plate."

"Yes ma'am, you got it. One flounder plate coming right up."

The waitress asked a few more questions about sides and

whatnot. Mason ordered shrimp, and then Ansley felt the need to bring up the subject about staying at his house.

"Mason, don't take this the wrong way," she suggested, "but I don't think it's fair for me to impose on you the way I have by showing up here out of the blue and expecting a place to stay." She didn't want to add that the more she thought about it, the more the idea of spending time in a stranger's home seemed rather careless.

Mason had been somewhat surprised when Ansley had agreed to stay at the log cabin with him and Callie. He'd mainly made the offer to be nice, and now he realized this was possibly his last chance to send her on her way, at least without feeling like a complete jerk. On the drive here, he couldn't help but think of how the last thing he needed was a woman throwing off his routines.

"It's the least I can do for you since my dad sent you all the way to Oriental on a wild goose chase," he responded against his better judgment. "Plus I don't know how to wash dishes so I could use someone to help around the house a little," he suggested with a slight chuckle lining his voice.

Ansley had already taken notice of Mason's dry sense of humor, and even though the comment could be taken as degrading toward women, she didn't expect that he intended it that way. Plus it was probably the most he'd said at one time since they left the house, so she didn't want to give him a hard time about it. His joke actually made her think of Cleve telling her about how differently men used to treat women, and she was thankful that expectations had changed over the years. Even though she didn't mind washing dishes, most likely because she hadn't been forced to as a child, she didn't want any man to expect her to do all of the housework. This reminded her of the date night story Cleve had shared with her about the first meal he'd had with Violet, the evening her father had told him that men don't do housework.

Violet had ever so humbly told me that she was a good cook, but I must say that she drastically underestimated her abilities in the kitchen. When we sat down at her parents' dining room table with all that food lining the center like a buffet at a fancy restaurant, my eyes nearly began to water. Maybe that's because having supper with Violet and her parents made me about as uncomfortable as a pig out of mud, but I'd like to think it was only because the food smelled a bit like I expect the aroma in heaven to resemble.

When I'd pulled the slip of paper from The Date Night Jar that read: Enjoy A Meal Together, *I wasn't sure exactly where or what we'd eat. At the time, Mother had been sitting there with me at our kitchen table, and I asked her what she thought would be best.*

"Well, that's up to Violet's parents, son," she reminded me. "I know they're relatively strict so they might not be comfortable with the two of you dining at a restaurant in town on your own or even with her visiting our house for supper just yet."

Mother was as sweet as a Georgia peach, and the soft sound of her voice resembled her personality. The moment she spoke those words about Violet's parents, I knew me and Violet would end up sitting at a table with her mother and father. Sure enough, that Saturday evening, I found myself in their dining room. Don't get me wrong, if having dinner with Violet meant having her father at the head of the table with his wife sitting across from him, I had decided it was well worth the feeling of butterflies flying around in the pit of my stomach all week long.

Their rectangular table was surrounded by six chairs, and Violet and I had been instructed to sit across from one another in the two chairs closest to the man of the house. I figured he wanted me close by in case he needed to kick me under the table for letting my gaze linger a bit too long on his beautiful daughter.

The other thing that made the dinner a bit awkward was that the other two chairs at the table weren't empty. Father was sitting next to me, and Mother was sitting beside Violet. When I'd made the phone call to ask Violet to have dinner with me, her parents had not only demanded that we eat at their house but also that my parents be invited for the occasion.

Thankfully, my parents and her parents seemed to get along just fine. Coming into the evening, they all four already knew one another due to living in our small village, but I guess you could say they were acquaintances rather than friends. Violet's family's farm produced primarily corn and my family's farm at the time specialized in tobacco. Boy, was tobacco farming hard work! If hell was hotter than working in a tobacco field or a tobacco barn, I didn't want to take any chance at ending up in that place.

"Owen, how are your crops holding up in this dry stretch?" Violet's dad asked Father.

Father shook his head east to west. "If rain don't come soon, we're gonna be up the creek with a paddle but no water."

Everyone at the table other than me and Mother burst into laughter. That was Father's favorite farming joke, one he swore he came up with on his own. Mother and I chuckled like we always did when he told it, not because we thought it was funny but because it was corny and we enjoyed watching other people's reactions. Some we figured just gave the joke a courtesy laugh and others actually found it amusing. In a way, I guess it was, and that evening I thanked God that Father's dry sense of humor eased some of the tension previously present at the table.

The best part of the meal, other than my calculated eye contact with Violet's charming blue eyes, was that she'd made my favorites. When we'd had the conversation on the phone to make plans for this particular evening, she had been so thoughtful to ask what foods I fancied most. At that moment, I had imagined her father in the background rolling his eyes as we talked briefly on the rotary phones in the living areas of our respective homes. That was the downside of telephone conversations back then, everybody within earshot heard every word of your business. Which when it comes *to two hormonal teenagers falling for one another, well, I guess in hindsight it wasn't necessarily a bad thing. Of course, as mine and Violet's relationship progressed, we hated that our parents overheard every conversation we had on the telephone. At home, I'd stretch that chord as far as it would go and talk as softly as possible without attracting too much attention. Violet would tell me that she often did the same, but her father would make sure to remind her that she wasn't allowed to whisper on the phone, so she didn't dare break that rule.*

"What do you think of this meal Violet prepared for us?" her mother asked me as I swallowed a bite.

I can't say that I'd eaten many meals back then that I didn't enjoy. Food was a bit harder to come by in those days especially when the fields were dry and the harvest was less than plentiful. Those were the times that the table often looked bare come mealtime. So, needless to point out, we delighted in whatever Mother put on the table, and the same rang true on the rare occasion that I ate a meal at a friend's house. As for the food Violet prepared—fried chicken, homemade French fries, string beans, and cornbread—I had nothing but the best compliments.

"It's quite delicious," I applauded with a grin as genuine as the table made of hardwood on which our plates were resting.

My parents verbally agreed, and we each made sure to thank Violet and her parents several times before, during, and after dinner. I did my best to use my manners when it came to using the utensils that had been provided even though Mr. Horne was gnawing at his chicken like a hungry dog on a bone. Like me and Father, he'd been hard at work all day. The only day of the week we took off from farming was Sunday, but on Saturdays, we did sometimes finish up our work before the sun fell out of the sky. Of course, that all depended on what needed to be done, so needless to say I busted my butt during the week in hopes of a shorter day on the weekend.

"Our Violet will make some man a good wife one day," her father guaranteed. "Not only can she cook, but she pulls her weight taking care of the house and a woman's responsibilities on the farm, too."

The way he said some man stuck out to me like a sore thumb, but I tried my level best not to wear my emotions on my sleeve. I didn't expect him to have penciled me in as Violet's husband quite yet since we'd just begun courting, but the comment almost came across as though he didn't think I was good enough for her. In his defense, he probably didn't think any boy was good enough for his one and only daughter.

I sure was glad when Father chimed in and said, "I think you are absolutely right, Mr. Horne; we've heard nothing but great things about your daughter." Father paused to acknowledge Violet's mother with a quick glance and a nod. "We sure are proud of both Cleve and Violet for completing high school," he declared.

I loved to hear our names side by side in a sentence, and it was a big deal that we'd both finished high school. In that era, college really wasn't an option for most high school graduates, and only about half of the classmates I'd started grade school with actually earned a diploma. The rest had dropped out at one point or another along the way but not because they were losers like most of the dropouts today. Instead of quitting to contaminate their bodies with drugs, alcohol, promiscuous sex, and so on, the kids that quit school back then used their abled-bodies to work on the farms, in the boats, at the lumberyards, and other places where they could help make the money needed for their families to survive.

That night after dessert—chocolate pie with meringue floating on top like an edible cloud—Violet and her mother excused themselves from the table to clean up and wash dishes. Mother offered to help, and the ladies allowed her to bring some of the dishes over to the sink as Violet began to scrub them. Even though the dinner table was in the small dining room, we could see right through into the kitchen. Using my manners, I asked the ladies if they needed any help in the kitchen, and in that instant Violet's father shot me a look I've never forgotten.

"In this house, men don't do housework," he declared.

I could feel my face turning red, but thank God, Violet didn't turn around to look at me. Neither of our mothers reacted to the comment either. They just went on about their chores as if he'd made a common remark that had nothing to do with them or what they were doing. Father pursed his lips and ever so slowly shook his head up and down even though both me and him had helped Mother with housework on many occasions. It wasn't something we did on a daily basis, but we weren't too proud to scrape crumbs into the trashcan or put away a dish. In hindsight, I don't think Father was agreeing with Violet's daddy, I think he was merely showing his respect for the man's beliefs.

"Let's retire to the living room," her father suggested next.

To be honest, I didn't want to leave the room we were in because I wanted to be in Violet's presence, but at the same time it might have been the best thing for me at the moment. The entire time she'd been standing with her back to me at the sink, I'd been very carefully allowing my eyes to dart in her direction when Father and her father were caught up in conversation. I inserted a comment here and there, but as the waistline of her blue dress swished back and forth to the rhythm of her motions in the dishwater, I couldn't help but want to stare at her like the television set the three of us men ended up in front of moments later. Every feature on Violet's body was like a magnet to my eyes, always had been. She had the same effect on all the other boys who had ever set eyes on her, but I tried to block out thoughts of any of them ogling her.

When Celia set Ansley's and Mason's meals on the rectangular table between the two of them, Ansley realized she'd only been half present since the last time Celia was at the table. Thankfully, Mason hadn't said much—not that Ansley expected him to—as her mind had drifted to his father's date night jar story. She imagined he'd probably enjoyed the lull in what had mostly been a one-sided conversation.

When he closed his eyes to give thanks for his food, Ansley figured, she took in her first steady look at Mason Fields. Based on Cleve's age, she had expected his son to be about the age of the waitress, but, if guessing, she would say that Mason was only a few years older than she. She didn't really find him attractive, but he was ruggedly handsome in his own way. His hair was a mess, and his face looked like it hadn't been shaven in a week. His eyes were mysterious like his father's, but they were a bluish-gray color rather than brown.

As they began to eat, Ansley felt the need to make sure that Mason knew she wouldn't be a nuisance while she was in town. "I'll make sure to stay out of your way while I'm here," she promised as she rested her fork on her plate.

He shook his head. "Callie and I will be out in the fields all day, so you'll have the house to yourself," he ensured.

"What is there to do around here?" she probed.

Mason smiled. "Not a whole lot if you're expecting excitement like what you could find in Myrtle Beach." On their trek into town, she hadn't really explained why she'd decided to override plans to visit one of the South's favorite tourist destinations, but it was another subject that had come up.

"What would you do if you were here on vacation?" she queried.

Mason fiddled with his napkin then tossed it onto the table next to his round plate. "I'd probably sit on the porch and take in the view."

"Is it a good one?" Ansley probed, noticing but trying not to eye the scrunched up napkin. If her mother were here, she would be having a panic attack right about now. Ansley's napkin was resting on her lap, *where napkins are meant to be kept*, she'd heard her mom say hundreds of times.

"It's magnificent and different every single day."

Ansley nodded her head. "That sounds pleasant."

She waited for a response from Mason, but he didn't say anything, so then she found herself wondering what the view from his porch might look like. Earlier, it had been too dark to take in the surroundings.

"What would you do next?" Ansley finally asked.

"Well, there's a small lake on the property, so I'd probably spend a lot of time out there," he imagined. "You're welcome to venture out that way if you'd like. There's a canoe you can help yourself to, and I have fishing gear in the barn, but you don't strike me as the fishing type."

"I've fished before," Ansley combatted, deciding against telling him that the only fishing she'd attempted had been at a booth at the state fair where Wanda had taken her one time when her parents were out of town—another secret she'd kept from her mother all these years.

Mason was surprised to hear that she'd fished, but he decided not to ask what type of fishing she'd done like he would have if she were a guy. "Well, the rods and lures are out there if you get the urge to cast a line." He paused, highly doubting she'd lay a finger on any of the equipment.

"Anything else?" she probed.

"You can also pick strawberries if that interests you," he offered. "Strawberry season on the farm officially started today, so there's plenty to choose from."

"I might have to try some of your suggestions," she said thinking of how each of the activities he mentioned would require a shower afterward. Thankfully, she had skipped out on having her nails done with her mother earlier today.

"If you want to venture into the village, you might enjoy walking along the waterfront or taking a historical tour." For some reason, a sign stating that Pamlico County Schools offered the first motorized school bus service in 1917 popped into his mind. "There's also a handful of restaurants down here and some shopping but not much."

Ansley couldn't help but think that these things seemed more like her style. "All of that sounds fun," she said.

As their late evening meal wound down, Mason didn't offer any other suggestions. When they walked out to the truck, Celia locked the door behind them, and Ansley shrugged when she spotted Callie sitting in pretty much the same spot where they'd left her.

Mason figured Ansley would talk most of the ride home, and she did. At least she didn't ramble on and on about people he didn't know, he decided. For the most part, her conversation had a purpose, and he had to admit that he found her relatively interesting. She was easy on the eye too, but, unfortunately, not really his type. A little too proper, he figured, and probably uppity. He'd noticed how she looked at his napkin when he tossed it on the table and how, while eating, she resembled a robot more than a human. Her posture was as straight as a two-by-four, and everything appeared to have a specific place—silverware, her hands, her beverage, condiments.

Back at the house, Mason helped unload Ansley's vehicle. Like the gentleman she'd met on the side of the road in Kinston, he wouldn't allow her to carry any of the luggage. Once inside, he showed her to a bedroom that she figured used to be his childhood room. She thought he might mention as much, but he didn't. He merely flipped on the light switch, pointed, and said, "There's your bed."

It quickly became apparent that Mason didn't care to stay up and chit chat. Ansley respected the fact that he would have farm work to attend to early tomorrow morning, so she didn't expect a tour of the house or ask him questions about where to locate certain things. But she did appreciate that he took a moment to show her where to find the bathroom as well as a towel and a washcloth for when she needed to shower. After that, each of them retired to their respective bedrooms.

Concerned that the sound of water spitting from the showerhead might keep Mason awake, Ansley decided she would wait until morning to shower even though she usually preferred to wash-up before climbing into bed. If, as a child, her mother had ever caught her beneath clean sheets without a bath, she would have had a conniption.

As Ansley lay in bed listening to the critters outside her window, she couldn't help but wonder how she would sleep in a foreign place with a somewhat strange man and a dog just down the hallway. She also wondered what she would do to occupy her time tomorrow. Even with these thoughts rummaging through her mind, she couldn't help but notice that the sheets rubbing against her bare feet were not very soft, or fresh for that matter, but she tried to disregard those concerns.

Lying in bed with the moonlight peeking in between the curtains, Mason wondered why Ansley had come to Oriental. Wondered what she wanted. He didn't feel too uncomfortable with her being in the house; he just wasn't sure how the days ahead would play out. He even speculated that once her car had a new tire put on, she might decide to head back to Raleigh or maybe even venture off to Myrtle Beach where she could find more entertainment options than what she would soon come to realize this place had to offer. She could easily visit every shop downtown in one afternoon, he knew.

As Mason and Ansley drifted off to sleep in separate bedrooms, what neither of them realized, is that they'd both wake up to a surprise tomorrow morning.

8

ason's morning routine was completely thrown off the very first day he woke up with Ansley Stone in the house. Last night, he'd had enough sense to know things would be different with her here, but he hadn't imagined waking up more than an hour earlier than usual.

When Mason climbed off his mattress and into his clothes, Callie glared at him from her soft bed on the hardwood floor as if he was insane. It was apparent that his companion had an internal time clock.

"What, girl?" he whispered being cognizant that Ansley was probably still sound asleep in the bedroom down the hallway.

Mason had something on his mind that he felt a strong desire to take care of before his regular day began. It had been the last thing he'd contemplated before falling asleep and the first thought that hit him this morning.

Callie trotted into the kitchen behind Mason where he pulled on his boots and headed out the back door after starting the coffeemaker. Callie made a stop at her bowl, glanced up at Mason who was holding open the door, and then looked back down at the empty container.

"Come on," he encouraged waving his hand. "We'll eat later."

Somewhat reluctantly, Callie followed suit.

A little more than an hour later, Mason and his sidekick waltzed back into the dark house. He gently filled her bowl and even tossed Callie a treat for following along with his plan, then he poured himself a cup of coffee. Glancing at the clock, he realized it was nearly the exact time that he would have had coffee on any other morning, but today he already felt tired from rising early, and he recognized he might need a second cup before heading up to the market.

As he and Callie wandered onto the front porch in the dark, he made sure to pull the door shut slowly so that he wouldn't wake Ansley. Doors seemed to have a way of rattling the walls of a whole house. Then, when he and Callie began to walk toward the rocking chair, she stopped in her tracks, and Mason immediately sensed that something was off-kilter.

A moment later, a voice drifted across the porch. "Good morning," Ansley greeted, holding a coffee mug in her left hand.

Startled, Mason's mug began to dance in his fingers, and a moment later a splotch landed in the same spot on the porch where Ansley had temporarily set The Date Night Jar last night. Now, the jar was on the dresser in her room since Mason hadn't seemed to want to have anything to do with it after finding out his father was alive.

"Mornin'," Mason obliged, completely surprised to find her sitting on the front porch—occupying *his* rocking chair.

"I'm sorry to have caught you off guard," Ansley apologized, realizing she had caused him to spill the coffee. "I would have said something sooner, but the moment you walked out the door, I was in the middle of taking a sip of my coffee."

After recognizing Ansley's voice, Callie wandered over to her regular spot next to the chair as if Mason were the one rocking, and as Mason watched, he shook his head when Ansley reached down to pet the soft fur on Callie's neck. *Traitor*, he thought, sitting his coffee cup on the wooden rail at his waist.

"That's okay," Mason said. "I just didn't expect anyone to be out here."

"I guess not," Ansley agreed, "but last night, you mentioned the views that could be taken in out here, so I wanted to make sure I didn't miss the sunrise."

Mason smirked. "It might be the best view of all."

"How about the sunset?" Ansley challenged.

"That might be the best one, too."

Ansley laughed in the darkness, and Mason could see her just well enough now to catch a glimpse of her perfectly aligned teeth. His, on the other hand, weren't quite as straight or white, but they weren't necessarily in bad shape either.

"Did I take your seat?" Ansley asked, suddenly putting it together that this was the direction in which Mason was heading when she'd caused him to spill some of his coffee. There weren't any other chairs on this side of the porch.

"It's okay," he replied. "I'll get the one from over here," he said as he walked to the opposite side of the porch.

When he set a second rocking chair on the other side of Callie, Mason's mind shifted to the two women he had thought about yesterday while sitting out here alone. Obviously, Ansley wasn't like the one who'd wanted to stay in bed all day, at least not based on this first impression, but he was fairly confident her word count would be able to rival the lady who'd talked his and Callie's ears off.

"How long have you been out here?" Mason asked while settling into an unfamiliar position. He wasn't necessarily upset that Ansley had taken the best seat in the house—or, technically, outside of the house—but if she was going to be out here with him, he had to admit that he wished there was a polite way he could ask her to switch rocking chairs.

"Long enough to know that I need to say thank you," she

uttered with an appreciative grin covering a face that had yet to be touched with makeup.

At first, Mason furrowed his brow, but then it hit him that she must have been watching him this morning.

"For changing my tire," Ansley added as she took another swig from her mug.

Mason stared at his bootstrings. "Oh, you caught me red-handed, huh?"

"Sure did."

"So if you were sittin' up here the whole time while I was changing your tire, why didn't you say something?"

Earlier, while kneeling on the ground next to Ansley's vehicle, a battery-operated spotlight had allowed him to see through the dark as he jacked up the car and made the switch. Callie had sat guard, but she hadn't done that great of a job, Mason now realized since she had failed to spot Ansley sitting on the front porch.

Ansley shrugged her shoulders. "I usually try not to interrupt a man while he's working," she said. Honestly, one of the reasons she'd chosen not to say anything was because she hadn't wanted to startle him, but so much for accomplishing that this morning, she recognized after the coffee incident. Looking down now, she noticed a few wet splotches on his dirty boots. "Plus, I'm not much of a talker in the mornings," she added.

"Really?" Mason snickered, letting the words slip out of his mouth as rapidly as the lug wrench had spun this morning after he loosened the lugs from the spare tire.

Ansley laughed out loud and nearly spewed her coffee all over the porch railing between them and wide-open space.

"I didn't mean it like that," he blurted out promptly, trying to cover himself.

"It's okay," Ansley encouraged. "I know I talked a lot last night."

Mason's pinched cheeks lifted as he shook his head slowly. "Kind of," he agreed.

Ansley could feel Mason loosening up just a bit, and she didn't mind that it was somewhat at her expense.

"You weren't talking much," she pointed out. "So I didn't want things to be more awkward than they already were for either of us," she mentioned.

Mason nodded, and it was at that moment that both he and Ansley recognized the first signs of the morning sun beginning to filter through the trees at the edge of the field. Neither muttered another word for quite some time as the glow began to wake up hundreds of rows of strawberry plants.

Ansley held a peaceful grin on her face as she took in the view for the first time—a scene that Mason was able to savor every morning of his life. She had to admit that she was a bit jealous especially as she watched two splotchy fawns follow their mother across the field, their scrawny legs toddling as if they were stepping on shards of glass. The little ones couldn't have been walking for more than a week or so, Ansley assumed, as she found herself nearly breathless at the sight.

The three animals would stop every so often to nibble, and then at the slightest sound, their necks would jolt upward, and they'd cautiously survey the surroundings. When the deer gazed toward the porch from a distance, she wondered if they could see her, Mason, and Callie watching them. Ansley recognized that Callie had also spotted the deer, probably well before she had, but Callie didn't seem very interested in the creatures. It was like her years on the farm had brought about a pearl of particular wisdom that reminded her to watch the animals rather than bark or run after them like many dogs would.

Mason had taken note of the doe with her fawns a few moments before Ansley. He knew this because when he was about to point them out, he saw her glance in that direction, and then the edges of her lips rose just a hair when she made them out in the distance. Nature, in the form of animals, was always present out here in the country especially in the early mornings and late evenings when human activity was minimal. On the days when Mason didn't see deer, he would spot rabbits or a fox or, on rare occasion, a black bear. A wide variety of birds were always chirping early in the mornings even before the sun rose, but once the horizon became visible, he would watch them fly about as if they were putting on an aerial song and dance show.

Surprisingly, Mason was the one who eventually broke the silence. The bottom of his coffee mug had become as bare as a dry field in the heat of the summer, and soon he would have pickers and customers expecting him at the roadside market. He hadn't felt a strong desire to leave the porch view for a refill, but now he figured he might fill an enclosed container and take it with him to sip on as his workday began.

"Well, it's time for me and Callie to head up to the market," he announced.

"The one up by the road?" Ansley inquired. She had noticed it before turning into Mason's driveway last night and then again when the two of them ventured out for dinner—the three of them, if she counted Callie. Before now, the market hadn't come up in conversation, or better put, she hadn't asked about it.

"Yes."

"Do you spend most of your day there?" Ansley inquired, interested in knowing more about a farmer's daily routines, especially as she overlooked these flowing fields where so many stories had transpired.

"The market is where we all meet in the mornings, and everyone disperses from there," Mason informed her. "I end up all over the farm, doing whatever needs to be done."

Ansley suddenly found herself relating his responsibilities on the farm to her own at the hospital. She imagined that like her, his goal was to take care of the tasks that only he had the expertise to handle, and delegate the remaining duties to others. In her field of work, that meant utilizing physician's assistants, nurses, and a variety of other people who were amazing at their jobs. Some of them were smarter than she, and it definitely took the whole team to take care of the many needs of patients.

"I see," Ansley responded. "Well, I won't hold you up."

"I'll see you later on then," Mason mentioned.

"I might still be sitting right here when you get home from work," she declared, letting her eyebrows rise with the idea.

Mason smirked. "I told you," he reminded her, glancing out over the horizon where the air was crisp and clear.

"Thank you," Ansley offered.

"Thank God, he's the one who made the view," Mason told her. "Well, the best part of it anyway."

"I'll make sure to do that," Ansley replied. "However, I was actually thanking you again for changing my tire."

"My privilege," Mason said sincerely. Where he came from and the way he was raised, helping others was merely a way of life. Plus, if she wanted to leave, he wanted her to have that opportunity.

"By the way, how much do I owe you?"

With his back to Ansley as he began to walk toward the door, Mason spoke over his shoulder. "I'll add it to your bill at the end of your stay," he proposed with a grin.

Ansley breathed out a laugh. There went his dry sense of humor again. "That's perfect," she agreed as he neared the door with Callie in tow. "And," she wondered aloud as he reached for the door handle, "where in the world did you get a new tire at such an early hour?" she inquired. The thought had been baffling her ever since she'd watched his pickup pull into the driveway this morning then come to a halt next to her vehicle, where he parked and hoisted the tire from the truck bed.

"How about I'll tell you over dinner?" he asked.

"Fair enough," she said at the moment without thinking much about the proposal. "Sounds like a plan."

As Mason and Callie disappeared into the house, Ansley began to wonder what just happened. Were they supposed to have dinner together based on the fact that she was staying at his home? Maybe. Or had Mason Fields just asked her on a date?

She didn't get the vibe from him that he was interested in that way, and she wasn't interested in him like that either. Although she had to admit that after what he'd done for her this morning, maybe she had been quick to judge him last night. Only time would tell, she figured, as she heard an engine start in the distance, and in a matter of moments a four-wheeler whizzed into view with Callie trotting along beside it. Ansley kept her eyes on the two of them until the dust settled and she could no longer hear the buzz of the motor.

A few minutes later, she glanced down when her phone dinged. The text message was from her mother, and it included a photo of a cute guy.

As Ansley studied the picture and the message, she quickly figured out who he was and why her mother sent the image. The good-looking man with a boyish face was the lawyer that her mom wanted to set her up with—had set her up with—kind of, anyway.

What time should Price pick you up this evening??? the message read.

Nibbling on her knuckle, Ansley was grinning at the same time. She set the phone down on the arm of the rocker. Then picked it back up. Then set it down again.

Price, she thought, what kind of name was that? When she'd first heard it come out of her mother's mouth yesterday, she had laughed out loud, and her mother had scolded her for poking fun at her future husband's name. Of course, in her mother's eyes, every man she attempted to set her up with was her future husband. Ansley had to admit, though, this was the first attractive guy that her mother had ever picked out. Some of the others were decent, but this man was as close to a ten as any of the men whom she had scrolled past on the dating website that Cleve liked to tease her about.

Thinking of the site, she reached for her phone and began to open the app to find out if she had received any new interests. She then decided she didn't want to bother with men on her vacation. The dating site hadn't worked up until this point so what was the use in wasting her time on it while here in Oriental. Plus, she already had a date tonight, she reminded herself, laughing for her own amusement. Two dates, technically, she remembered, laughing harder now. One with a man named Price whom she had never met and one with Mason whom she'd first met last night. How odd, she thought to herself. Of course, dinner with Mason wasn't really a date. They'd had dinner last night, and she hadn't considered that a date. Just an outing with a new friend, she guessed, was the best way to put it.

But, Price. She could pack up her things now, hop in her car that had a newly installed tire, and be back in Raleigh in time to prepare for a date with a sexy, successful man.

She reached for her phone and began to type with her thumbs. When she looked up, she realized that daylight was now in full effect and she could see people starting to wander into the fields that surrounded the log cabin. She assumed that they were hired workers rather than customers, but she didn't know for sure. They were all moving fast like ants on a mission.

Within thirty seconds of the time that Ansley touched the send button, her phone began to ring. It was her mother; of course, Ansley should have known that responding would signal to her mother that she was awake which meant she would call since she didn't care much for texting.

"Hello, Mother," she answered as she watched the pickers in the fields begin to fill their buckets with strawberries. They weren't close enough for her to have a conversation with, but if she yelled, they'd probably be able to hear her voice. She looked around for Mason, but she didn't see him anywhere.

"Ansley, what time should Price pick you up?" her mother inquired.

At the sound of her mother speaking the lawyer's name again, she remembered previously asking, "Price is his last name, right?" Her mother had gone on to tell her that Price was the man's first name and that it was a family name passed down for three generations, making his full name Price Wayne Johnson, III. He was an heir in a prominent line of attorneys, her mother made sure to add.

"Mom, I'm in—" Ansley halted in midsentence, remembering at the last second that her mother had no clue of her whereabouts at the time being.

"You're in what, Ansley?" her mother questioned, then paused, making it obvious that she was waiting for a response. When she didn't get one within the normal amount of time, she huffed, "Don't tell me you're in love with someone else—it's the man who was at your house yesterday morning, isn't it?"

Ansley giggled. "Mom, you searched the house high and low for that man, and you didn't find him, remember?" What a funny moment that had made.

"That doesn't mean that he wasn't there before I arrived," she concluded.

In the distance, the spitting sound of a tractor coming to life became apparent. Ansley wasn't sure if she'd heard it start or if it had just now become close enough to register in her eardrums.

"Mom, I can't go out with Price this evening," she conveyed bluntly.

"How come?"

As Ansley searched for an appropriate answer, she watched the old tractor come into sight as it made its way around the outskirts of one of the fields, and she was almost positive that Mason was the one behind the large round steering wheel. She recognized the button-up flannel shirt—blue this time—that he was wearing when he'd been sitting next to her. He'd also had on a pair of jeans that appeared to have seen better days, but from her vantage point, she couldn't really see those at the moment.

"I'm busy," she said simply.

"Doing what?" her mother interrogated. "And what is that awful noise?"

Attempting to cover the phone's mouthpiece with her fingers, Ansley rose to her feet and walked across the porch toward the door.

"Is that a tractor?" her mother inquired. "Where in God's name are you, Ansley?"

Ansley made it safely into the house before the roar of the tractor became more prominent. She could still hear it through the walls of the house, but she was almost certain that her mother could no longer hear the engine on the other end of the line.

"Are you shacking up with a farmer?"

Ansley nearly dropped the phone. *Yes*, she thought about blurting out just to elicit a response from her mother.

"No, Mother, I am not shacking up with anyone," she clarified. "Listen, I am free this weekend. Why don't you ask Price if he would like to take me out for dinner Saturday evening?"

Her mother's voice suddenly became cheerful. "I knew you'd come around," she acknowledged. "You just better hope he is free, and that come Saturday he is still single. A lot can happen in a week's time, you know?"

9

When Ansley was finally able to get her mother off the phone, she dialed the number to the hospital to check in on her patients. As she imagined might be the case, the nurse who answered the phone informed Ansley that her colleague Dr. Tanya Roman was currently in with a patient, but that she'd have her give Ansley a call back at her earliest convenience.

Dr. Tanya Roman pushed open the door that led into Cleve Fields' room and found him as still as a statue, his eyelids closed. Sometimes, patients in this state appeared dead, but the fortunate aspect about them being hooked up to medical monitoring equipment was that it not only displayed vital signs, but the system would also alert staff if a patient was flatlining or having complications that would require attention.

Nearing Cleve's bedside, Dr. Roman made sure to stand back far enough where she couldn't reach him and, more importantly, where he couldn't reach her. She had heard stories of the fake sleeping trick before, and she wasn't going to end up being the talk of the hospital for not following protocol. This man frightened her even though Dr. Stone swore he was as harmless as a baby kitten.

Over the years, Ansley had earned her trust regarding just about anything and everything related to the medical field, but Tanya didn't trust a single patient in this unit, and that's where she and Ansley differed. While Dr. Stone saw each of these men as patients first and prisoners second, she saw them as prisoners first and patients second. There was a reason why men like Cleve Fields were handcuffed to the railing on either side of their bed. They had done something terribly wrong, and although they had every right to the best medical attention available, they had to be treated differently in some regards than patients whose rooms weren't watched around the clock by prison guards. Therefore, in this hospital on the prison grounds, every patient posed a potential threat.

"Mr. Fields," Dr. Roman called out.

With an electronic tablet in her hand, she waited a moment for a response, but noticing that his body didn't even flinch at the sound of her voice, she spoke his name once again.

Ever since Ansley left for vacation, Tanya had been absolutely swamped, and this was only day two of her filling Dr. Stone's shoes. The nurses had been coming to her with more questions than usual, and the patients seemed to have required way more attention. Of course, the hospital had brought in a doctor to assist her during Ansley's absence, but he wasn't familiar with the charts, the staff, or the routines. He was doing an excellent job so far, but most all of the responsibility was weighing on her shoulders, and she truly believed she was thriving under pressure.

On a typical day at the hospital, she and Ansley basically split the patient workload. They would come to each other from time to time for a different perspective, but other than that they each flew solo and made their own decisions. On paper, Ansley was the lead doctor on the floor although she rarely pulled that card, and

Tanya was thankful for that. The two of them had always gotten along just fine, but she had been trying to get Ansley to loosen up for as long as she could remember. She often asked Ansley to join her and some of their coworkers for drinks after shifts, but Ansley always found a reason to decline. She would say she needed to take care of things at home, wanted to stay after hours to catch up on paperwork, or visited with Cleve—with whom Tanya was becoming frustrated at the moment.

Even when awake, Cleve had been giving her the cold shoulder since Ansley left for Myrtle Beach, and she had the suspicion that he was only pretending to be asleep right now. She finally decided she didn't have time for his games, so she walked out the door without having a conversation with her patient for the time being. Later, she would make sure to have a nurse check in on him. Mr. Fields gave her the creeps anyway since he reminded her of one of the old rich men who used to frequent the gentleman's club where she danced during college. When that man would tip her for a private dance, he would always slide the cash beneath one of her straps and let his fingers linger on her skin just a little too long.

Tanya had always chosen to be an open book about her time spent as an exotic dancer, but she could tell that those conversations made Ansley uncomfortable. She really did wish Ansley would let her take her out for a night on the town sometime. The woman seemed to have very little going on in her personal life, unfortunately, and this thought sparked Tanya to wonder what Ansley was up to in Myrtle Beach. She figured her coworker was one of those women who would probably spend the evening sitting on a hotel balcony with a book rather than enjoying the nightlife. Oh well, she concluded, at least she had finally taken a vacation. When Ansley had first come to her and said she was taking a trip, Tanya nearly fainted. Most physicians put in long hours, but in her eyes Ansley was the definition of a workaholic. As long as the two of them had worked together, she had never known Ansley to take off more than a day here and there.

As soon as Tanya stepped back into the quiet hallway, a nurse handed her a note: *Please call Dr. Stone with an update on her patients.*

Once the nurse disappeared around the next corner, Tanya grinned and shook her head.

Mason spent almost two hours on the tractor before returning to the roadside market. One chore he often took care of during the early morning hours, after attaching the vacuum to the tractor, was navigating through the field rows to suck bugs off the strawberry plants. This particular accessory had proven to be one of his favorite because he felt like it helped reduce the amount of pesticides farmers were spraying on crops. Of course, it wasn't always one hundred percent effective, but overall he believed it made a noticeable difference. On his farm, he also made sure to keep all the areas around and between the fields as clean as possible, including the ditches. Weeds attracted bugs about as much as a porch light, and this thought reminded him again that he needed to replace the bulb above his front door.

The aspect of being up at the market that Mason disliked was dealing with the customers. He far more enjoyed working alone in the fields. The people buying fruits and vegetables wanted to talk and give their opinions, and ultimately, he felt like many of them were wasting his time. That's why instead of hiring an employee to run the market, all sales were based on the honor system. Each item was clearly labeled with a price, and there was a locked bucket where customers could drop money. Most locals were accustomed to this setup, so they always brought cash including correct change, and there were several large signs in the shop for new customers to read that explained the process. On the counter by the cash register which rarely got touched, there was a walkie-talkie available, for buyers who did need change, to call Mason for assistance which is what had brought him to the market now.

"Young man, I could have just walked out of here with these items and no one would have ever known," an older lady with gray hair and thick glasses informed Mason as he placed change for a fifty-dollar bill into her open palm.

When he had first walked in with dusty boots and a ring of sweat around his collar, she had shared with him that she was in town from Pennsylvania visiting her sister. She told him all about the bus ride here and the plans she'd made for her stay in Oriental.

"Most people around here are honest, ma'am," he explained.

"The way teenagers are these days, you better install cameras in here," she said, glancing at the four corners where the ceiling met the walls.

"It's never been an issue," Mason shared. "And I doubt that fruits and vegetables and so forth are at the top of a thief's list."

"They'll rob you blind," she concluded as if she hadn't processed a single word he'd uttered.

"Thank you for your business," he acknowledged walking toward the door, not only with the intention of opening it for her but also to invite her to leave so he could return to more pressing matters.

After a few more pieces of advice about theft prevention, the lady eventually waddled to her car and drove away.

After unpacking her luggage, Ansley took a long, hot shower. She'd been pretty tired last night, so she hadn't taken the time to remove all the items from her bags and put them into the drawers of the dresser that Mason said she was welcomed to use. Amid that process, she'd eyed The Date Night Jar off and on before heading into the bathroom, and she found herself wondering if it would sit there all week or if Mason would eventually decide to take it back.

Ansley nearly opted for a relaxing soak in the antique-looking claw foot bathtub, but instead decided to wrap the shower curtain around the metal rod that circled the tub. She'd always liked bathtubs like this that sat out in the middle of the floor rather than being attached to a wall. A silver pipe that led from the lower nozzle to the stationary showerhead was completely exposed, and it appeared to have been added on at some point. She wasn't a plumber by any stretch of the imagination, but it looked as though Mason may have tackled the task himself. The shower worked just fine other than the water stream being a tad weak and the piping assembly a little wobbly. On the floor, a towel which appeared to have been there for quite some time was positioned to absorb water from a slow drip at the base of the add-on feature.

Throughout the morning, Ansley had begun to notice little nuances about the house that revealed its age. In the bathroom, there wasn't an exhaust fan, so the area seemed even hotter than a standard bathroom after trapping the steam in the confined space. The mirror quickly became covered with fog, and to avoid sweating which would defeat the purpose of taking a shower in the first place, she cracked open the bathroom door and peeked into the hallway.

With a towel draped around her otherwise naked body, she listened for a few moments to make sure Mason hadn't come back into the house then made a beeline to the bedroom where she'd slept relatively soundly last night. After closing the door and twisting the lock, she fell back onto the bed figuring the ceiling fan would cool off her body a bit. But, upon doing so, she realized there was no ceiling fan in the room, only a small light fixture that she hadn't even taken notice of last night.

Once dressed, she applied a light covering of makeup and ventured back out to the porch with a book in her hand. The pickers were as busy as bees in the fields, and using the tractor, Mason appeared to be spraying something on the crops. She figured it must be pesticides which made her second-guess an earlier thought when she'd considered picking and eating strawberries at some point today. At the grocery store back home, she typically only bought pesticide-free, organic produce.

About the same time when she had watched Mason steer the tractor through a small opening in the tree line that apparently led back to the roadside market, Ansley put away her book. Inside, she took a moment to remove her flip flops and replace them with tennis shoes. On her way out the back door, she realized that the porch did indeed wrap entirely around the log cabin. After taking in the rearview of the cabin, which was gorgeous in a very natural way, she walked down the dusty driveway in a direction she had yet taken. This was the way Mason mentioned would lead to the pond. She wasn't quite sure what she would do once she made it there, but she at least wanted to take a look.

The dusty path beneath her feet wound around a couple of bends, and there were narrow openings between the lines of pine trees on either side that led into fields of crops. It was apparent by the marks on the ground that the tractor frequently traveled in and out of these spots.

It took several minutes to make it to another quaint opening through which water became visible as she neared it. Upon entering through a thicket of trees on either side of the walkway, the area opened up vastly, and with her mouth agape, she became pleasantly surprised as she took in the view.

The body of water in front of her looked more like a private lake than the tiny pond in which she envisioned Mason floating in a stable canoe with a fishing pole occupying his hands. Now that she was here, she could imagine how kayaking around the area would make for a good workout.

As she took a few steps toward the edge of the water, where it was evident the grass had been well-maintained, she estimated the circumference of the pond to be at least three acres. In some areas weeping willow trees dangled over the surface while other parts of the shoreline were grassy or sandy.

As her eyes wandered, she spotted a canoe on the bank with two wooden oars sticking out one end. On the opposite side of the pond, a small dock jutted out into the water. Near to where she was standing, an old wooden bench nestled at the water's edge was close enough where she could imagine sitting and dangling her feet into the pond. After having the thought, she decided to take a seat there and untie her shoestrings. The water felt nice and cool on her bare toes, and she just sat there for what seemed like an hour as she swallowed in this surreal atmosphere in the middle of nowhere.

Wildlife was ever so present. The calls of bullfrogs, which Ansley imagined were probably much more prominent at night, echoed throughout the area. Crickets and grasshoppers were dancing around the base of the bench, and the splashing sound made by fish jumping every so often caused her head to jolt in the direction of the splash. Birds hovered above the water, some dipping down for a drink or making an attempt to catch one of those acrobatic fish she was enjoying. In addition to the expected animals and critters, Ansley's mouth suddenly dropped open when she spotted a furry creature floating across the pond on the opposite side. It was too far away to make out clearly, but it had to be either a beaver or an otter. Neither of which she had ever seen in the wild, only at the aquariums where Wanda had taken her when she was growing up.

Taking in this magical scene reminded Ansley once again of another one of Cleve's date night jar stories. For a moment, she wondered if this pond was where the date had taken place, but then she realized the setting of his story was much different, and it was at Violet's family's property, she eventually remembered.

When I pulled the scroll from the jar that read: Enjoy A Day At The Water, my heart skipped a beat. Being a teenage boy, I instantly imagined Violet in a bathing suit. Of course, bathing suits in those days were made up of much more material than they are now. Violet's mother made all of her daughter's clothing, so being as conservative as her parents were, I should have known that her swimsuit would pretty much cover every inch of her skin. In hindsight, I'm surprised that her father even let us swim alone in the muddy pond out behind their house. I guess he and her mom could see most of the waterhole from their back porch where they just happened to spend a lot of time that day.

When Violet first jumped off the rickety dock, I followed making a splash a few feet from where her head emerged.

"Last one to the other side is a rotten egg," she called out and started swimming in that direction before I even had a chance to consider the competition.

"Hey, that's no fair," I combatted, but she couldn't hear me because her arms were already rotating as fast as a windmill on a breezy day.

I swiftly ducked my head beneath the surface of the water and started kicking like the bull I had seen my buddy Danny ride at the rodeo the previous weekend. There weren't many country boy competitions I was afraid to get involved with, but that was one I wasn't having any part of. I'd seen way too many grown men bounce off the back of one of those animals like a rock flung out of a slingshot. I was brave, but I wasn't stupid.

What Violet didn't know is that my family had a good-sized pond on our property, and I swam in it every chance I got. If our high school had a swim team, I was confident that I would have been the captain. We didn't have much time for sports back then, unfortunately. Don't get me wrong, us boys loved playing them. Baseball. Football. Basketball. Those were the main ones.

When I eventually came up for a breath, I expected to see Violet *a few yards behind me. At that point, I was probably about halfway to the opposite shore. The pond might have been fifty yards from one side to the other. When I caught a glimpse of her sailing like a gazelle in water, I quickly realized that I was going to be the rotten egg. At the moment it seemed like a big deal, but what does that really mean? I probably smelled better after jumping in the murky water than I did beforehand. I'd been working all day on the farm digging a trench with a shovel so that the rainwater could flow better through one of the tobacco fields.*

A rotten egg—Violet was always saying silly stuff like that. Things we had said when we were eight years old, but that she still found humor in at eighteen. I really liked that about her, and it was a side of her I hadn't seen much of at the schoolhouse. It was like she had begun to let her guard down around me, and that made me feel special, to say the least.

"Where did you learn how to swim like that?" I asked when I climbed onto the shore where she was sitting in her one-piece bathing suit which looked a lot like a pair of overalls—just not jean material—cut off below the knees.

"In this pond, silly," she answered as if the question was a no-brainer, and in hindsight, I guess it was.

"You're quite the swimmer yourself, Cleve," she acknowledged.

I'd been beaten by a girl, maybe for the first time in my life, so it didn't make me feel like the captain of the imaginary swim team when she complimented my swimming skills after beating the socks off me. I might as well had hopped back into the water, swam to the other side of the pond, picked up my socks laying there with my boots, and headed home with my tail tucked between my legs. I got over the defeat pretty quickly as beads of water dripped from Violet's wet hair. Her eyes seemed to sparkle even more when her hair was matted down like that—if that was even possible.

We spent the rest of the afternoon swimming and jumping from the dock. We had cannonball contests, diving competitions, and even timed each other to see who could hold their breath underneath the water the longest. It made me feel a little better about my manhood when I outlasted Violet by thirty seconds, but in the grand scheme of things, it didn't matter who won. We had a blast splashing around and acting like the teenagers that we were.

Surprisingly, her parents didn't come out to the waterhole a single time, and for the most part I forgot they were even in the vicinity though not enough to lay a finger on Violet Horne. Our feet did touch a few times beneath the surface of the water, and that was enough physical contact with an attractive girl to send tingles up my spine.

Boy, did I ever want to kiss her that day when we were sitting on the shore, our bodies dripping like a broken water faucet. I wanted to taste her lips when we sat near one another on the dock and talked about how much different it felt to be graduated from high school and knowing we'd never have another test or homework assignment. It felt like freedom, but in hindsight, we had more freedom when we were teenagers than we ever had as adults. It's funny how when you're young and foolish in so many ways, you have no idea that such will be the case.

When her parents called us in just before sunset, I realized how fast the time had flown by that day. I remember wishing we could go back out to the pond after dark so I could wrap my arms around Violet and kiss her tender lips.

Lying in my bed at night, I'd been thinking about that ever since we'd held hands in the cornfield. That's when I realized that I actually might have a chance to French kiss the most beautiful girl in the county one day. I was as lucky as a clover—a four-leaf clover. Maybe next time, I daydreamed, as we sat down at the Horne's table for my second dinner in their home.

10

The cloudy haze that dusk brings was giving into darkness as Mason twisted the key to lock up the market. This day had been a hectic one, but every day in farming was as busy as the honey bees on the backside of the property. There was rarely any downtime, and other than pausing for a quick bite to eat around midday, Mason had barely stopped moving since he lifted himself from the rocking chair this morning. For lunch, he'd scarfed down a peanut butter and jelly sandwich at the house. If he'd eaten one of those in his lifetime, he'd had a thousand. PB&J was his go-to for a quick meal. Most mornings, he packed the sandwich along with a small bag of chips in a brown paper bag before work and took it with him.

Today, he hadn't done that because of wanting to check in on Ansley, but when he walked through the front door while the sun hovered directly over the house, he hadn't found her inside. He glanced in the bedroom where she was staying—the room in which he grew up—but the only thing that looked different in there was that the bed had been made as if it were on display in a furniture store's showroom and her zipped suitcases were neatly arranged in one of the corners. It almost appeared as though Ansley was packed and ready to leave, which caused him to wonder if when he arrived back at the house this evening, he might find that the spot where her car had been parked since arrival was as empty as his stomach. All afternoon, he found himself wishing he'd eaten two sandwiches, but he really hadn't had time to make another one.

Before steering the four-wheeler around the corner of the log cabin where he habitually parked it for the night, Mason realized Ansley hadn't skipped town. Her vehicle hadn't moved an inch from the spot where it had sat when he changed the tire this morning. Once again, he couldn't help but wonder where she'd been when he'd come home for lunch. He was also curious about what she'd eaten.

Thinking about Ansley and, for some reason, the honey bees that had popped into his mind earlier, Mason made a mental note to warn her about the hives in case she was to venture to that area of the farm alone. As long as a person knew what he was doing, the bees were as harmless as the green snake Mason had watched slither across the path on his way to the house.

He liked having snakes around the farm because they ate the mice. Green snakes, on the other hand, only ate insects, which was nice, too. The only snakes Mason ever killed were the venomous ones because he was afraid that if he let them roam the property one would eventually bite Callie. She had cornered many snakes throughout her long life, and thankfully her insistent barking in those situations had always alerted Mason, and he'd been able to keep her safe.

When Mason pulled open the back door, an unfamiliar yet heavenly aroma flew into his face. He stood in the doorframe for a moment trying to figure out the smell, then he glanced toward the stove and found Ansley standing there in a pair of blue jeans and a light green shirt with three-quarter length sleeves.

As he took in the sight of her cooking in his kitchen with a cloud of steam rising above her thin frame, a smile began to creep onto his face. But, then, a sudden burst of sadness overtook him when he realized this was the first time he'd seen a woman standing in front of that oven since his mother last stood there with a checkered apron tied around her waist.

Ansley glanced over her shoulder and found Mason standing there with a confused look covering his face. Her attention was diverted when Callie squeezed between the door and Mason's legs before waddling toward the stove. The dog dropped her hind legs and sat at Ansley's side, her tail wagging as she peered upward.

Ansley reached for the top of Callie's head. "Hey there, girl," she greeted with a smile, noticing, for the first time, streaks of gray mixed in with the dog's dark brown fur. "Did you have a long day?"

Mason let the door close behind him.

A moment later, Ansley turned her attention back to Mason who had yet to say anything. "Did you have a long day?" she asked him, too. He didn't need to answer; she could see the tiredness shadowing his eyes, and his clothes were as dirty as those of a child who had spent the day making mud pies. "I hope it is okay that I decided to cook dinner for us," she said using a tone somewhere between one that would ordinarily be used for asking a question and one for making a statement.

Mason wasn't sure how to respond without hurting her feelings. He honestly didn't know how he felt about another woman cooking on his mother's stove. As he glanced between the stovetop and the counter, he saw the ingredients: noodles, sauce, and hamburger meat. *Spaghetti*, he assumed, as the steam continued to rise from the large pot on the back left burner.

"It smells good," Mason finally uttered. If she didn't ask any further questions, he'd leave it at that, he guessed.

Earlier in the day, when Ansley had come back to the house after discovering the pond, she had scoured through the cabinets in the kitchen and checked the refrigerator. At that particular time, she had been looking for something to make a picnic lunch to enjoy out by the pond. At first, she felt like she was snooping, but then she reminded herself that Mason had told her to make herself at home, so she decided it was okay. That's when she'd come across the ingredients for spaghetti and thought it would be a nice gesture to cook for a man who had not only given a stranger a place to stay but who'd also been working hard all day. To her knowledge, he rarely if ever had the opportunity to walk in the backdoor to a home-cooked meal.

"I hope you like spaghetti," Ansley mentioned.

"Of course," Mason answered. "Who doesn't?"

Ansley shrugged her shoulders. "It should be ready in just a few minutes."

Mason nodded his head. "I think I'll go wash up then."

When he headed toward his room, Ansley noticed that as Mason left the kitchen, he touched a hole in the wall that she'd spotted earlier in the day. It looked almost like a peephole, and she wondered if, at some point in this home's history, it had served a purpose. After a moment on that thought train, she turned back to the stove and began to add the final touches to the meal.

Based on Mason's demeanor, Ansley wasn't sure how he felt about her cooking for the two of them. It was possible that he'd had something else in mind for dinner. Perhaps he'd wanted to take her to a specific restaurant in town? Or maybe he didn't really like spaghetti, and he'd only said he did out of fear of hurting her feelings? She doubted he would tell her if he didn't, at least not once he saw she was already making it. The more she thought about it, the more she realized that just because a person has noodles and sauce in their cabinet and hamburger in their freezer, doesn't necessarily mean that they like spaghetti, but, like Mason said, *who doesn't like spaghetti,* she finally concluded.

She'd had to thaw out the frozen hamburger meat, and she'd even questioned whether something was wrong with it because it had a different appearance and consistency than the beef she was used to cooking.

As Ansley set plates on the table, she heard the shower come to life through the thin walls inside the old log cabin.

Mason took a step over the side of the tub and let the cool water rinse the grime off his body. Black lines quickly began to crawl toward the drain at his feet as his palms gripped the frame that stabilized the shower curtain. On the inside, he began to feel the emotional pain that accompanied memories of his mother cooking meals in their kitchen. Why had his dad done what he'd done? Mason asked himself for the millionth time since that tragic day. In some ways, it seemed so long ago, and in other ways, it seemed so vivid that he could have sworn it happened last week.

As his mind circled in a familiar pattern, he suddenly found himself wanting to punch the wall within arms reach on the other side of the curtain. He'd hit this wall before, even put a hole in it. The patch to remind him would always be there. But this time, he held in the anger that was causing his bones to rattle. If Ansley wasn't in the house at the moment, he was confident there would be another hole to cover. But, if Ansley weren't here, these memories of finding his mother in the kitchen after a day on the farm with his father wouldn't have flooded his mind.

Mason figured Ansley meant well, but he would have rather she asked if it was okay to prepare a meal in his mother's kitchen. What if he wanted to go into town for supper? Or what if he'd wanted to make dinner himself? He realized that he hadn't thought to give her his cell phone number, but she could have found him. The farm was rather large, but there were only so many places he could be, and it wasn't like she had been busy. She had been on the property all day. Somewhere.

These thoughts ran through his mind as he scrubbed his body

until he could see his skin again. Why was Ansley here? What did she want?

Ansley was standing next to the dining room table when Mason returned wearing a fresh pair of jeans, a plain white t-shirt, and wet hair. She had to admit that she found the look a tad bit sexy in an unfamiliar way, but she didn't let her eyes linger long enough for him to notice. He was husky, and she didn't usually go for husky men. She typically liked her man to be athletic and toned, clean cut. Mason was hairy and rough around the edges, not her type.

When Mason walked toward the table, he found Ansley there along with two plates of spaghetti and two glasses of ice. As he looked her in the eyes, he wondered what she was thinking.

"I didn't pour our beverages yet because I wasn't sure what you prefer," she acknowledged.

"Mountain Dew," he said without hesitation. "I can get one for myself," he added taking a step toward the fridge.

She waved her hand toward the chair at the head of the table. "Sit down, I'll get it for you," she offered. "You've been working hard all day."

Feeling a bit out of sorts, Mason wasn't quite sure how to react to such treatment. He figured he should be thinking about how he could get used to this kind of service, but he wasn't. Things were off, he couldn't help but feel as he let his body settle into the chair where he always sat. Then, he reached for the plate Ansley had set for him and slid it toward him. Steam was still rising from the meal at his fingertips, and he tried to focus his thoughts on enjoying a home-cooked supper for the first time in a long time.

Ansley retrieved a cold can from the refrigerator, and when she turned to walk back to the table, she tried not to furrow her brow upon noticing that Mason had moved his plate.

When she cracked open the soda, Callie's ears perked up, but she didn't budge from her spot on the kitchen floor—the one she'd claimed while Ansley finished cooking.

Out of the corner of his eye, Mason caught a glimpse of Callie's movement, and when he glanced in her direction, he lost sight of his glass for a moment.

Ansley was about to pour the drink onto Mason's ice when he turned back swiftly and reached out his hand to cover the rim of the glass.

"I don't want it in the ice," he declared firmly.

His comment, coupled with the gesture, somewhat took her aback, but she wasn't sure why. He had a right to his preferences, didn't he? Maybe it bothered her because at her parent's house a can of soda on the table would have been forbidden. Everyone was required to drink from a matching glass. However, this was his house and his rules, right?

"Okay," Ansley reacted, handing over the soda with a forced smirk.

Mason sat the green can next to his plate and watched Ansley pour sweet tea into the glass of ice on her side of the table. Before sitting, she returned the pitcher to the refrigerator. While she was doing that, Mason got up to fill Callie's bowl with dog food.

"Sorry, Callie, I almost forgot to feed you," he admitted sourly as she rose from her comfy spot to fill her stomach. His routines were all out of whack with Ansley being here.

Ansley watched the food trickle into the tin bowl, but she didn't say anything.

"Thank you for making supper," Mason expressed when he returned to the table.

"You're welcome." Ansley paused before picking up her fork. "Before we start eating, though, I want to mention that the meat seemed a bit different than what I'm accustomed to cooking."

Mason's face drew a familiar grin. He'd heard that said before. "It's good meat," he guaranteed. "It just didn't come from the grocery store like the meat you're probably used to seeing."

"Oh," she said simply.

"A bunch of us farmers trade food," he clarified, "so this meat came straight from a cattle farmer down the road. It might taste a bit different, too, but I promise you it's about the best quality meat you can get your hands on."

A few moments later, the two of them were eating spaghetti together. Ansley chopped her meal into little squares and began to eat them one by one. Mason twirled the noodles around his fork and sucked in each bite as if he were eating from a straw. Ansley tried not to glance up as his mouth made slurping noises, but she couldn't help but think about the reaction his eating habits would elicit from her mother if they were dining at the same table.

Her mother would never eat with this man. Maybe once, but she probably wouldn't endure the entire meal. If they were at her house, she would most likely ask him to leave if he wasn't going to use better manners at the dinner table. She had literally done that to a boy Ansley dated in high school. Needless to say, there hadn't been a need for another date after that meal.

"What did you do today?" Mason asked casually between bites.

Ansley told him about wandering out to the pond, watching the fish jump, and relaxing on the bench with a book in her hands. It had been a real treat, she thought to herself, as she relived the day in her mind. At home when she wasn't at work, she spent most of her days going, going, and going. Rarely did she ever just relax like she had today, but she had to admit that it felt good.

"What did you eat for lunch?" Mason eventually asked.

"I made a peanut butter and jelly sandwich."

"Me, too," he said.

"I know," she responded with a smile after taking a sip from her glass.

His forehead began to wrinkle. "How did you know that?"

"When I got hungry, I walked back to the house to see if I could figure out something for lunch, and I found the peanut butter and the bread you left on the counter. Thanks, by the way," she conveyed with a grin. "I wasn't sure if you'd left it out for me or if you were just in a hurry to get back to work."

At the mention of those items, Mason glanced at the counter and immediately realized she must have put them away.

"You're welcome," he said with a grin.

She decided not to mention how prior to making the sandwich she had rummaged through his cabinets and refrigerator looking for something that might sound more appetizing. As she had searched, it became evident that he must not have been to the grocery store recently.

"So," Ansley reminded Mason, "you're supposed to tell me how you found a brand new tire for my car so early this morning."

"Oh, yeah," he recalled. "You know how I just mentioned that I trade with other farmers; well, there's a mechanic down the road that I trade with also. My crops for his services and parts—at least the services that are beyond my level of understanding. Changing a tire is simple."

"To you, maybe," Ansley quickly assured him. She had never changed a tire in her life.

"You could do it," Mason claimed. "It's easier than most people think."

Ansley gave him the *I don't know about that* look. In the past couple of days, she had watched two strong men change a tire, and it hadn't come across as a simple task either time. Maybe to them, but not to her.

"So this mechanic was in his shop before daylight?"

Mason shook his head side to side. "No, at least not today."

"So . . . how did you get the tire?" she quizzed. "Did you wake him up or break into his shop?"

"Neither," Mason clarified. "I just walked into the shop and picked out the tire I needed."

"What? That's crazy. His door wasn't locked?"

"Most people around here don't lock their doors, Ansley," he informed her. "When the temperature is right, we leave our windows open at night, too," he said with a snicker.

"Really?"

Her reaction to this idea reminded him of the lady at the market earlier although Ansley's response was a bit more conservative. "Sure. The crime rate in Oriental is almost non-existent." *Unless you count mailbox bashing as a crime,* he thought to himself.

"Why do you think it's like that?"

"Probably because we all have shotguns and we ain't afraid to use 'em," he suggested.

As soon as the comment flew out of Mason's mouth, it triggered a memory from his past, and from there the conversation continued at a slower pace. Similar to last night, Ansley began to do the bulk of the talking as the food on their plates dwindled. Eventually, Mason got up for a second Mountain Dew, and when he did, he made sure to ask Ansley if she wanted more tea.

"No, thanks. I don't normally drink caffeine at dinnertime," she mentioned. "That one glass of sweet tea will probably keep me up all night." As she made that comment, she reached for the glass of water sitting next to her empty glass. It was a habit to pour everyone at the table a glass of water in addition to any other beverage of their choice. However, throughout dinner, she noticed that Mason hadn't touched his water, and the ice in his other glass had slowly melted away.

"Okay," he responded.

"Having all that soda won't keep you awake?"

"Not after all the energy I exerted today."

As a sign of understanding, Ansley nodded her head. "What are your plans for the rest of the evening?" she inquired. "I don't want to keep you from your routines."

Too late for that, Mason thought to himself. "I don't know," he replied. He wasn't sure if he was supposed to entertain her or just go about his night as if she wasn't there. "How about you?" he asked, hoping for some clarification of what she expected. Maybe she would say she needed to do something in particular, and then he could just do whatever he wanted without worrying about her.

"I'm flexible," she mentioned.

"I can barely touch my toes," Mason responded with a straight face.

"Huh?" Ansley inquired, a confused expression settling in on her face. A moment later, the comment sank in, then Ansley cackled and almost snorted. His humor. It reminded her of his dad, and she was never sure if she was laughing at the joke or at the person who told it. "You're . . .," she almost said *just like your dad* but then decided against using the reference for the time being, ". . . funny," she uttered instead. "Want to go out somewhere?" she quickly asked, attempting to cover up the words she had nearly fumbled.

"Like where?"

"I don't know. It sounded like a good question."

"There aren't many places to go on a Tuesday night in Oriental," he assured her.

They sat in silence for a moment, and then Ansley jumped up from her chair in excitement and said, "I have an idea!"

"You do?" Mason inquired, his eyebrows rising as he watched her hustle away from the table and then skip down the hallway.

When she returned, he was shocked when she set The Date Night Jar on the table.

Mason sat back in his chair and swallowed slowly. "What are you doing?" he asked, openly less excited than her.

"Let's pick something from the jar," Ansley suggested with a grin.

11

*T*he first time I set *The Date Night Jar* on the table between Violet and myself, her eyes lit up like a Christmas tree. Honestly, I had been surprised when Mother and Father agreed to allow me to take the jar to Violet's house that particular evening. To my knowledge, the family heirloom had never left our home since being passed down from my grandparents to my parents.

Mother had said, *"Make sure you don't forget to bring the jar back home with you."* This was mentioned just after she wrapped it delicately with newspaper as if she was swaddling baby Jesus before laying him in the manger. She then placed the glass jar ever so carefully into a square cardboard box in which it fit ever so snugly.

"Why did you consider for one moment that I would think The Date Night Jar was odd?" Violet asked me.

I hadn't initially clued Violet in on *The Date Night Jar.* Even though all of our date ideas had come from within it, she didn't know that, at least not until after our previous date when I spilled the beans.

In the beginning, I was afraid she would find the concept weird. I guess I thought this because, to me, it was awkward, but at the same time I had to admit that it made coming up with interesting dates a bit simpler.

"Well," I stuttered. "I've never heard of anyone else's family having a date night jar," I shared honestly.

"I love it," she told me. "I absolutely love it!"

Once she knew about the jar and realized I had been plucking the ideas for our dates from it, she expressed how eagerly she wanted to be involved in the process. She wanted to reach her hand through the rim, pick out one of the little scrolls wrapped in twine, and be the first to read the words written on the inside.

"That makes me happy," I exclaimed.

"So, how does it work?" she asked. "Is there a special way to pick?"

"Not really," I informed her. "You just twist off the top, reach in, and pull out a piece of paper," I explained. I'd already given Violet a brief history of the jar. Of course, it hadn't always been called The Date Night Jar although that's what I'd known it as during my lifetime. Over time, the word dating had become more prominent than earlier used terminologies such as courting, wooing, and other titles that described a man and a woman getting to know each other in the interest of marriage. Therefore, the name of the jar had evolved.

"This is so exciting," she said for about the tenth time.

"Well, there is one rule," I mentioned as her hand hovered above the jar.

"What's that?" she inquired, letting her fingers fall onto the lid and rest there, waiting impatiently for my response.

"You can only pull out one date idea."

She smiled. "Of course, silly."

So, at her parent's kitchen table, I watched her tiny wrist slide through the glass rim as a big smile stretched from one side of her face to the other. Her mother was washing dishes—smiling, too, because she had overheard every word being spoken between me *and her daughter. Her father was in the den watching television, and I remember hoping that he hadn't heard any of our conversations. I figured he would think The Date Night Jar was absurd. I even wondered if he'd say something akin to "A real man comes up with his own ideas for a date with a woman."*

I had come to learn her parent's nightly rituals, and her dad rarely ever stepped foot back into the kitchen after he finished off his supper. Violet's mother would sometimes fill a wooden bowl with ice cream and take it into the den for him to enjoy while relaxing. Sometimes she would end up sitting with him, but more often than not she would end up on the other side of the room knitting.

Violet's mom was sweet, and she talked to me a lot. Asked me questions about my day and my plans for the future. Her father, on the other hand, didn't say a whole lot to me. He was stern and only talked when he felt like something needed to be said. Looking back, I guess I could have tried harder to get to know him, but the man frightened me. I just knew I'd say the wrong thing and he'd forbid me to date his daughter.

Violet twisted the tin top around the grooved rim then set it quickly on the tabletop. Before reaching in, she glanced up at me. "Anything else I need to know?" she asked.

I shook my head east to west. "Nope."

"Here goes," she said grinning.

I watched the excitement travel all over her body, and I wished I had a photograph of her face at that moment. She closed her eyes and tightened her lips.

A moment later with her eyes still shut, she untied the twine and used her thumb and pointer finger on each hand to stretch out the piece of paper so she would be able to read it easily. Then, she opened her eyelids and whispered out the words written in cursive: Build A Campfire For You And The Lady And Roast Marshmallows.

"Ansley, we're not dating," Mason explained.

"So?"

"So—that's The Date Night Jar," he said pointing at the glass mason jar she'd set on the table in between them.

"Yeah, I know that, but we don't have to be dating to pull out a suggestion."

"Dating is the whole point of the jar," Mason reminded her, "and it's silly," he added.

She nearly blurted out, *It worked for your parents, and your grandparents, and . . .* but she decided that these words would only add fuel to the fire. She also thought about saying, *Maybe if you had used this jar for dating purposes you wouldn't still be single.* But who was she to talk? The two of them were about the same age, and like Mason, she was as single as a dollar bill.

"Have you ever tried it?" Ansley decided to ask.

"No," he assured her, his cheek rising, pinching his eye as he nodded as if to express the thought of *Why would I?*

"It might be fun," she suggested. "It's not like it's going to say you have to hold my hand or kiss me or anything like that," she clarified.

"How do you know?"

"Because your dad tells me stories from The Date Night Jar all the time, and he's never once said anything about the date suggestions being physical."

"Well, anyway, what's the point?" Mason queried.

"What else are we going to do?"

"I don't know," he responded. "Maybe we should just watch TV," he suggested.

Now, Mason found himself wishing that when Ansley first asked about his plans for the evening, he'd told her that he usually watched TV at night. That's what he would be doing if she hadn't shown up here with this Date Night Jar in the first place. Anyways, she had some nerve bringing it out after his reaction to it last night.

"How about this?" Ansley offered while pointing at the jar. "If the jar tells us to watch TV, then we'll watch TV."

"You make it sound like it's a Ouija board when you say it's going to tell us what to do."

Ansley grunted. "Semantics," she uttered. "If the slip of paper we pull from The Date Night Jar reads, *Watch TV*, then you can pick the show. How about that?"

"I'd pick sports," he reeled off.

"Ugh."

"The Date Night Jar isn't going to have a slip of paper that says *Watch TV*. It's old school," he reminded her.

"TVs existed when your parents started dating."

Ansley's mind had jumped into some of the stories that Cleve had told her, stories that included what he called television sets. As soon as she had let the comment about his parents trickle out of her mouth, she realized she probably should have kept it to herself. She knew that the subject of his parents was a touchy one.

Mason drew in a deep breath then exhaled slowly. He was on the verge of telling her to carry the jar back to the bedroom or maybe even to take the jar and leave. He'd spotted it earlier on the top of the dresser that he'd told her she could use for her clothes, and as he stared at it then, he thought about throwing it up against the wall.

Ansley could see the frustration mounting on Mason's face, so she decided to attempt to defuse the situation rather than give him an opportunity to reply to her last comment. "How about if you don't want to do whatever it is that's on the piece of paper we pick out, then we just do something else?"

"Like watch TV?" he huffed.

"Sure," she agreed. "But not sports," she said holding up her pointer finger to accompany her serious look.

"What?" he snapped. "Why not?"

"Fine," she grunted. "It's your TV so we can watch whatever you want." She paused for a short moment. "Except for football."

"Okay," he agreed, wondering how he had let her talk him into this. As for the football part, they wouldn't be able to watch football anyway because the season ended in January and wouldn't start back until September. But there wasn't any need in revealing that piece of information, he decided.

"Can I pick it out?" she requested, her hands folded, the tips of her knuckles touching the smile on her face as her elbows rested uneasily on the table.

"I don't care," he said wearing a facial expression that precisely matched his choice of words.

Ansley felt giddy inside. She had been wanting to pull a sliver of paper from The Date Night Jar for as long as she had known about it. Every time she listened to one of Cleve's stories, she imagined making a similar memory of her own. Of course, things were different in this situation. She and Mason weren't dating, which had been a valid point that he'd made as soon as she'd brought out the jar. They weren't even interested in one another like that. To be honest, they didn't even know each other. But still. There still seemed to be something magical about reaching her hand into this jar that had guided Mason's descendants to true love, and this might be her only chance to experience it firsthand since Cleve had asked her to leave the jar with Mason.

Mason watched as Ansley twisted the cap and set it carefully on the table. Then, her fingers slid through the rim of the glass before flirting cautiously with the slivers of paper on the inside. When he glanced at her face, he noticed that her eyelids were shut and her cheeks were flushed red, making her long blonde hair stand out even more. In that instant, he nearly laughed out loud. She was way too into this, he thought.

A moment later, Ansley loosened a thin string of twine and began to stare at the scroll-like paper between her fingers. When she read the words, her hand slipped toward her mouth covering it as it gaped open.

"Oh, my goodness," she uttered.

Mason furrowed his brow. All of a sudden, he found himself wanting to know what was on the paper, but he didn't want to ask. He didn't want to come across as interested because he wasn't. Well, maybe a little, but only because of the suspense being created by the person on the other side of the table. In the grand scheme of things, it didn't really matter what the paper said. He doubted it would be anything he'd want to do anyway. It would probably advise them to frolic in the flowers or dance in the living room. No—he wasn't doing anything silly like that. Absolutely not.

Ansley was speechless. Cleve had told her about this particular date. It had been a special one, and she held the story close to her heart. She suddenly found herself wanting to share her thoughts with Mason, but she knew he wouldn't understand.

"What?" he asked. "What does it say?"

Ansley heard his voice, but she still felt frozen. That screen inside her head was playing in black and white, and she was watching Cleve and Violet fall in love beneath a star-filled sky on a clear night in Oriental.

"Earth to Ansley," Mason projected.

Ansley shook her head slightly to clear her mind from the daze. "Sorry about that," she said.

"So," Mason asked again, "What does it say?"

Ansley let the edge of her tongue slide across her lips before speaking. "It says: *Build A Campfire For You And The Lady And Roast Marshmallows.*"

12

"Seriously?" Ansley asked Mason for the second time. "The name of your grocery store is Piggly Wiggly?"

Laughing hysterically, she pressed the sole of her shoe against the brake pedal on her vehicle, forcing the car to come to a halt at a stop sign in the middle of nowhere. As the engine idled, she let her head fall into the steering wheel while the humor in the local store's name nearly brought her to tears.

"Yes, I promise," Mason answered, chuckling at how tickled she was to find out about the Piggly Wiggly.

"This is one of the funniest things I've ever heard," Ansley exclaimed as she spoke through the space below the horn. "It sounds like a strip club where heavyset women would dance," she spewed, laughing in between almost every word in the sentence.

As soon as the comment escaped her mouth, she thought of Tanya whom she had ended up chatting with earlier today while feeding the edges of her bread to the fish at the pond. Tanya wasn't heavyset by any means, but anytime a strip club reference surfaced, Ansley's mind automatically went to Dr. Roman.

Mason began to laugh at Ansley's comment, then he turned to glance out the back window to check for approaching headlights since her attention at the present time was anywhere but on the road. "You do know the stop sign isn't going to turn green, right?" he mentioned as he turned back around after realizing no cars were coming up behind them.

Ansley lifted her head out of the steering wheel and forced a semi-serious face. "Really?" she inquired. "You're telling me this town has a Piggly Wiggly and the stop signs don't turn green?"

Mason fought the smirk growing on his face, but when Ansley burst into laughter once again, he couldn't help but laugh all over himself. He knew they could probably sit here at this stop sign for five minutes before another car would come into view. He wasn't sure what had made him think of the green stop sign wisecrack, but he had to admit it was a good one. The joke by itself wouldn't have made him chuckle, but Ansley's response seemed to have pushed his laugh button.

She fell back onto the headrest with water in her eyes from laughing so hard and then turned to face Mason. This was the first time she'd seen him let go, and it looked good on him.

"We're not quite as advanced as you city folk," he explained, chuckling as he made the comment. Some people from big cities liked to make fun of this place's small-town feel, but Mason didn't get the sense that such was Ansley's intention. He was pretty sure that she just found the name Piggly Wiggly amusing, and he had to admit that if he hadn't heard mention of it hundreds of times throughout his life, he might be rolling around in the floorboard right now.

"You're going to have to teach me how to drive out here in the sticks, then," Ansley cackled.

"That's why I offered to drive my truck," he reminded her.

Not long after Ansley had dug her hand into The Date Night Jar and plucked out the slip of paper about building a campfire and roasting marshmallows, Mason realized that he didn't have marshmallows at the house. That's when Ansley suggested an impromptu trip to the grocery store. She made mention that she needed to pick up some items for the next few days anyway, and then she was somewhat surprised when Mason became interested in her idea about getting graham crackers and chocolate so they could make s'mores.

Ansley twisted her shoulders and glanced into the backseat. "I think Callie likes my car better," she teased, reaching her arm between the two front seats so she could pet the dog.

"She just likes your heated leather seats," Mason observed. Honestly, he'd been shocked to find out that Ansley didn't have a problem with a dog riding in her vehicle. Maybe she wasn't quite as particular as he'd initially thought, he considered.

When the sun had gone down before dinner, the temperature of the air cooled off quite a bit. Ansley recognized this immediately when they stepped out the back door to head for the grocery store. Moments later, Callie hopped into the backseat with very little hesitancy, and now she was sprawled out with one eye half-opened, looking at the two people in the front seats like they were bonkers.

"These seats are the best," Ansley admitted as she attempted to rub the leather with her free hand while continuing to pet Callie with the other.

A few moments later, she let her foot ease off the brake as she began to turn the steering wheel. "I am allowed to turn right on red here, correct?" she asked playfully, giggling again as she spoke.

"Funny," Mason responded. "Yes, right on red at stop signs is allowed."

"Good because I don't need to get pulled over by Barney Fife."

"Watch it, city girl," he warned.

For the remainder of the drive to Piggly Wiggly, Mason and Ansley laughed off and on about their time spent at the stop sign. Ansley became a laughing box again when she turned into the grocery store parking lot and caught a glimpse of the cartoon-looking pig's face in the middle of the words Piggly and Wiggly above the store's entrance.

Callie dozed off in the backseat while Ansley and Mason filled what he called a *buggy* with groceries.

"What do you call it?" he asked Ansley.

"A shopping cart," she answered.

It was evident to both Mason and Ansley that they were from two different worlds, but it didn't seem to keep them from having fun on this particular outing. Even though she drove a foreign luxury automobile and he owned a hand-me-down pickup truck, they laughed in the same language. If they had been at her townhouse and wanted to build a fire, they would have ventured along a well-lit path to the patio out by the swimming pool where a bricked-in fire pit awaited. Once they made it back to Mason's, though, he led her through the dark to a burn pile where three metal-framed lawn chairs looked like they had been sitting since the 1990s.

Ansley sat down cautiously as Mason wandered a few steps over to a nearby stack of firewood from which she watched him pluck enough pieces to start a campfire.

When they had been inside putting away the groceries, she noticed that Mason hadn't grabbed a match or a lighter, and he also hadn't fetched lighter fluid or a gas can to fuel the fire. Yet, in a matter of moments, she witnessed a spark become a flame, and before she knew it, the blaze was climbing toward the stars twinkling above their heads.

"You must have been in the Boy Scouts," Ansley mentioned as she watched him work his magic.

"Nope," he answered. "I just grew up in the country."

"Who taught you how to build a fire?" she inquired.

Ansley hadn't intended for the question to be a loaded one, but once the words came out, she realized it most likely was.

Mason was squatting in front of the fire like a baseball catcher about to receive the ball from the pitcher, except he was holding a small stick, poking the deep orange flames at the base of the teepee-like structure he'd built with his calloused hands.

"My dad," he answered slowly, staring directly into the burning wood.

It wasn't cold out, but it was certainly cool, and Ansley felt relief when her body began to absorb the heat from the flames as they warmed her feet and legs.

Callie was laying in the dirt about fifteen feet from the blaze, and she seemed carefree about the brisk air and the warm fire.

"It looks like he did a good job," Ansley noted.

"Yeah," he answered simply.

Ansley rearranged herself in the chair, pulling her upper torso closer to the warmth. "Can I ask you a question that I've never been able to ask your dad?"

Poking around in the fire, it took Mason a moment to respond. He was thinking, wondering if he should just say no or maybe shift the conversation in another direction. But, at the same time, he was curious about what she wanted to know. "Sure," he finally agreed.

"How come no one visits your dad?" she probed. She didn't want to ask him why *he* didn't visit his father. She figured a question that direct might turn him off from discussing the subject altogether if, in fact, he would even consider entertaining it in the first place.

The heat was almost too intense for Mason to remain in his current position, but he didn't want to step back and have to look at Ansley, or better yet, allow her to look at him as he responded. "Do you know why my dad is in prison?" he finally asked.

Ansley bit down lightly on the insides of her lips before responding. "No," she answered honestly. Truth be told, she didn't know why any of her patients were in prison. Not knowing was a choice she'd made early on in her career. She wanted to see each patient as a person not as a prisoner.

Mason spoke softly yet directly. "My dad went to prison for killing my mom," he revealed.

As the heat blanketed Ansley, she suddenly felt a cold chill run up her spine. She had never imagined that Cleve Fields could be responsible for killing another human being, much less his own wife. At that moment, as she processed Mason's statement, she reminded herself not to judge Cleve. She wasn't naïve, and she knew that on any given day she could be treating a patient who had murdered someone. But Cleve? How could he have possibly killed Violet? His Violet. The woman whom he held on such a high pedestal in every one of The Date Night Jar stories he'd shared with her.

The campfire continued to illuminate an otherwise dark sky, and as the moon hung above, unaffected by the depth of this conversation, the crackles and pops inside the burning wood made the only sounds present. Quietly, Mason and Ansley each wrestled with the thoughts in their respective minds. The ones traveling through Mason's brain were thoughts that he often had, and the ones present in Ansley's were foreign and unsettling.

"I'm sorry," she eventually uttered in the most sincere tone her voice was capable of producing.

Softly, Mason dropped back onto the seat of his pants, unconcerned about the dirt particles that would attach to his jeans. As he held onto the stick with a death grip, he folded his arms across his lifted knees. "Thanks," he finally muttered.

Callie's eyes had darted in Mason's direction when he fell back, but otherwise, she had remained as still as a photograph.

"I know that doesn't make it any better," Ansley exclaimed. "But I really am sorry," she offered again. "I had no idea."

At that moment, she wondered if she would have come here if she had previously known what Mason just shared. Now, how could she possibly try to convince a man, whose father had killed his mother, to go see that father?

The question Mason posed next caught Ansley entirely off guard. "Why are you friends with him?"

The quiet of the night seemed to swallow Ansley as she pondered an honest answer. She thought about saying something vague such as, *I like everybody.* But that was a cop-out response, and she knew it. In all of her life, she wasn't sure if any human being had ever asked why she was friends with a particular person, but it was a great question, she thought, and Mason deserved a genuine explanation. "Ever since the first time I met Cleve," she began, remembering the frightened look on his wrinkled face when he was wheeled into Room 112. "He has treated me like his friend, not his physician," she finally divulged.

Ansley could see the left side of Mason's face, and she thought she saw his head nod ever so slightly, but she wasn't certain. The light from the fire was casting shadows on him and all around both of them as the flames danced to music rising from beneath.

"Did you come here to find out what he did?"

"No," Ansley answered hastily.

"He went to prison for shooting my mother," Mason made sure she knew. He wanted her to know exactly why his father was there so that the next time she looked into his eyes, she wouldn't just see Cleve—the man who treated her like his friend. He hoped she'd also see Cleve—the man who was the reason why his mother was dead.

Ansley felt the insides of her throat tighten, and her bones began to tremble even though they were oozing with the warmth being spread by the campfire. Never once had she imagined Cleve capable of killing a human being. But this—this was the reason she didn't want to know why her patients were incarcerated. She wanted to see a person, not a crime.

"I can't imagine—" she mumbled, letting her words trail off.

"I lost all of my parents that day," Mason uttered in a voice much smaller than himself.

Ansley could feel her chest rising and falling, and she felt tears welling inside her as she watched a single drop of sadness slide down Mason's left cheek. The light from the flames caused the trail from his tear to glisten slightly, and she found herself wanting to reach over and wipe the pain from his face.

Instead, she reached her hand toward his shoulder and let her fingers linger there. She could see Mason's jawline tightening, and she knew he was trying hard to hold back his emotions. He was a farmer, a rough and tough country boy. He wasn't supposed to cry. He was supposed to bottle up his sorrow and press on. Anyway, that's what she assumed a man in his shoes was expected to do; however, Mason's boots were dirty and torn and had been beaten by the weather and the shaky ground on which he'd walked for years on top of years.

Ansley wondered if . . . if anyone had ever held him in her arms and told him that it was okay to cry and that feeling pain was being human. She didn't ask, though, she just slid out of the chair and onto his shoulder, the weight of her body causing him to have to catch her with his sturdy arms.

As the stick that had been in Mason's grip since he'd started the fire slipped from his fingers, his knees gave way. He garnered every ounce of strength in his body to keep Ansley and himself from toppling toward the flames, and before he knew it, the two of them landed together on the soft dirt surrounding the campfire.

13

he weekend following the evening when Violet pulled the campfire date from the jar, her parents allowed her to visit with me at my house for the very first time. They dropped her off at five o'clock in the evening with the understanding that Mother would drive her home later that night.

When I opened the front door to greet Violet, Mother was in the kitchen and Father was outdoors in one of the fields checking on a patch of crops that were being invaded by insects. I was somewhat surprised, yet relieved, that her parents didn't walk her to the door.

Not long after her arrival, we sat down for supper with my parents which for me was much less stressful than eating a meal with her folks. Although I had to admit that I felt a different kind of nervousness that night—for Violet—since she hadn't spent much time with Mother and Father at that point in our courtship.

I probably shouldn't have been concerned. That evening, I watched her charm my folks just like she'd been charming me since grade school. I knew all along that Father would love Violet, but mothers aren't always as easy to win over when it comes to a woman courting their only son. However, Mother took to Violet like the moths to the flames by the campfire that Violet and I found ourselves sitting around after a delicious meal and a pleasant conversation with my parents.

Father allowed us to slip out the back door together while he helped Mother tidy up the dinner table and wash the dirty dishes. Violet offered to help, but Mother told her to enjoy her time with me out by the fire.

When we walked out behind the log cabin in the dark, a warm fire wasn't waiting on us, but all I needed to do was ignite the teepee-like structure I'd taken the time to construct earlier in the day. Thankfully, Father had allowed me to retire from work a bit sooner than usual so that I could prepare for the evening and have plenty of time to shower before Violet arrived.

An assortment of logs made up what would become our campfire. Some were skinny, some fat, and others in between. Our family always kept a stack of firewood out near the barn which was typically used in the fireplace inside the cabin during the winter months. Father and I sharpened the axes often since we would chop down trees from random patches of woods on the farm pretty much year-round. We cut oak and pine and everything else we could find that would burn. We knew which wood was best suited for starting a fire and which would burn the longest. You learn these things when the temperatures dip down into the teens, and your life depends on having a warm fire to nestle around. At those times, the chimney pumped out smoke like a train that runs on coal. Of course, Eastern North Carolina has always been known for relatively warm weather, but there are a couple months out of the year when you feel like you're in the North Pole, minus the snow.

I'd made sure to toss in twigs in just the right places where I knew they would help spread the fire quicker than a virus in a Sunday school room filled with toddlers. Within a matter of moments, the patch of crunchy leaves nestled beneath the twigs took to the spark I created for them. When I stepped back, me and

Violet stood side by side and watched an orangey glow work its way toward the top of the pile.

It was so dark and cloudy outside that we couldn't even see the stars above our heads, but the flames quickly lit up the entire area behind the house. All of a sudden, we could vividly see the barn and the edge of the closest field, and, more importantly, Violet's face became much clearer.

Gazing into Violet's eyes was one of my favorite things to do. It just didn't seem to get old, neither did touching her, whether in the form of a simple brush or having her fingers wrapped in mine.

As we let the fire warm our bodies, I reached down for her hand, and we stood real close. There must be something magical about a campfire because I felt her squeeze my hand a little tighter than she had before. It caused me to turn and face her, and that's when she took my other hand in hers and used her toes to push off the ground, so our faces became nearly even. I'll never forget the smile on her face or the way my heart rattled like the engine of the tractor I'd spent most of the day driving, as she closed her eyes and let her lips touch mine.

Ever so softly, we kissed.

I can remember how our lips barely moved. They just kind of embraced. Mine were chapped from being outside all day, and hers might have been, too, but neither of us seemed to take notice. We just let our lips linger there for what seemed like a lifetime or maybe it was only one second. Either way, I felt like I'd died and flown straight to heaven.

That was the first time I ever kissed Violet Horne, and I prayed it wouldn't be the last. I prayed we'd kiss every single time we saw each other from now until eternity—over and over and over again. I hoped I'd never kiss another woman in my entire lifetime. Violet was the only woman I wanted to be with, and I knew that like I knew how to start a fire.

Back then, I would have never in a million years told my guy friends that Violet Horne was the first girl I ever kissed. Most boys had kissed a girl or two, maybe even a handful, by the time they turned eighteen. Or at least they said they had. Some of them were lying through their teeth, and I knew that, and some of them didn't even still have all of their teeth. But not me, I hadn't kissed a girl. It was like I'd been saving that special moment for the girl of my dreams.

When our lips finally pulled apart, my heart was still thumping. Hers was, too. I could feel it when her body was pressed against mine. I hoped my parents hadn't caught us kissing, and I immediately found myself glancing out of the corner of my eye toward the house.

"Did they see us?" Violet asked.

Her eyes were locked on mine, and she knew exactly who I was looking for at that moment.

"I don't see Mother or Father at the windows," I said relieved.

"Would they be disappointed in us?" she asked, her brow crunching, showing me that she wanted to remain in their good graces.

"I think they'd understand," I answered honestly. "It's not like I have my hand up your dress," I whispered real low.

Violet's face immediately became flush, but she then burst into laughter, and at that moment I knew her mind had instantly jumped back to our first date when we ended up in the cornfield.

That night as we spent the evening around the campfire, we kissed three more times. We tried to find a spot where my parents couldn't see us even if they were looking, just in case. We also roasted marshmallows, but I can't remember how a single one of them tasted. The only taste on my lips was the taste of Violet Horne, and I was addicted to her more than a child is to chocolate.

With her eyes closed, Ansley vividly remembered the story Cleve Fields had shared with her about his and Violet's first kiss.

She wished she could tell Mason—whose body was flush with hers at the present time—but she didn't dare interrupt this moment with a single word.

Mason wasn't sure how long he and Ansley had been lying on the ground next to the fire, but he knew he didn't want to move. He didn't want to let go of her embrace. They were wrapped in each other's arms as if holding on for dear life, and he would have never imagined that they would have ended up this way tonight. In this moment, he realized he needed this. He needed someone to hold. Someone whose shoulder he could cry into. He hadn't wailed by any means, but he'd let years of pent-up tears flow from his bluish-gray eyes. He doubted that Ansley even knew he'd been crying unless she'd heard his quiet sniffles, which, come to think of it, she probably had. But, for some reason, that seemed okay.

It wasn't until Ansley felt her body become unbearably uncomfortable in its current position—wedged against the hard ground and Mason's left side—that she slowly pulled away from him. At that moment, she caught a glimpse of the waves circling around his eyes. He didn't say anything; he just looked at her as she pressed her elbow into the ground to hold up her torso. She thought about leaning forward and kissing him tenderly, but she didn't want to ruin the moment. Didn't want to make things awkward if he didn't want to kiss her back. Part of her wanted to jump on top of him and let her own emotions run wild, but another side of her told her to be still.

Mason swallowed as he gazed into Ansley's blue eyes. He wondered what she was thinking, both now and when she'd fallen onto him. He wanted to close his eyes and kiss her lips, but he couldn't. When he looked at her, he saw someone else. So, instead of letting down the barriers that stood between him and whatever lie beyond the walls he'd built, he lifted his body off the ground to sit up.

"How about those s'mores?" he said in the same fashion that a sports fan trying to change an awkward subject might say *How about those Cowboys?*

Ansley smiled. "They sound delicious," she declared, trying to force herself to become as excited about the idea as she had been earlier.

As they had lain on the ground, Callie had slowly and quietly scooted closer to them using the army-crawl technique. Now, Mason reached down to pat her on the head, thanking her for showing emotional support in her own way. Ansley smiled, thinking nearly the same thing as Mason about Callie's silent gesture. Dogs were so in tune with people's feelings, she thought.

While Mason added wood to the fire, Ansley grabbed the marshmallows, chocolate, graham crackers, and roasting sticks. A few minutes later, she slid a marshmallow onto a stick for him and then one for her. Rather than sitting in the chairs, they sat on the ground in the same spot where they'd been lying not long before. Ansley felt comfortable sitting close to Mason now, but they weren't so close that they were touching.

He took the roasting stick when Ansley handed it to him, and at the same time, they held their marshmallows above the flames. Moments later, Ansley pulled hers away and stabbed the opposite end of the stick into the ground. Mason kept his in a bit longer, and when he pulled it out, he had to blow out the fire that had overtaken the marshmallow.

"You like yours crispy, huh?" Ansley asked as she grabbed two graham crackers from the box and set a piece of chocolate on the bottom one as she used them to make a sandwich around Mason's toasted marshmallow.

When he felt her clamp down, he pulled the stick out of the marshmallow. "Yes," he said. "It's the only way."

Ansley snickered. "If you say so," she responded, then it took him by surprise when she pushed his s'more into her mouth.

"Hey," he began, his mouth gaping open. "You thief," he teased.

With pieces of graham cracker and gooey marshmallow and melted chocolate clinging to her lips, Ansley attempted to cover her mouth with her other hand as she laughed at his reaction.

Instinctively, Mason plucked her stick from the ground and held it into the fire to blacken the marshmallow.

When he removed his roasting stick this time, Ansley had just finished eating her s'mores—or, better yet, his s'mores—but then she once again went through the whole process of helping Mason make another one. This time, when she pinched it off the stick, she gave it to him, and they both shared a chuckle as he quickly snatched it from her hand and took a bite.

The rest of the evening followed a similar pattern. Ansley would say or do something funny, and Mason would respond in his own quirky way. He had to admit that he liked being around her, and he now understood why his dad was friends with her. She was special. Beyond special, actually; Ansley Stone was nothing short of a miracle. As Mason put out the campfire that he'd built, he realized that over the course of the past two days, he was pretty sure he had figured out exactly why his dad had directed this woman to Oriental.

Back in Raleigh, Eleanor Stone was beginning to get worried about her daughter. She had been trying to call Ansley all evening, and after hours of failed attempts, she'd even made a trip to Ansley's townhouse even though her husband advised against the idea. After knocking on the door for a few minutes, she realized that her daughter wasn't home. She hadn't been able to find Ansley's vehicle in the parking lot either, which was a simple task since the residents were given assigned spaces.

Sitting in her own car, Eleanor had called the hospital to find out if Ansley was on shift.

"Sorry, ma'am, Dr. Stone ain't workin' tonight," Betty relayed.

"Do you know when she is scheduled to work again?"

"I'm not allowed to share the doctor's schedules," she answered politely. It wasn't a lie, but Betty also knew that Ansley didn't want her mother to know that she was off this week.

"Betty, I am her mother," Eleanor huffed into the phone.

"I understand that, ma'am," Betty responded calmly.

"Is Dr. Roman available?" she demanded to know.

"One moment, please."

The line went blank, and for a few seconds, Eleanor wondered if Betty had hung up on her. If she had, she'd sure enough call right back and give that woman a piece of her mind even if she was Ansley's friend—especially because she was Ansley's friend. Then she'd ask to speak to her supervisor. It wasn't like Ansley not to respond after this much time had elapsed. Even when her daughter was working, she'd text her back within an hour or so.

"Hello, Mrs. Stone," Dr. Roman's voice chimed. "I hear you are looking for Ansley."

"Yes, that is correct," Eleanor responded in a chirpy tone. "Do you happen to know where I might be able to find her?"

At the other end of the line, Dr. Roman grinned mischievously. She had met Eleanor Stone and even been around her on several occasions at social functions. The lady was high strung, but Tanya liked her nonetheless. She found her amusing and enjoyed her candid banter. The woman had enough money to say whatever she wanted and get away with it amongst almost any crowd. Tanya also realized that this lady often drove her own daughter crazy because she was so involved in Ansley's business.

"Ansley is on vacation," Tanya shared without hesitation. "Didn't she tell you?"

The air between them fell silent for several moments, and while Tanya waited for a response, she held the mouthpiece away from her lips so that she wouldn't accidentally giggle into it. It had quickly become evident that Ansley hadn't told her mother that she was going on vacation, and Tanya couldn't help but feel like she was back in high school and one of her friends had just gotten busted for withholding the truth from their mom.

"I didn't realize that was this week," Eleanor finally replied, fudging. "I can't recall where she said she was going, though. I'm so forgetful sometimes, dear."

"Myrtle Beach," Tanya offered willingly.

Another moment of silence. Another held in snicker from Tanya. As soon as she'd taken this call, she'd shewed away Betty so that she wouldn't overhear this conversation and tell on her. All of the nurses liked Ansley. Everyone liked Ansley. Some of them a little too much, Tanya thought.

"There aren't tractors in Myrtle Beach—"

Tanya tilted her head. "I'm sorry?" she inquired.

"Oh, nothing." Eleanor hadn't even realized that she'd spoken the tractor thought out loud until Dr. Roman replied.

The conversation pretty much ended there, and Eleanor Stone found herself furious with her daughter. Why would Ansley not want her own mother to know she had gone on vacation? Her mind wandered for a moment . . . back to her daughter's behavior the last time they'd been together. Now that she thought about it, something had seemed off from the instant Ansley opened the door that morning. Of course, she'd had a hunch that a man had been there, and now she knew she must have been right even though Ansley swore otherwise. *Ansley must be off with some man she doesn't want me to know about,* Eleanor decided. That must be why her daughter had put off meeting Price Johnson, one of the most eligible bachelors in the area.

Where were her daughter and this secret friend now? She had to find out.

14

nsley closed the bedroom door and then let her back fall flush against it. Her eyelids swallowed her eyes as her mind wandered back to when she was lying on top of Mason Fields on the cool dirt surrounded by a warm fire. If the door wasn't behind her at this very moment, she would lift her foot and kick herself in the butt for not kissing him or at least letting her eyes linger a bit longer to see if he might initiate a move.

Reliving the feeling of Mason's body pressed against her own, she clasped her hands together atop her breasts and then, pressing gently, slowly guided them down her torso before letting them fall apart near her midsection.

Leaning against the door, she felt as though she'd just experienced the act of making love. Her body was relaxed yet tense, and at the same time, she wanted more . . . more of Mason Fields.

Just moments ago, they'd said goodnight in the hallway and walked to separate bedrooms. She wondered what he would have done if she had followed him or grabbed his hand and led him into her room. It just hadn't felt right, though. Kind of like the idea of kissing him next to the fire had seemed inappropriate for some reason, as if she would be crossing some invisible boundary.

The only line she had crossed, though, was letting herself get too close to Cleve. She knew she was risking her career by spending her personal time with him. If her superiors knew about her extracurricular trips to Cleve's room, they'd be outraged. All of the nurses on the floor had kept quiet about it. It was like a silent pact they had even though they didn't understand it. Of course, Ansley always made sure to make up a reason why she needed to check on Cleve, but she knew her colleagues saw right past it.

As she thought about Cleve, her mind drifted to a comment Mason made earlier in the evening. What had he meant when he said, *I lost all of my parents that day*? A person could only have two parents, biologically, at least. You didn't have to be a doctor to know that.

Ansley had no reason to assume that anyone other than Cleve and Violet was a parent to Mason. Cleve had never mentioned anything different. She'd found herself wanting to ask Mason for clarification, but at the time she didn't want to stir up another tender subject. There was definitely something she didn't know about this family's makeup and the circumstances that had led Cleve Fields to prison.

Mason climbed into bed with two people on his mind. Ansley had shown up at his house just yesterday, and she had already flipped his world upside down. He was still wondering why she had fallen on him the way she did next to the campfire. If it had been an accident, she would have pulled herself off him as soon as they landed safely on the ground, but she hadn't. She had kept her arms wrapped around him, and she had held him tightly, which he had to admit he enjoyed rather much. There wasn't anything quite like the feeling of a woman's body pressed up against him, especially for the first time. Her being attractive helped things out even more. But, he still couldn't seem to get past whom she reminded him of, and that thought brought his dad back to mind.

Mason hadn't spoken to his father since he was eighteen years old, but he suddenly wanted to call him. There was one question in particular that he wanted to ask, and if he was honest with himself, there were many more.

Betty picked up the phone at the nurses' station on the fourth ring, stating her name as always. She didn't normally let it ring that long, but she had been elbows deep in the file cabinet at the other end of the closed-in area when it began ringing.

"Hey, Betty, do you think it would be possible for me to talk to Cleve Fields tonight?"

Betty glanced into the quiet hallways surrounding her. One led straight to the double doors that she was staring at in this very moment. The other two created a "T" from that hall, heading in opposite directions from where she was sitting. As usual, an armed prison guard was stationed in each hallway on either side of her desk. One was writing notes on a pad, the other twiddling his thumbs and humming to himself.

"How you expect me to do that, child?"

On the other end of the line, Ansley smiled. Betty's favorite nickname for everyone was child. She was a seasoned nurse who'd been at the hospital for as long as anyone could remember. She'd been talking about retirement, and even though Ansley was happy for Betty, she would hate to see her go when that time came.

"Betty, if anyone in that hospital can make this happen, it's you."

"He ain't got no phone in his room, Dr. Stone," she reminded Ansley. "And this phone I'm talking to you on has been in the hospital almost as long as I have been. I can't just stretch the cord all the way down the hallway, child."

At any other time, Ansley would have laughed out loud, but

right now she wanted to talk to Cleve. She had some questions to ask.

"You have your cell phone with you, right?"

"You askin' me to use my personal phone to let you talk to that man?"

Ansley knew that Betty liked Cleve almost as much as she did. The two of them joked around like they'd known each other since high school. Ansley would always laugh when Cleve would say, "Woman, quit calling me child. I'm as old as you." Their banter was amusing, and it reminded her of how a brother and sister might talk to one another at that stage of life.

"You're right," Ansley said. "It's not fair of me to put you in that situation."

"If I go in that room and hand that man my cell phone and he decides he ain't gonna give it back, we both in trouble."

"You know Cleve wouldn't do that," Ansley countered.

"Probably not, but child I'm 'bout to retire and I ain't taking no chances like that," she declared. "I could put you on speaker phone, but then if that guard who whistles all the time stops whistlin' and hears an extra voice in that room, he's gonna come chargin' in like it ain't nobody's business," she pointed out. "You know they bored, they just waitin' fo' some action."

This time Ansley let out a tempered laugh, but she made sure not to laugh too loudly in case Mason had drifted off to sleep already.

"Plus, Tanya been actin' real funny ever since your mama called up here."

"What? My mother called?" Ansley barked, confused at first, but then after thinking the situation through for a moment, it didn't surprise her at all. "Why?"

"Your mama was lookin' fo' you."

"What did you tell her?" Ansley was suddenly interested in knowing.

"I told her you weren't workin' tonight, but that wasn't good enough for her. You know that. Then she wanted to talk to Dr. Roman."

"You let her?" Ansley rumbled.

"Child, you know I regret it now."

"What did Tanya tell her?"

Betty glanced down the hallways again and swiveled her chair to make sure the doors that led to the offices behind her were shut. She was pretty sure Dr. Roman was in a patient's room, but just in case, she wanted to be real quiet.

"Well, I didn't hear everything because Dr. Roman shewed me away like a stray cat and then she was talkin' real low like I am right now," she muttered. "But I think she told your mama you were in Myrtle Beach," Betty shared. "Where is you, child?" she asked.

"I'm in—"

Before Ansley could finish answering, Betty butted in abruptly. "Don't you tell me, I don't want to know what you up to. I shouldn't have asked in the first place. It ain't my business, and if I don't know, cain't nobody ask me."

"That's true," Ansley agreed. "Can you write a note and give it Cleve for me?"

"Child! That's evidence. Ain't you ever watched them detective shows on the television set?"

"I don't have time to watch TV," Ansley spouted, laughing intentionally in an attempt to suppress her nervousness.

"Listen, child," Betty said real straight-like. "You give me five minutes, and I'll call you back on my cell phone."

"What do you mean?"

"Me and Cleve gonna call you back."

Mason couldn't fall asleep. He wasn't sure if it was because his mind was reeling through thoughts about Ansley and his dad, or if he'd eaten too many s'mores and the chocolate was keeping him awake.

He sat up in bed and decided to do something he never imagined he would do.

❧

"Ansley," a voice whispered real low into her ear as she lay in bed daydreaming in the dark.

Ansley furrowed her brow. She could barely recognize the voice, but she immediately knew who it was and she was happy to hear from Cleve as she pressed the phone tightly against her ear.

"Hey," she whispered back.

"Is everything okay?" he asked.

Betty was holding the phone a few feet from Cleve's bed. Close enough that she didn't have to put it on speaker but far enough that he couldn't reach it.

"I can barely hear you."

"I know, I can barely hear you, too," Cleve confirmed. "Betty doesn't trust me to have her phone."

Betty instantly furrowed her brow and shot Cleve the evil eye as she balled up her fist and shook it in the air at him.

"Betty," Cleve said looking up at her. "My arms are cuffed to this bed," he reminded her. "What am I going to do with your phone?" he asked rhetorically. "Just lay it on my pillow next to my ear so that Ansley and I can hear each other better," he requested.

Betty breathed in real hard and cocked her head while pressing her lips together tightly. "Fine," she agreed between her teeth as she set the phone next to him. "But, child, if you try to keep my phone, I ain't callin' that guard in here. I'm gonna come onto that bed and show you a whoopin' a good ole' country boy like you ain't never seen," she threatened, shaking her finger like it was on fire.

"Can you hear me better now?" Cleve asked Ansley with his eyes still set on Betty.

"Much."

"Why are you calling me?" he inquired, concerned. "You know by doing this you're putting your job and Betty's job at risk."

Ansley grimaced. "I know," she admitted. "I just need to ask you something."

"What?"

"Are you and Violet Mason's biological parents?"

The telephone at the nurse's station began to ring as Dr. Roman walked out of a patient's room a few doors down the hallway. She was about to walk toward another patient's door when she noticed that Betty wasn't sitting at the desk. In fact, no one was.

As the phone continued to ring, she marched toward it with purpose. While she was in charge of this unit, her team wasn't going to drop the ball in any area. When it came time for a promotion, she wanted to be the first one in line.

"Hello?" she answered on the sixth ring.

"Hello, ma'am," a shaky voice on the other end uttered.

"How may I help you?" Tanya asked, somewhat surprised the caller hadn't given up on someone answering the phone especially at this time of night.

"Um," he rattled. "I am calling to see if I might be able to talk to my dad."

Tanya furrowed her brow. "Who is your dad?" she inquired. None of the men who worked in her unit were on shift tonight, except for the guards.

"Oh, I'm sorry—Cleve Fields," Mason mumbled, shaking his head, thinking of how dumb he must sound and suddenly feeling stupid for making this call.

Tanya hesitated before responding. Protocol instructed that she should tell the caller that prisoners—technically, patients— weren't allowed to receive phone calls. But, answering the phone wasn't her responsibility, it was Betty's, who was missing in action at the moment.

"May I ask who is calling?" she inquired out of curiosity.

Not wanting to share his name, Mason froze for a moment. If he didn't answer her question, she most likely wouldn't allow him to talk to his father. "This is his son," Mason responded weakly.

"I see. And what is your name, sir?"

Mason closed his eyes and slowly knocked the back of his head against the headboard two times. Sleeping next to him on top of the covers, Callie lifted her head to examine the noise further just as she'd done when he'd started talking on the phone. Once again, Mason rubbed her head, and she lowered it. "Mason," he eventually revealed.

Tanya jotted down the name on a scrap piece of paper.

"Sir, I'm sorry, but I'm not able to process your request at this time," she responded generically. "Is there a message you would like me to relay to the patient?" she inquired.

Mason hesitated. He wasn't at all prepared to respond to a question like that. He just wanted to talk to his dad to confirm why he'd sent Ansley to Oriental. "Not really," he finally uttered.

"I believe your name is on the list of authorized visitors," Tanya mentioned, making that up entirely. "But I am sure that in your communications with Dr. Stone, she has informed you of that," she added, fishing for evidence. Earlier, she had red-flagged it when Ansley's mom mentioned tractors . . . Tanya was almost certain that she'd read or heard that Cleve's family owned a farm. There was a slim chance that Ansley was at that farm instead of in Myrtle Beach, but something odd was going on here, and she wanted to get to the bottom of it. Security was the number one concern in this unit.

"Thanks," Mason said simply, imagining that Ansley wasn't supposed to have non-medical related contact with him, and certainly there had to be a rule against her staying at his house.

134

"What is your name?" Mason asked.

Tanya froze. She hadn't expected him to ask for her name. He'd been so off-kilter from the moment she'd first heard his voice. "My name is . . . Betty," she finally mumbled. "I'm Dr. Stone's nurse," she added. "She's told me about you."

"She has?" Mason asked.

"I probably shouldn't talk about that, though."

"What has she told you?" Mason inquired, curious to know what Ansley might have shared with her coworkers, and why, and when?

"I really can't say," Tanya—pretending to be Betty—offered. "She thinks a lot of your dad, though."

"I know," Mason said without even realizing at first that he was admitting more than he probably should.

You do? Tanya thought, smiling. From there, she probed a little more, but she couldn't get him to say anything else that would give her ammunition against Ansley, even though she tried her best to get him to crack.

"I'll make sure to let your dad know you called," was one of the last things she said.

"No," Mason said. "Please don't."

Cleve wondered why Ansley was asking the question about whether he and Violet were Mason's biological parents. But he didn't have anything to hide from her or anyone for that matter. Well, maybe one thing, but that wasn't an issue, at least not right now. Although ever since he'd last seen Ansley here in his room, he'd been worrying that she might just be wise enough to figure out a family secret that wasn't supposed to be told. That scared him more than being in prison. He'd even second guessed asking her to visit his son, but he prayed that in the end, her time spent there with Mason would be worth the risk.

"I'm not Mason's biological father," Cleve admitted for the first time in his life. Before he could explain the situation further, he heard the door handle at his back twist. Instantly, he glanced up at Betty whose face became ghostlike as her eyes darted in that direction. She was facing the door, and he was facing her and the window, in a position where he could turn slightly and possibly lean into the pillow without causing any alarm.

The door flung open, and two prison guards burst into the room ready for action.

Betty jumped back then glanced down at Cleve who had immediately rolled his head over onto her phone. From her viewpoint, she could no longer see the phone, and she prayed that the guards couldn't either.

When Betty glanced back up, Dr. Roman emerged from behind the guards.

"Betty, what are you doing in here?" Dr. Roman demanded to know.

"I'm checkin' on Mr. Fields," she responded with a frog in her throat and wrinkles between her eyebrows.

"Then why did you jump when we opened the door?"

Betty felt a sudden surge of confidence. "Because you bust in here like you was raidin' the room," she snapped. "Scare an ole' woman all the way to death, cause I'm well over halfway there already, child."

"Why aren't you at the nurses' station?" she demanded to know.

"I just tol' you, and cain't you see it with your own two eyeballs?" she asked. "I'm in here checkin' on Mr. Fields," she said real slowly this time.

"Why didn't you ask Felicia to check on Mr. Fields?"

"She's in with another patient, so I just ran down here for a minute."

"Well I need you at the nurses' station immediately," Dr.

Roman instructed, taking full advantage of her authority.

"Yes, ma'am, I'll be right there once I finish checkin' the patient," Betty responded.

"Immediately means immediately," Dr. Roman clarified. "As in right now," she demanded. "I'll finish checking on Mr. Fields for you."

"You know he don't like you, Dr. Roman," Betty reminded her. Dr. Roman had been complaining to her earlier in the evening about how he faked being asleep. "Soon as you walked in here he fell back asleep. He ain't gonna let you check on him."

"Well," Tanya replied, making sure to be careful what else she said in the presence of the guards. She didn't want to alarm them any more than she already had since nothing extracurricular seemed to be going on—at least not at the moment. "If I need your assistance, Betty, I'll come to get you, but I am confident I can handle Mr. Fields," she said wandering toward his bedside.

Moments later, Betty and both guards exited the room, and Tanya was occupying the space where Betty had been standing earlier. Cleve's head hadn't moved a hair. Beneath his right ear, the phone was still connected to Ansley, and she had heard nearly every word that had been said from the moment the commotion started.

"Mr. Fields," Tanya said real sweetly. "I didn't come in here to disturb you," she clarified. "I just wanted to let you know that your son Mason called and he wanted me to give you a message."

Back in Oriental, Ansley's eyes were wide-open in the dark. Her mouth was agape, but she made sure not to make a sound because it was apparent that somehow either Cleve or Betty had managed to hide the phone. Otherwise, the guards would have taken over the situation, and Tanya wouldn't be alone in the room with Cleve.

Cleve wanted to smile. He wanted to smile real big because in all these years this was the first time that anyone had told him that his son had called him. He also wanted to ask Dr. Roman what Mason had said, and at the same time, he wanted to speak into the phone beneath his head and ask Ansley what in the world was going on in Oriental. Why were both she and Mason calling him at the same time on the same night? What was wrong? That was his next thought.

Standing over Mr. Fields, Tanya watched a tear slip out of the corner of his left eye and then slowly work its way down his wrinkly face. As she stared at him, she noticed that the tear seemed to follow the lines as if it knew exactly where it was headed. She watched his jaw clench, and even though she knew without a doubt that he was wide awake, she stepped away from his bedside, and a moment later, closed the door behind her without saying another word.

15

Cleve sniffled.

"Ansley," he finally uttered after turning ever so slowly to make sure that Dr. Roman had in fact exited the room like he thought.

Ansley didn't answer.

Cleve then rolled his face closer to the phone. "Ansley," he whispered again.

"Cleve," Ansley murmured real low into her phone just in case anyone was still in the room with him even though it sounded like everyone had exited.

Cleve didn't respond.

Ansley removed the phone from her ear to look at the screen, then she shook her head side to side when she recognized that she and Cleve were no longer connected.

Cleve frowned when he figured out that he must have somehow hung up the phone when he rolled over onto it. For the longest time, he was confident that he could hear Ansley's breath seeping through the speaker as he prayed that neither the guard nor Dr. Roman would spot the phone beneath his head. Thank God, they hadn't.

The last time he remembered being able to hear a presence on the other end of the line was when Dr. Roman told him that Mason had called. That's when he'd tried to hold in his emotions, but he'd let a tear slip out of his eye, and he'd felt his jaw clench. That was the moment, he bet. When his jaw had tightened, it probably pressed against the phone and hung up the call.

Leaning against his headboard, Mason kicked the mattress beneath him with the heel of his foot. He did it again and again. *Did you really think they'd let you talk to him?* Mason scolded himself. He was angry about the decision to make the phone call on a whim. He should have waited. Given it more thought. All these years had gone by, and he'd never made an attempt to reach out to his dad, and now all of a sudden he'd tried to call him as midnight was approaching on a Tuesday night.

Frustrated, he dug his fingers into his hair. The room was dark with only a few slivers of moonlight seeping through the blinds. In addition to feeling like an idiot, he was afraid he might have just gotten Ansley into some hot water at the hospital. He didn't know the rules of a doctor being involved with a prisoner's family, but he was pretty sure that she shouldn't be at his house right now. Thankfully, he hadn't revealed anything of that nature to the lady he'd spoken with on the phone, but he knew he'd said too much. He wondered why she was so interested in knowing about his communication with Ansley.

For a moment, Mason considered walking down the hall and asking Ansley about the situation, but he wasn't sure if that was a wise idea. She would probably be upset with him for revealing the information he had given to someone named Betty from her department. The only good thing was that it sounded like Ansley and Betty were pretty close. But why had Ansley been talking to her nurse about him, he found himself wondering, and what had she been saying?

⚶

Why had Mason suddenly decided to reach out to his dad? Ansley wondered as she sat in bed listening to the thoughts in her mind along with the sounds of the country critters chattering outside the windows on either side of the bed. She could get used to the chirps and the howls—it sure beat the noise of passing cars and slamming doors.

Other questions were also circling her mind right now. Why had Mason thought that anyone at the hospital would let him talk to his dad? Didn't he realize that patients in his dad's predicament weren't allowed to receive calls? That was common knowledge, right?

Ansley's mind suddenly shifted to Tanya, and she instantly slammed her phone onto the hard mattress. Why had Tanya been the one who answered the phone when Mason called? Doctors rarely ever attended to phone calls unless the caller specifically asked for them. On top of that, why had Tanya told Cleve that Mason called? She wasn't supposed to share such information. In a situation like that, she was supposed to file a report that a caller had made an attempt to reach a patient. In the department in which they worked, that was a red flag.

Fidgeting with the covers and her phone, Ansley realized there was no way she could lie here all night and let her mind run free with these questions. She would never be able to fall asleep. But there was only one way to get answers.

A moment later, she climbed out of bed wearing nothing but a long t-shirt that covered her underwear. She ripped open the door leading out of her bedroom before barreling down the hallway to knock on Mason's door while at the same time twisting the knob and then barging in uninvited.

"What were you thinking?" she demanded to know, her voice cutting through the dark as she came to a halt just inside his room. Two things suddenly stopped her in her tracks: Callie's vicious growl and the realization that she had absolutely no idea where Mason's bed was situated, nor any other furniture. She didn't want to trip and fall trying to find him, and she definitely didn't want his dog to bite her.

Mason, who was still sitting in the upright position against his headboard, was so startled that he nearly jumped out of bed to grab his shotgun. The butt of the gun was nestled on the wooden floor next to the bedframe, the barrel resting against the wall. As soon as he recognized Ansley's voice, the threat level diminished—for both him and Callie—even though he could tell his houseguest was furious about something. He sighed and subconsciously thanked God that he didn't have to touch that gun.

"Excuse me?" he responded, unsure of what she was asking, but he had a good idea where this might be leading.

As she spoke, Ansley couldn't help but wonder if she had awakened him, but at the moment she really didn't care. "You called my hospital," she accused.

"Yeah, okay," he acknowledged, realizing he had no reason to hide the truth although he still wished he could go back to the moment when he'd transitioned from checking tomorrow's forecast on his phone to looking up the number that might lead to a conversation with his dad.

"Okay," she cried out. "Just okay?"

"What do you want me to say?" he probed.

"I want to know why?" she questioned, peering through the dark in the direction of his voice. "And where are you?"

Mason asked a question that was off the subject but completely legit in his mind. "Why did you barge into my room?"

Ansley placed her hands onto her hips as if he could see the gesture.

Mason's focus remained on Ansley's silhouette which he could barely make out in front of the doorframe.

"I thought I'd made that clear, Mason Fields," she articulated sharply. "I want to know why you called the hospital to talk to your dad."

"What if I was naked?" Mason randomly asked.

Ansley's head shuttered. "What?" she asked rhetorically before expressing her next thought. "Then I guess I'd be having this conversation with you in the nude," she countered.

Mason stretched his fingers toward the lamp on the nightstand next to his bed. When the light flickered on, the brightness took Ansley by surprise. She'd been in the dark for the past thirty or so minutes. Instantly, she found herself covering her eyes, partially because of the brightness and also due to Mason's comment.

"Are you really naked?" she asked.

"I'm under the covers," he informed her, "so I guess it doesn't matter." As an adult, he'd been sleeping naked for as long as he could remember. It wasn't something he normally shared with people because it wasn't anyone's business.

When Ansley removed her palm from in front of her eyes, she discovered Mason sitting against the headboard, covers up to his bare stomach. As she would have assumed based on the rest of his body, his chest was covered with dark hair. For some reason, she'd imagined that with his shirt off he'd look a bit chunkier, but the first words that came to mind to describe his body were sturdy and solid.

As Ansley glanced back and forth from Mason's face to his chest to the covers, wondering for some odd reason if he really was naked, she could tell that Mason was also giving her the once over.

Holding the covers tightly as if a random wind might blow them off his body, Mason couldn't help but notice Ansley's legs, long and lean, as the light beneath the lampshade traveled across the room. The shirt draped over her narrow-framed upper body barely covered her skin beyond the underwear he assumed she was wearing.

"So?" Ansley finally barked, breaking the silence.

"So what?" Mason asked, his brow furrowed.

"Why did you call?"

"I wanted to ask my dad a question?" he revealed. "How did you know I called, though?" he inquired, squinting his eyes.

"It's a long story," she admitted.

Mason sat up a little straighter, pulling the covers to match the movement of his body. The springs in his old mattress grumbled as they always did when he would toss or turn.

"Oh, so I'm supposed to answer your questions, but you don't have to answer mine?" he jabbed.

"My job is on the line here," Ansley exclaimed.

"Listen," Mason argued, "you put yourself in this situation by showing up at my front door out of the blue."

Ansley took a deep breath. "Fair enough," she agreed. "But what did you tell Tanya?"

"Who's Tanya?"

"The lady you spoke to on the phone."

Mason shook his head east to west. "The woman I talked to said her name was Betty."

A puzzled look fell across Ansley's face. How could he have talked to Betty? Betty was in Cleve's room when Tanya had burst onto the scene, and then Tanya had told Cleve that she had a message for him from Mason.

"Did you call more than once?" she found herself needing to know. That was the only way she could imagine that he might have possibly spoken to Betty.

"No."

Ansley shook her head from side to side.

Mason was taken aback by her body language. "What? You don't believe me?" he quizzed.

Ansley shook her head again in the same manner. "Oh, no, it's not that," she explained as she followed a trail of thoughts before sharing her assumption with Mason. "I'm pretty sure you talked to Tanya," she informed him. "What did she sound like?"

Mason's brow suddenly became as wrinkled as the covers on top of his body. "What do you mean?"

"I mean, did she speak properly or—" Ansley began, but paused, searching for the appropriate words to describe a woman whom she adored. "Was her speech, less educated sounding?"

"I'm not sure," Mason admitted. "I wasn't paying that close of attention to the sound of the woman's voice."

Ansley wished she could call Betty now even though she was almost positive that Mason hadn't spoken to her friend. But it was probably in everyone's best interest for Ansley to lay low for the time being. At this point, there was no telling who would answer the phone at the nurses' station if she called, and there was absolutely no way she was attempting to call Betty's cell phone while it was in Cleve's room. At least she hoped it was still in Cleve's room.

What if the guard had come in to search the room and found the phone after Betty and Tanya left? *Oh, God, help us all*, Ansley thought as she closed her eyelids for a moment and took a deep breath. The authorities would find her number to be the last one called and then she and Betty would both be fired and, possibly, prosecuted. She was in over her head, she knew. Maybe she should have listened to her mother's voice of reasoning that had been speaking loudly and clearly in her mind as she made her way to Oriental and even after her arrival. *Shoot!* Ansley suddenly shouted inside her thoughts, remembering that she had missed calls and text messages from her mother, but she had neglected to respond to any of them. She'd been so focused on calling Betty to see if she could talk to Cleve that she hadn't taken the time to even check the messages. Now, her phone was in the other room, and she had bigger things to worry about.

"I think Tanya just told you that she was Betty, but I'm not sure why," she rambled attempting to take her mind off the other thoughts ravaging her mental state. "Did she use words like ain't and cain't?"

Mason shrugged. "I don't remember," he answered. "I'm from the country, and we really don't care how anybody talks as long as we can understand what they mean."

Ansley felt the tension between her and Mason dwindling, but now she was even more fired up at Tanya. She knew that Tanya had it out for her, and her colleague had already been asking questions about her relationship with Cleve. All it would take was a little bit of evidence that something outside the boundaries was happening, and Tanya was sure to go to their supervisor. To have been a stripper, the woman played by the rules more closely than anyone she had ever worked with. Ansley knew how excited Tanya had been about taking charge while she was away, and a situation like this would be the perfect opportunity for Tanya to take her job right out from under her.

"It doesn't really matter," Ansley finally concluded. "But what did you say to whomever it was that you talked to?" she asked. "This is really important," she made sure to explain.

"I just asked if I could talk to my dad."

"How did she respond?"

"She said that she could take a message for him."

Ansley shook her head and made a comment geared more toward herself than toward Mason. "She's not supposed to do that," she uttered. "But, anyway, what did you ask her to tell your dad?"

"What if I don't want to talk about this?" Mason proposed.

"Mason, please!"

"Fine," he mumbled. "I told her I didn't want to leave a message for my dad."

"You did?" Ansley questioned. She'd personally overheard Tanya telling Cleve that she had a message for him from Mason, which meant one of them wasn't telling the truth.

"Yes."

"Are you sure about that?" she double-checked, praying that Mason wasn't the one lying.

"I'm certain," he conveyed then asked a question of his own. "Who have you been talking to about all of this?" he inquired.

"Betty," Ansley acknowledged. "Well, kind of—"

"What do you mean by *kind of?*"

"It's a long story."

"Oh, that again." Sighing, he paused, waiting to see if she would elaborate, but she didn't. "Well, I have all night," he offered. "I've stayed up this late, so I might as well not even sleep."

"If you must know," Ansley said in a huff, "I called Betty so I could talk to your dad."

Mason interrupted. "Why did you want to talk to my dad?"

"I needed to ask him a question."

"What question?"

Ansley crossed her arms at her chest. This *was* going to take all night. They were both trying to call Cleve, but it was apparent that neither of them wanted to admit to the other why they'd been trying to contact him.

"He's my patient," Ansley declared. "I needed to check in on him."

"So you can call prisoners at the hospital but I can't."

She corrected him. "Patients."

"He's a prisoner, Ansley. He's in prison. Just because he's in your hospital doesn't mean that he's no longer a prisoner."

"You sound like Tanya," she snarled.

"Well, Tanya's right," he reeled off.

Ansley stepped closer to the bed and threw up her hands. "You don't even know her," she spewed.

Mason said nothing in response, and he tried to look away as Ansley's underwear became exposed when she lifted her arms.

A moment later, Ansley spoke again. "Did you say anything to Tanya about me?"

Mason wasn't sure exactly how to respond. He needed to choose his words carefully. "Technically, no."

Ansley squinted her eyebrows, the skin between them crunching as she spoke. "I don't like the sound of that," she admitted. "What do you mean?"

"The person I talked to mentioned you."

"Oh, my God," she grumbled, raising her hand to her forehead as if checking for a fever. "What was said?"

Mason had been so overwhelmed at the time of the call that he honestly couldn't remember what all was said. He just knew that he'd basically admitted to knowing how Ansley felt about his dad.

"The lady who said she was Betty told me that she was your nurse and that you had talked to her about me."

"What?" Ansley exclaimed.

"Yes, I'm pretty sure that's what she said," Mason assured her, digging through his memory, hoping to be as precise as possible.

"What did you say?"

"I think I just said, *She has?*"

"Then what did she say?"

As Mason breathed in a deep breath, his stomach sunk in and his bare chest rose. "She said she probably shouldn't talk about that."

"What else?"

"The only other thing she said is that you think a lot of my dad."

"And how did you respond?"

Mason dropped his head.

Ansley quickly asked the same question using different words and a heavier tone of voice. "Mason, what did you say?"

"I think I said, *I know.*"

16

The following morning life seemed abnormally normal again. Mason was the first to awaken, and after brewing a pot of coffee, he settled into his rocking chair on the front porch. He'd barely slept a wink last night, and neither had Ansley he found out when she joined him on the porch. She smiled when she realized he had beaten her to the chair she'd occupied the previous morning. She'd had a hunch that it was *his* chair, and today, she was happy to sit in the one he'd dragged over yesterday. She had quickly caught onto how much Mason liked his routines, and she imagined it had driven him crazy when she'd taken his spot.

Before pouring a cup of coffee and walking onto the porch, Ansley had taken a moment to text her mother. She'd purposefully kept the message simple: *Mom, I am okay, but I need a little space right now. I am on vacation, which I realize I should have told you about, and I will come to see you once I return home at the end of the week.*

Late last night, Ansley had been afraid that she might have to travel back to Raleigh sooner than planned if someone found Betty's cell phone in Cleve's bed. But, thank God, Ansley had been awakened this morning by a phone call from Betty letting her know that she'd been able to retrieve the phone during the middle of the night. Betty had even provided a timely laugh when she said, "Child, I didn't know how on God's green earth I was gonna sneak back into that man's room without Tanya callin' the authority. She was on me like white on rice all night long. But as soon as her filter-free mouth tole' me she was going to take a number two, my fat-self scurried down to that room like a chocolate cake was waiting on me."

Betty had gone on to tell Ansley how relieved Cleve had been when he saw her enter his room—alone. "I thought y'all were about to join me in prison," he shared with a therapeutic laugh of his own. He then told her that he had been fighting sleep in fear that he'd accidentally nudge the phone far enough away that he wouldn't be able to cover it when someone came in to check on him, or even worse, that it might fall off the bed. Then Betty had said to Cleve, "Child, I gotta get out of this room, I cain't stick around and chitchat with you like usual."

Last night, when Ansley was in Mason's bedroom, she had gone on to enlighten him about the cell phone incident, and like her, he thought they were all going to end up in trouble. He definitely didn't want investigators breathing down his neck again. This morning, he felt a sigh of relief when she shared the details of her and Betty's most recent phone conversation. "Oh, and Betty said she was definitely not the one who talked to you on the phone when you called the hospital," Ansley clarified.

Mason, Ansley, and Callie spent the next thirty minutes watching the sunrise together for the second morning in a row. As a group of wild turkeys wobbled across one of the strawberry fields, they glanced at one another and smiled. As usual, birds were flying, chirping, and reminding everyone that daylight had arrived. They sounded much more peaceful than a rooster, Ansley thought, but she decided to give Mason a hard time about his farm not having such a bird that served as a natural alarm clock.

"How can you call this place a farm without a rooster?" she teased.

Mason went on to tell her that his family owned a rooster when he was growing up. "Chickens, too," he added.

After consuming two full cups of much needed coffee, Mason made his way toward the roadside market beneath a cloud-covered sky. The lack of sun made it feel a bit cooler out, and Ansley decided to spend some time indoors reading instead of venturing out during the morning hours. Eventually, she caught herself glancing through the online dating app on her phone, but after scrolling through the profiles of a few of the guys that had *liked* her profile, she found herself comparing each of them to Mason. She wondered if Mason Fields liked her. For some reason, she just couldn't get a feel for what he might be thinking. What if he didn't like women with blonde hair? What if he was a breast man rather than a butt man? She wasn't naïve enough to think that curves didn't matter to a man. Of course, every woman wanted to hope that personality was more important, but the truth of the matter was that looks mattered, especially to men.

Mason spent the morning packaging strawberries as the pickers brought them into the market, and when lunchtime came around, he went home to take a nap. When he walked in the front door, he found Ansley lying on the couch with a book covering her face. He and Callie tiptoed across the floor and ended up in his bedroom. When they came out an hour later, his hair was matted, and Ansley hadn't budged.

About thirty minutes after Mason and Callie left the house, Ansley woke up from a two-hour nap. Hungry, she headed for the kitchen where she found a brown paper bag with her name written on it with a black marker. Inside, she discovered a peanut butter and jelly sandwich and an individual bag of chips. She grinned real big. *I think he likes me*, she thought to herself as she read a note on a piece of paper that had been tucked inside the bag:

Thanks for making dinner last night! I thought I'd return the favor just in case you end up needing a picnic lunch again today. Maybe when I get home this evening, we can pull another slip of paper from The Date Night Jar. That was fun!

With another evening brought on by The Date Night Jar bouncing around like a pinball in her mind, Ansley took a walk down the dusty driveway toward the pond. The thought crossed her mind that if she had grabbed the fishing poles that Mason had mentioned the first night she was in town, and if she had a little boy walking alongside her, this would feel just like the opening scene of *The Andy Griffith Show*. Life out here seemed to bring her back to a different era, and she had to admit that she relished the feeling.

She probably wouldn't have chosen to eat a PB&J again today, but after Mason had gone through the trouble to prepare one for her, how could she pass it up? She couldn't, she decided, and as she watched the ducks float around the pond, she was glad she had come here. Even though there had been some rough patches during this trip, this place was therapeutic just like Cleve promised.

Mason's afternoon was divided up between tending the fields with the tractor, repairing some equipment in the barn, and handling a few customer questions at the market. Thankfully, today, no one had made any complaints or silly suggestions. He noticed that Callie seemed a little sluggish, and he figured that she was probably just as tired as he was. He'd been yawning all day, and if he hadn't taken a power nap at lunch, he wasn't sure if he would have been able to keep his eyes open as he drove the tractor.

After lunch, when Ansley was sitting on the bench overlooking the pond, she had spotted a trailhead on the far side of the open area that led into the woods. She was surprised that she hadn't noticed it yesterday, but she realized there was a lot of nature to take in out here. Curious, she wandered into the opening and quickly found herself beneath a canopy of trees. Some of them appeared to have been there for hundreds of years, and others were much more youthful. There was relatively little underbrush which made the view on her walk absolutely serene. The trail winded through a wide variety of hardwoods and pines that dotted the forest, and she could tell that Mason must ride his four-wheeler out here from time to time because the path was very clear.

On the outskirts of the pathway, she noticed carefully placed branches that outlined the trail. It was also obvious that fallen trees had been cleared from the path with a chainsaw. She figured that old age or wind storms must have gotten the best of them. Hurricanes frequented this part of the state, too, so that might have been the cause of some of the downed trees and branches.

Mason's last task of the afternoon had taken him and Callie to the backside of the farm beyond the area where the pond was situated. On the way back to the house as he drove the tractor past the opening that led to his favorite fishing hole, he glanced in as if looking through a window, wondering if Ansley had spent time there again today. When he turned his head back to the dusty path in front of him, something caught his attention out of the corner of his eye, but by the time he turned back to look through the opening, he could no longer see into the pond area.

Ready to get home, he decided to keep driving the tractor even though something inside him was whispering for him to go back. Then, to his surprise, Callie suddenly bounced off the moving tractor and shot through the opening to the pond like a ball of fire. Mason instantly shut off the engine, and that's when he heard someone screaming. A moment later, he was running as fast as possible as the hollering continued to grow louder.

When Mason made it through the opening, he spotted Ansley on the far side of the pond, running and flailing her arms as she yelled out for help.

He couldn't figure out why she was running or what she was trying to get away from, but he continued to run around the outside edge of the water in her direction.

"Help," Ansley hollered when she spotted Callie and Mason heading her way. "Help!"

Mason could tell she was freaking out, and when Callie made it to her, he watched his collie jump into the air around her, swatting at something with her paws.

In that instant, Mason figured out exactly what was going on—bees!

A few moments later as he was closing in on Ansley, he realized she wasn't going to stop running, and she didn't need to because the bees would then sting her repeatedly. At this point, Mason knew he only had one option. There was no way to instantly calm down a swarm of angry bees. So, as his and Ansley's paths crossed, Mason lowered his shoulders like a linebacker making a tackle in football. He snatched his new friend by the waist and in the same movement lifted her into the air like a dancer would his partner, letting the momentum carry them in circles.

At the water's edge, Mason released Ansley, letting her body soar through the air before splashing into one of the deepest parts of the pond. He hadn't noticed the cell phone in her hand until he'd flung her with all of his might, not that he would have done anything differently if he had, but he caught a glimpse of the device flying through the air before making a small splash of its own. Hoping to lose the bees, he made sure not to stop moving, and he dove right in behind her.

Once underwater, Mason swam rapidly up to the surface, wanting to make it there before Ansley. When his head popped out of the water first, he began to swat at the bees in the air above him as he waited for Ansley. Soon after, he watched her head rise above the waterline.

When Ansley came up, she immediately spotted Mason slapping at the bees that had followed them.

"Go back under," he quickly instructed, "and swim as far out into the pond as you can."

As soon as the words came out of his mouth, both of their heads ducked beneath the brackish water. As Mason suggested, Ansley swam as far as she possibly could and stayed under water until she couldn't hold her breath a moment longer. She prayed it was long enough, but she didn't have much energy after running through the woods for what seemed like several minutes. She wasn't sure if any of the bees had stung her—adrenaline had kicked in, and she knew that if she had been stung she probably wouldn't realize it until she calmed down.

Mason knew he could remain underwater for nearly two minutes if he needed to. When he was a teenager, he and his parents used to have regular contests to see who could hold their breath the longest. Of course, during those competitions, he wasn't wearing boots that at the moment felt like they weighed about twenty pounds. Unfortunately, the bees hadn't allowed him to kick off his shoes and socks at the shoreline.

His mom almost always won any type of swimming-related matches, and it drove his dad crazy. He knew this because his dad was the one always asking for a rematch. Both of his parents were terrific swimmers, and they'd taught him how to swim at a young age. As a kid, he spent time at this pond nearly every day during the summers, and he had continued doing the same as an adult. Back then, he would play games and try to make big splashes like the ones he and Ansley had made moments ago. Nowadays, he enjoyed swimming laps from one end to the other as many times as he could. It was a great workout and quite refreshing after a long day in the sweltering North Carolina heat and humidity. He also liked to sit out here on the canoe and take in the calmness of the world around him with a fishing pole in his hand and nothing on his mind.

Today, however, calm wasn't the word to describe the scene out at the pond. Holding his breath while swimming like a frog, Mason decided that he better pop up to see if Ansley had surfaced, and as soon as he did, he realized she was treading water about twenty yards from him. He wanted to make sure he could help her if the bees had been able to follow them. When those creatures locked onto a scent, they were like heat-seeking missiles.

"I think we lost them," Ansley gasped as Mason began to swim toward her. "And my cell phone," she screeched.

When Mason made it to her side, he began to tread water also. "Are you okay?" he asked hastily.

"I think so," she conveyed, looking down at her arms for the first time to see if there were any visible bee stings.

"Did you get stung?"

Ansley didn't notice any whelps. "I don't think so," she revealed, surprised that she managed to escape without any real harm—thanks to Mason and Callie, she thought, as she suddenly felt a surge of weakness throughout her entire body.

As soon as Mason realized Ansley was going to be okay, his attention immediately turned to Callie who had apparently been running circles around the pond ever since the two of them jumped into the water. She was a smart dog, the most intelligent he had ever known, and he had no doubt in his mind that she had purposefully drawn the attention of the bees to herself by leaping into the air next to Ansley and pawing at them.

"Callie," Mason yelled as he watched her four legs move as fast as they ever had. "Come here, girl," he screamed. "Jump in the water!"

He could tell by her relentless speed and consistent barking that the bees were still chasing her, but it was like she was waiting to make sure that he and Ansley were safe before she took care of herself.

On Mason's command, Callie leaped into the water near the opposite end of the pond, and as she did, both he and Ansley watched her dip under like a duck.

"Mason," Ansley suddenly relayed with fright lining her voice. "I can't stay—"

Before she could complete her cry for help, Mason turned just in time to watch her head collapse beneath the surface. Instantly, he followed his first reaction and lunged in her direction, and as he did, he thanked God that he was close enough to reach below the water and grab ahold of her body.

Once he was able to pull her back up, she attached to him even tighter than she had last night by the fire. A moment later, he felt one of her shoes kick against his shin. He'd never had to save anyone from drowning, but his parents had taught him how to in case an emergency ever happened out here or in any other body of water.

Mason loved Ansley's arms wrapped around him like this, but he knew what he needed her to do in order to make sure that both of them didn't end up drowning. "Let go, Ansley," he instructed as he continued to kick his feet beneath the water. "I need you to turn around and lay back onto me so that I can swim us to the shore," he explained.

Thank goodness she listened, and in a matter of moments they were cruising toward the opposite edge of the pond from where they'd jumped in. Either side was about equal distance, but Mason didn't want to go back to where they'd come from just in case the bees were still swarming in that area.

When they made it to the edge of the water, Mason drug himself and Ansley just far enough where they could collapse onto the grassy bank.

Once they landed, Ansley rolled over, but her shoulder was still on Mason's chest, and her arm was wrapped around him and so was one of her legs. Both of them were completely beat.

"I might need mouth to mouth," she teased, breathing hard and rapidly as she made the comment. The moment the thought had become vocal, she realized how silly it sounded. There were probably a million better ways to ask a man to kiss you, she figured. Or, she could have just taken advantage of the situation and kissed him.

Mason smiled, took a deep breath, then said, "I'd be happy to if you'd let me." Just like Ansley, the moment the line left his lips he realized how corny it sounded.

Ansley smiled back at him and, to his surprise, said, "I'd love that."

Without thinking about anything else, Mason lifted his head off the ground, and as he felt his lips touch Ansley's, both of them dripping wet, he let his eyelids collapse. He reached his hand up to wipe the water from her hair and face as he continued to kiss her for the first time.

There was something special about first kisses, and Mason knew that this was a first time that he would never forget. What a story this would be, he thought to himself.

Ansley let her body slide further onto Mason Fields as their lips moved like two bodies dancing to a slow rhythm. In a way, she felt like she was in a movie where the hero had just saved the damsel in distress. She nearly laughed as the thought crossed her mind, but she was thankful that she was able to hold in her amusement because she knew it would ruin the intimate moment. Then, a second later, Mason abruptly pulled back and all of a sudden their first kiss had ended much too soon.

"Callie," Mason clamored, "I have to check on Callie."

Ansley twisted her body and began to search with her eyes for his dog. Caught up in the moment, she had somehow forgotten all about Callie.

Mason lifted himself from the ground. He didn't see Callie anywhere, and he felt a brick of guilt slam down on his chest as he imagined the possibility that Callie may have drowned while he was kissing Ansley. But, Callie was a good swimmer, he reminded himself. She loved being in the pond with him. Yet . . . she had been running so hard . . . and she was an old dog. All of the energy spent may have been too much for her, just like it had been too much for Ansley. Who knows what would have happened to Ansley if he hadn't been right there beside her to pull her to safety a few minutes ago?

"Callie," Mason hollered, and he was just about to jump back into the water to begin searching beneath the surface when he spotted her lying motionless on the opposite side of the pond.

"There," Ansley called out, pointing as she located Callie about the same time as Mason. Callie's body was as still as the water they'd just climbed out of.

17

Mason immediately kicked off his soaking wet boots and dove back into the water, once again swimming with all his might, hoping to get to the other side of the pond before it was too late.

Soaking wet, Ansley picked herself up from the ground and took off running next to the edge of the pond. As her legs moved as fast as they had when she'd been trying to escape from the bees, she kept glancing back at Mason as he swam as if competing for an Olympic medal.

Ansley soon circled the edge of the pond near the opening that led back to the dirt drive and then began the trek back up the other side. When she was about thirty yards from where Callie was lying, she watched Mason climb out of the water and fall at his dog's side.

Ansley was nearly in tears when she made it to Callie, but she instantly dropped down beside the dog on the opposite side as Mason.

With his arms wrapped around his best friend, Mason looked up hopelessly at Ansley. "Is she dead?" he uttered. Callie hadn't made a single movement since he'd first laid eyes on her from the opposite shore.

As soon as Ansley's knees had hit the ground, her fingers had begun to search for a pulse.

A dog's body was different from a human's, but the concept was the same. It didn't take her long to realize that two separate issues were going on with Callie, and time was likely the biggest obstacle. In the water, Ansley had let Mason take charge, but now it was her turn.

"Move back," she instructed.

Without speaking a word, he did.

As she began to perform CPR for the first time ever on a dog, she gave out quick and concise directions to Mason just as she would to one of the nurses in an emergency at the hospital.

"Go to my car. Bring the black bag from the floor behind the driver's seat. Hurry."

Something in the tone of Ansley's voice told Mason that there was no time for questions, but there were at least a dozen circling his mind in addition to the one he'd already asked. As he sprinted, these questions pounded on his brain as his bare feet pounded on the ground. He flew right past the tractor, knowing he could make it to Ansley's car faster on foot than he could driving that massive piece of machinery, especially since he'd have to start the engine, shift the gear, and get moving. Unlike sports cars, tractors weren't made for zero to whatever speed.

Was Callie going to die? Mason had decided that she must not be dead or Ansley wouldn't have started CPR and instructed him to get her bag. What was in the bag? Medical equipment, he assumed. But what? What exactly did she need? It wasn't like there could be an oxygen mask in there, right? Regardless, he kept his feet moving as fast as he could even though the roots were taking a toll on them.

Ansley continued with the compressions, and after each set, she checked for a pulse. "Come on, girl," she yammered. "You can do this," she demanded. "Breathe. Just breathe for me."

About halfway to the house, a new string of thoughts hit Mason: Was Ansley's car unlocked? What if it wasn't? Where were her keys? Did he have time to search for them? What if they were in her pocket? What if they had fallen out when she was running? What if they were at the bottom of the pond with her phone?

It didn't matter, he finally told himself. If he needed to, he'd break the window. He'd pay for a new one if that were the case. Callie was more important than a window. Heck, she was more important than the whole car, and the thought of losing her kept him running when his body told him to stop.

Ansley hadn't taken the time to mention it to Mason, but in the very beginning, she had found a pulse. That didn't mean that Callie would make it, and she didn't want to get his hopes up. She didn't want him to think about anything other than what needed to be done to save his dog, and the more desperate he felt, the better. Adrenaline had a way of giving humans a temporary surge of superhero strength and endurance.

Mason snatched the handle and breathed a deep sigh of relief when the rear driver's side door flung all the way open with one forceful tug. He seized the bag as if he'd done so a hundred times and left the door wide-open as he retraced his steps—or rather lunges. As he ran, he prayed that Callie wouldn't be gone when he got back. There had to be hope or Ansley wouldn't have sent him to fetch this bag. He hadn't taken the time to open it to see what was inside, but he sure hoped it was something that would help save his dog.

Ansley was in the middle of a set of compressions when water suddenly spewed out of Callie's mouth. Ansley instantly grinned from ear to ear. "There you go, girl," she encouraged as Callie gasped for air. "Keep going," she encouraged. More water erupted out then came more gasps for air and a string of coughs. "Good girl," Ansley uttered, smiling even bigger.

Obstacle one was out of the way. Now, where was Mason? Ansley needed her bag. Now. When she'd been feeling for a pulse, she had felt the whelps on Callie's body, and while she'd been doing the compressions, she could see some of the places where the bees had stung the dog. From the looks of the spots, it was evident that Callie was allergic. On top of nearly drowning, the poor dog was having an allergic reaction. Her tongue was swelling, and her throat was contracting. Thank God, the water she'd swallowed had made it out before her airway became too constricted.

When the tractor came into view, Mason knew he was nearing the end of the race for his dog's life, but he had to tell his legs to keep moving. Now wasn't the time to let up.

When he finally reached Ansley and Callie, he slid in next to them like a baseball player sliding into home plate to score the winning run. The bag dropped next to Ansley who was sitting on her legs.

With precision, Ansley popped open the bag and reached in knowing precisely what she needed. A moment later, she stuck the sharp end of an EpiPen into Callie's skin. Thank God, a dog of this size could handle the same epinephrine dose as a human. Otherwise, they would have another issue on their hands.

Upon arriving with the bag, Mason had been relieved to discover Callie's open eyes, and he could see her chest rising and falling, although at a much faster pace than normal, and she seemed to be gasping for air. He didn't know if that was because she had water in her lungs or if something else was going on. Whatever Ansley had just stuck into her seemed to help almost immediately.

"She's going to be okay," Ansley explained, locking eyes with Mason.

He wanted to hug her and thank her for saving his dog's life. He also wanted to finish the kiss that had started on the other side of the pond, but when Ansley said, "You can love on her; she probably needs that right now," he did exactly what she suggested.

"Callie, everything's alright. I'm right here," he let her know as she lifted her eyes at the sound of his voice. "I love you," he reminded her. "I love you so much."

Letting the two of them have their moment, Ansley smiled as she watched. She loved these moments. This was what being a physician was about, and she truly believed she had been created for this. This time, though, she didn't have to remove her scrubs and gloves and follow all the other protocols after saving a life. She was just able to watch—to enjoy Mason holding onto his dog who was now licking him in the face like a kid licking a lollipop.

The seat on the tractor was wide enough for both Mason and Ansley to sit with Callie sprawled out across their wet laps. Mason steered the machine carefully up the dirt drive trying his best to avoid the occasional pothole or bump. This road that led through his property was too long for one person to keep perfectly maintained. On most days he didn't even notice the imperfections, but today he didn't want to jolt Callie.

Once at the house, Mason carried his dog inside and gently rested her body with its matted fur on top of the covers on his bed. "She'll need some rest," Ansley had prescribed earlier as Mason carried his girl from the pond area to the tractor. Ansley had walked next to them, toting her physician's bag and Mason's wet shoes that she'd been kind enough to retrieve. He made sure to thank her for that.

"You can take the first shower," Mason offered after Ansley

checked over Callie in the house.

"Thanks," she obliged appreciatively. "I think I'll take a bath, though."

"That sounds nice," he admitted.

"I love taking baths," Ansley shared.

Her comment drew a smirk from Mason, and at first, Ansley wondered why. Then he said, "Don't tell anyone, but I do, too."

Ansley smiled. "Who am I going to tell?"

"I don't know, your girlfriends, maybe."

"They'd think that was sweet."

"Well, I would say don't tell my guy friends, but I don't really have friends these days."

Ansley tilted her head ever so slightly as she asked, "Why not?"

"I stay busy with work, and when I'm not working, I just do my own thing."

Ansley showed understanding through a simple nod. "Farming is hard work, huh?"

Mason shook his head. "Definitely, but it's worth it."

"That's how I feel about being a physician," Ansley shared.

"I'm sure being a doctor requires a lot of long hours, too," Mason mentioned, continuing to rub Callie as he spoke.

"It does."

"A lot of responsibility as well, I would imagine," he added.

"Yes," she agreed. "It's my job to keep people alive," she said loosely as she reached her hand out to pet Callie. "And dogs, too," she added with a wink.

"Thanks," Mason offered. "If you hadn't been here, I'm not sure what I would have done," he admitted.

Ansley lowered her head in self-disgust. "If I hadn't been here, you and Callie wouldn't have had to save me from those bees, and she wouldn't have had to go through that trauma."

Mason had nearly forgotten about the bees. All of his attention had shifted to Callie ever since the moment he spotted her lying on the opposite side of the pond. Now, as he watched Ansley's head lift, their eyes met, and he remembered what else had happened at the pond . . . that kiss.

"How long had you been running from those bees?"

"It felt like I ran for a mile, but I'm really not sure."

"I've meant to warn you that there are honey bees back there on the backside of the property beyond the pond," Mason mentioned, and he watched Ansley's eyes begin to widen as her mind absorbed the information. "When Callie first started jumping in the air and pawing at them, I thought, *oh no, she's disturbed their colony.*" He paused for a moment. "But the bees that were chasing you weren't honey bees," he assured her.

"How do you know that?" she asked inquisitively. It wasn't his fault that the bees chased her, regardless of whether it was honey bees or some other type of bees. Granted, it would have been nice to know they were out there, but at the same time, she should have been paying more attention to her surroundings. Honestly, she wasn't sure where the bees had come from. She had been leisurely walking that trail and then she remembered feeling a tapping sensation on her legs. When she glanced down, bees were swarming all around her.

"I think they were ground bees," Mason guessed based on the buzzing sounds he'd heard, but he couldn't be certain. Everything had happened so fast.

When Ansley explained how the chase had begun, Mason figured his hunch was most likely correct.

Callie coughed a few times deeply, and the conversation about bees quickly dwindled away as Mason became concerned about his dog's health. Noticing his expression, Ansley promptly assured him that Callie was okay and that she'd probably cough off and on the rest of the night.

After answering a few more questions about Callie's current state, Ansley gathered the items she needed for a bath. "Just let me know if you need me," she told Mason before leaving him alone with Callie.

It felt refreshing to Ansley when she lowered her body into a bathtub full of hot water where she let her head rest on the rim of the claw foot tub as her arms dangled over the sides. A few moments after sinking below the surface, she found herself wishing she had a book in her hands, and a glass of wine would have been quite nice as well, she thought.

She wished she could just call out to the farmer down the hallway: *Hey, Mason would you mind fetching my book and bringing me a tall glass of wine?* Dreams.

Better yet, she wished she and Mason could have crawled into this tub together. Not because they would both be naked and there would be something very sensual about that, but because it would be nice to relax in the bath while having a pleasant conversation with a person sitting across from her. *That's a date night I'd love to pull from a jar*, she thought with her eyelids resting as her mind wandered.

Thirty minutes later, after Ansley slipped on her clothes, she ventured to the room where she found her new dirty farmer-friend still sitting on the bed with his best friend. She felt guilty knowing that he had been waiting there all this time, but she was happy to discover that he had at least taken off his wet clothes and replaced them with an old pair of shorts and a ratty t-shirt.

"I'm glad to see you changed out of those wet clothes," she mentioned with a smirk.

"They felt like they were stuck to my body, and they didn't smell so good."

"I know what you mean," Ansley agreed, having felt the same way before stripping off her soaked clothes in the bathroom. "I'm sorry I took so long," she admitted. Time had kind of gotten away from her.

"That's okay, I wanted to be here with Callie anyway," Mason confirmed as he massaged his dog's head.

"Well, I can take over now if you want to hop in the shower," she offered. "Or the bathtub," she mentioned with a wink.

"The shower will probably work best this time," Mason answered, knowing there most likely wouldn't be any hot water left. He then grabbed a stack of clothes that he'd taken the time to set out while Ansley had been soaking in the tub.

"We can skip The Date Night Jar this evening if you'd like," Ansley suggested. She figured that revealing the thought that she'd had in the bathtub about a perfect date, which had reminded her that they were supposed to pull from the jar again this evening, wouldn't be appropriate to share with him at this point in their . . . whatever it was that was going on here.

"It's up to you," he said. "I know you seemed excited about it." He wasn't going to admit that he'd thought about The Date Night Jar off and on all day.

Ansley figured her face probably looked a little puzzled at the moment. Although their date night jar activity last night had gone quite well, and even though the two of them had shared an amazing kiss at the edge of the pond this evening, she had imagined that Mason would be looking for any reason possible to get out of seeing that jar again.

"I know what we could do," Ansley mentioned, thinking back to the way many of Cleve's and Violet's date nights had been selected. "We can pick a date from the jar now, but if it's something we're not feeling up to tonight, especially something that would mean leaving this old gal," Ansley clarified as she scratched Callie with the tips of her fingernails, "we can just save it for later."

"I'm not sure that's how The Date Night Jar works," Mason mentioned.

When did you all of a sudden become an expert on the rules of

The Date Night Jar? Ansley wanted to ask but knew better.

"I'm pretty sure it's okay. Cleve mentioned that when he and your mom first started dating, he would pick out a date during the week and then they would have their date that weekend."

Mason mulled over the comment for a moment. "Yeah, I guess you're right." He paused, thinking back to the guidelines his parents had shared about The Date Night Jar. "But, in the beginning, when he pulled out the dates, they weren't together at those times because mom didn't know about the jar yet," he reminded Ansley.

Ansley thought back to the campfire date which was still fresh on her mind—both Cleve's and Violet's as well as hers and Mason's. "I vividly recall Cleve telling me that he and your mom were together at her parent's house when she plucked out the campfire date, which they went on at a later time."

Last night, when Ansley had read the sliver of paper that she pulled from the jar, Mason had instantly recalled the story his parents told him about their night at the campfire and their first kiss. They hadn't gone into the details, but he remembered his mother laughing about being afraid that they'd get caught. He found himself wishing she were around to tell him one more date night jar story. "You're right," he finally said.

Ansley tilted her head slightly and grinned. "So you want me to fetch the jar?"

"That's fine, but you're not a dog," Mason laughed, and Callie cocked her head at the comment as if wondering why the word dog had been mentioned.

"Ha, ha," Ansley commented instead of actually laughing.

A few moments later, she returned with the jar. "You want to pick it this time?" she asked.

In all of his life, Mason had never picked a sliver of paper from The Date Night Jar. He'd always wondered if one day he'd want to give this thing a shot, but he honestly doubted that he ever would—

all the way up until last night when he thoroughly enjoyed the time he spent in the backyard with Ansley Stone. He wanted more of that. "Sure," he agreed, figuring it *was* his turn since she'd picked last night.

Ansley handed the glass jar to Mason as he plopped down on the bed next to her. Holding it with one hand, he used the other to twist off the lid. His eyes didn't light up like Ansley's had, and he didn't take his time; instead, he just dug right in and snatched out the first roll of paper his fingers touched.

Then, he read it aloud: *Play A Board Game.*

The word *Monopoly* instantly flashed into Mason's mind. Not because he wanted to play that particular game now with Ansley, but because Monopoly was his mother's favorite board game. Also, it wasn't just her favorite board game, it was the first game that she and his father played together when they were dating. She'd told him that story once. Maybe twice. Somehow, he suddenly remembered it almost word for word.

Son, when your daddy pulled the scroll from The Date Night Jar that said to play a board game, I was as giddy as all get out . . .

170

18

*O*f course, when he pulled that date from the jar, he wasn't your daddy. You weren't born yet. He and I weren't even married. We'd been courting for a short time, and, truth be told, I was falling head over heels for him. Believe it or not, he was the first boy I ever dated. Technically, he was a man, and I was a woman because both of us had recently turned eighteen, but he still seemed like the same boy I'd known since grade school.

He had stringy brown hair and brown eyes to match it. He was handsome and strong and smart, and I'd had a crush on him for as long as I could remember. All the girls at school had eyes for your daddy. I'm not sure he knew that, but he could have courted any one of them that he wanted, so I felt quite special when he chose little ole' me. Enough about that. You're a boy, and you don't care about that mushy-gushy stuff.

The reason I was so excited about that particular date was because I absolutely loved playing board games. My parents and I played games at the kitchen table often, and we'd played Monopoly so many times the board was worn out on the edges. So were all the different cards that go with the game.

We were sitting at your daddy's parents' kitchen table when he pulled out the game night date. The two of us smelled like smoke *because we had just finished roasting marshmallows over a bonfire in the backyard, which was our date on that particular evening, and it was the first one I'd ever plucked out of the jar. I'll never forget that moment.*

The previous week, your daddy had introduced me to The Date Night Jar—a family courting tradition that I was quite excited about being a part of since it was passed down to him.

The first time we made a selection from the jar together, he'd been sweet enough to let me pick. He has always been that type of man. The one who holds the door for me, lets me use his hankie when I am crying, and takes good care of me when I am sick. It's the little things that mean so much to a woman. Always remember that, Mason.

Don't get me wrong, he's always been a man's man, which you know because you work with him every day on the farm, but he knows how to treat a lady.

Sorry, I realize I'm babbling about this lovey-dovey stuff again. One day you'll understand, though.

Anyways after I picked out the first date, we made a decision that we would take turns pulling from the jar. Technically, it wasn't the first date because he had been pulling them out by himself until he built up the nerve to tell me about The Date Night Jar. He thought I would think it was silly, which was why he waited to tell me. We also decided that the best time to pick our next date was at the end of the one we were having that particular day. That way we could always choose together and look forward to our next opportunity to spend time with each other. We both worked long hours on our parents' respective farms, so free time was hard to come by, which made us cherish the moments we had together that much more.

The following Friday, your daddy came to my house to play Monopoly. Well, I should say he came to my parents' house. Father often told me that his home was my home for as long as I wanted to live there, so I've always called it my house, too. Back then, a woman didn't typically move out of her childhood home until she married. Most men didn't either. It helped keep us grounded and made a lot of sense from a financial perspective.

Monopoly is all about money and property, and I've always thought it's more fun when you have a group of people involved, so I talked Mother and Father into playing with us. Father was a little hesitant, but he finally gave in when I twisted his arm with my puppy dog eyes. I think your daddy would have rather it just be me and him playing because he was really nervous around Father. I'd told him that the man was a big teddy bear, but your daddy was terrified that one day he'd roar at him.

As usual, Mother prepared the board, setting out the game pieces, money, and cards. Father always used the car piece; Mother used the iron; and I used the thimble.

"Which piece would you like?" Mother asked, and all eyes turned to your daddy as we waited for a response.

"I'll be the—" He hesitated as he glared at the pieces sitting loosely in Mother's palm. "Shoe," he finally picked.

He later told me that when he played Monopoly, he would almost always choose the car. I laughed, knowing that Father would have definitely roared if your daddy tried to take the car from him.

Over the next few hours, we took turns rolling the dice and moving our pieces around the board. Father was the first to make it around the entire square; Mother bought the first property; and I earned money for winning the beauty pageant.

"You are beautiful," Father said proudly after I read the card aloud.

Your daddy glanced at me out of the corner of his eye and grinned. Then, a turn later, he ended up in jail. Not because Father caught him smiling at me, but because that's the card he picked out of the pile situated in the middle of the board. We all *laughed out loud, and even though it seemed to embarrass him, I think it loosened everyone up a bit.*

That night, your daddy ended up beating the pants off all of us. I was afraid that Father was going to be irritated because he always won at Monopoly. I think in some weird way it made him regard your daddy a little higher, probably because he took note of the wise decisions he made when buying properties and adding houses and hotels to them.

I'll never forget watching Father stand from the table after losing and shake your daddy's hand. "Good game, son," he complimented. "Let's play again next time you come over to the house to visit with Violet."

Your daddy grinned quite proudly not because he'd won the game, but because he realized he'd just earned a little more respect from Father. Later, he told me that his hand was sore for two days after that handshake, but he also admitted that he enjoyed playing the board game with me and my family. That meant the world to me. I was very close to my parents, and I wanted so badly for him to like them and for them to approve of him.

That night, Father let me walk your daddy to the car in the dark for the very first time. Things couldn't have worked out more perfectly because your daddy had something important he wanted to tell me. Something he would have never said in front of my parents.

As we stood in the doorframe of his pickup truck, I gave him a quick kiss on the lips. When we opened our eyes, our gaze met, and he whispered, "I love you, Violet Horne."

"Mason," Ansley called out for the second time as he sat across from her but seemed to be a world away.

Mason blinked his eyes several times. "Yeah," he finally responded not even sure what Ansley had just said, but he thought he'd heard his name.

"Are you okay?" she investigated. He looked like he was in a trance.

"Yeah," he assured. "Yeah, I'm fine. I was just thinking about something," he added, trailing off.

"Do you want to do it?"

"Do what?"

"Play a board game," Ansley clarified. "We could do that and sit here with Callie."

"Oh, yeah, definitely," he uttered. He wondered how long his mind had been in another place.

"What about dinner?" Ansley mentioned. "Want me to make us something?"

"Let's just order pizza," Mason suggested. "Well, if you like pizza, that is."

"Who doesn't like pizza?"

Mason shrugged. "When I get out of the shower, I can order it and go pick it up if you'll stay here to keep an eye on Callie."

"Why don't we have it delivered?" Ansley inquired, then she snickered. "Are we too far out in the country for delivery?"

"You're funny," Mason responded with a grin. "There's a local place that will deliver here, but they charge a delivery fee, and the driver will expect a tip."

Ansley furrowed her brow. She couldn't remember the last time she'd ordered a pizza for carryout. "I'll pay for it," she offered, recognizing that he was extremely frugal with his money. She figured footing the bill would be much simpler than debating about how much it would cost him in gas to drive into town, especially with the gas mileage for that truck of his.

"No, I can't let you do that," he combatted. "I'll pick it up, it's no problem."

"Mason, please, let me pay for the pizza," she insisted. "You're letting me stay at your house, so it's the least I can do." She'd figured out early on that he was the type of man that felt the need to pay for everything when a woman was involved. He had persisted about paying for dinner the night she arrived in Oriental, and he'd paid for the groceries last night, too. She appreciated the gesture, she really did, but she wanted to help, and she was accustomed to paying her own way.

"How about I'll pay for the pizza, and you pay for the delivery charge and the tip?" Mason proposed.

"That's a deal," she agreed with a smirk. She found it amusing that he didn't want to pay for delivery and a tip. He was old school, though, just like his dad, she realized. Most likely, that's how he'd been raised so he'd gotten it honestly.

Mason was in and out of the shower in less than five minutes. Not because he wouldn't have found pleasure in indulging in the hot water like Ansley had, but because all the hot water was indeed gone. He didn't hate cold showers, but he didn't feel like taking one today. He usually saved those for the summertime. Plus he wanted to be out before the pizza delivery guy showed up so that he could make sure Ansley didn't pay for everything. She had been kind enough to offer to call in the order for the pizza while he hopped in the shower.

When the doorbell rang, Mason was dressed, and he was surprised when Ansley didn't race him to the door so that she could try to pay for the pizza. She stayed behind with Callie in the bedroom where they'd been talking.

A young man wearing a funny-looking hat handed Mason a hot cardboard box, and Mason asked how much he owed. He'd forgotten to ask Ansley if the pizza place had given her a total over the phone, but it didn't really matter because he had plenty of cash in his wallet. He knew Ansley would pay her part, which he kind of felt bad about agreeing to earlier.

"Nothing," the pizza delivery guy answered.

"What?" Mason inquired. "You're not charging us for the pizza?"

"The lady on the phone paid for it already," he informed Mason.

With a grin on his face, Mason cocked his jaw to one side and shook his head. "I see," he acknowledged, reaching into his back pocket for his wallet. "Well, let me give you a tip then." This would be the first time he'd ever tipped a pizza delivery person, but it was also the first time a pizza delivery guy had ever been at his front door.

The young man held up his hand. "Sir, I appreciate the offer, but your wife already paid a tip as well."

Mason was caught off guard to the extent that the words *your wife* didn't even register to begin with. "She did?" he double checked. "I mean, she's not my wife," he explained when he realized what the pizza delivery guy had said.

"Well, you should definitely consider marrying her," he advised.

Mason furrowed his brow. "What? Why?"

"Please tell her I said thank you for the twenty dollar tip," he said over his shoulder as he began to hustle back to his car with its engine running and headlights shining toward the house.

A moment later, Mason walked into the bedroom with the pizza, two paper plates, and a glass of sweet tea for Ansley.

"We got free pizza!" he said with a serious face.

"Really?" Ansley responded, fighting to hold a serious face of her own.

"Yeah, I tried to pay the guy, but he said we didn't owe him anything."

"Well, that was mighty nice of them," Ansley mentioned, going along with Mason's theory. "Maybe you've ordered nine pizzas this year and the tenth one is free, or something like that," she suggested.

"Nope, I haven't ordered that many pizzas."

Mason walked out of the room and came back a minute later

with a can of Mt. Dew and napkins. When Ansley opened her napkin, a twenty dollar bill fell out.

"What is this?" she asked, pinching the money between her thumb and forefinger as she held it in the air.

"That's for the free pizza," Mason announced with a smile stretching across his face as he clumsily maneuvered a slice of pizza into his mouth.

Ansley tried her best to hold in the laughter bubbling up inside of her, but she couldn't. She threw the twenty dollar bill at Mason. "Your money is no good here," she demanded, enjoying the moment.

"Why did you pay for it all?" he asked somewhat seriously but still finding the scenario amusing. Truth be told, she'd gotten him good. He'd been absolutely clueless when that guy said he didn't owe anything for the pizza.

"Because I wanted to," she answered simply, smirking.

"You're something else, Ansley Stone."

Ansley's smirk grew into a smile. She was pretty sure that was the first time she'd heard him say her first and last name together, and she liked the way it sounded coming out of his mouth even if it was filled with pizza.

They continued to chat over pizza and beverages in Mason's bedroom as Callie rested. When she began sniffing at their dinner, Mason remembered that she hadn't been fed like normal after a long day of work. So, in between slices, he ventured to the kitchen and brought a cup of dog food into the bedroom. Ansley thought it was cute when he began to hand-feed his canine companion. Callie was completely worn out from the events that had transpired earlier, and even though Ansley knew the dog would be fine after some much needed rest, she felt terrible for her. However, with the kind of treatment Mason was showing Callie, Ansley began to think that maybe she should have shown more signs of fatigue herself. In all honesty, her muscles were beat from the running and the swimming.

In general, she felt like she was in relatively good shape. She still played tennis regularly and often worked out at the private gym inside her gated neighborhood. As she thought about what her body had been through today, she realized that she was one event short from practicing for a triathlon. Mason laughed when she mentioned as much.

"I think I could handle the swimming and the biking, but the running would get the best of me," he divulged.

Ansley smiled then changed the subject. "So, what board games do you have?"

Mason named off all the games that he could remember being stacked in the closet in the spare bedroom the last time he looked in there, but he hadn't played any of them in years.

"I had forgotten all about Battleship," Ansley revealed with enthusiasm after hearing his list. "Do you like that game?" she asked. "We should play it," she suggested before giving Mason a chance to respond to her question.

He couldn't help but grin at her childlike excitement. "Sure, it's fine with me," he agreed.

Ansley appreciated when Mason asked her permission to go into the bedroom where she was staying so that he could retrieve the game from the closet. A few moments later, each of them opened their respective game boards and began to strategically place their plastic ships.

The empty pizza box was now laying on one corner of the bed, and Callie was sprawled out on the other one with her eyes closed. Mason's back was flush against the headboard, and Ansley was sitting next to him with her legs crossed and her body angled so that neither of them could see the other's board. They soon began to call out shots and place the coordinating pegs on their grids.

"Did you play board games a lot when you were growing up?" Ansley asked.

"Yeah, I played with my parents quite a bit," Mason answered. "How about you?"

"My parents didn't really care for board games," Ansley revealed with a hint of sadness lining her voice. "I did go through a stage of life when I played with my friends, though, and that was a lot of fun."

"I can't remember the last time I played a board game," Mason admitted.

"Really?"

Mason shook his head.

"That's sad," Ansley said. "But at least you're playing now," she added before calling out her next shot.

"Oh, no!" Mason exclaimed. "That's a direct hit."

It didn't take long for Ansley to determine the direction of the ship's placement and ultimately sink it with a victory grin covering her face.

As the two of them continued to fire shots back and forth, she began to realize how nice it was to live in the moment without cell phones and other distractions. Mason rarely looked at his phone, and hers was at the bottom of his pond, probably buried in the muck by now. It had been tucked into the back pocket of her jeans when she'd started running from the bees, but as she ran, she'd been able to reach for it like a sprinter stretching for a baton. At that time, her plan was to call for help, but then help arrived out of the blue, and she hadn't even thought to drop the phone before it went flying along with her into the pond.

Fortunately, she'd been able to talk with her mother before the incident. She still hadn't shared her whereabouts or any information about what she had been up to, but nonetheless, she felt like her mother would at least call off the search for her missing daughter. That might change if her mom couldn't reach her the rest of the week, but she decided she wasn't going to let it bother her anymore.

Ansley had also carried on another conversation with Betty, and they'd both agreed that it wouldn't be a good idea for Ansley to try to talk to Cleve over the phone while she was in Oriental. Betty promised to let her know if Dr. Roman attempted to stir up anything at work following the events that had transpired last night. Ansley was afraid that she was going to, but there wasn't much she could do about that, especially from afar.

Now, as she played Battleship with Mason, she was trying to build up the nerve to ask him the question that she'd asked Cleve last night.

Her body was trembling inside when she finally uttered the words. "Is Cleve your biological father?"

19

"I've never told a single soul who my real father is," Mason shared in a tone of voice much lower than normal.

Ansley was looking him in the eyes as he spoke, but then she purposefully glanced down at her game board, hoping he would feel less intimidated by the gesture. "You don't have to tell me if you don't want to," she made sure he knew as she fiddled with her pegs.

Over the past few days, she had really begun to enjoy spending time with Mason, and, at this point, she didn't want to ruin that by twisting his arm for information that might or might not matter in the grand scheme of things.

"The guest cabin that my dad told you about . . . it didn't burn down."

Ansley furrowed her brow. *But you told me it did*, she almost reeled off, wondering why he would have lied about it.

Noticing her expression, Mason realized he should probably provide further explanation. "Well, technically, it did burn down, but not randomly like it may have sounded when I first mentioned it," he clarified.

Ansley felt as confused as she had the first night when standing on Mason's front porch. "Huh?" she finally queried.

"I burned it down," he confessed. "On purpose."

Why? Ansley wondered, unsure if she should solicit further information or wait to see what he might willingly divulge. "Why?" she asked anyway.

"That's where *he* lived."

Without intention, Ansley pursed her lips, and her head tilted slightly to the right. "Who?" she inquired.

Now, Mason was staring at the ships and all the white and red pegs on his board. "My biological father."

Ansley couldn't control the reaction that suddenly forced her eyeballs to enlarge. *Your biological father once lived here on the property?* All of a sudden there were dozens of puzzle pieces dancing to a rapid beat in her mind. *Who was he? Why did he live here? When did he live here? Did Mason know that this man was his biological father? If so, how long had he known? Where was this man now?*

"So, Cleve isn't your biological father?" she asked for clarification purposes.

"No," he admitted. "I've never told anyone that either."

Wow. Ansley gently placed her hand on his leg just above his knee, hoping it would comfort him some. "Thanks for sharing that with me. I'm sure it wasn't easy."

"I just don't understand it," Mason murmured.

"Understand what?" Ansley asked.

"Why no one told me," Mason exclaimed.

Here came the confusion again. "Why no one told you what?"

"That my dad—Cleve—wasn't my real dad."

Ansley let her mind work for a moment before responding. Mason had just informed her that Cleve wasn't his biological father. In fact, he'd said so twice in the past sixty seconds. So, if he knew that to be true . . . someone must have told him, right? "If no one told you, how did you find out?" she reasoned.

"Well, no one told me until it was too late," Mason shared with a look of disgust overshadowing his face.

Too late for what? "What do you mean?"

"Too late for everything."

Suddenly, Ansley felt more like an investigator than a friend or a physician or a person of any other role she'd ever played in anyone's life. "Like what?" she questioned.

"Too late to ask questions," he started and considered stopping right there, changing the subject. He could feel everything bubbling up inside of him, and he had to pour this out as fast as he possibly could before he boiled over. All of these things had been circling in his mind for the past seventeen years, and he'd never spoken them out loud, at least not where another human being could hear him—maybe help him make sense of why his life had to turn out this way. "It was too late to ask how it happened. To find out why my dad—Cleve—raised me if I wasn't his son. Too late to have a relationship with my real father."

"When did you find out?" seemed like the best question to ask first, Ansley decided as she attempted to process everything Mason had just shared straight from the depths of his heart.

As soon as the question rolled off Ansley's tongue, Mason's eyes closed and his head dipped. He fought back the tears that felt like they were trying to form in his jaw so that they could work their way toward his eyes. Why did tears always seem to start with a tightened face? "I found out the day that he was killed."

Oh, my, Ansley thought. She could see the tension on his face trying to work its way out. "The day your biological father was killed?" she checked.

"Yes."

"When did this happen?"

"On my eighteenth birthday," he revealed.

As soon as he mentioned that bit of information, she couldn't help but wonder if his eighteenth birthday played a significant role in the death of his biological father. What were the chances that

184

those two events coincidentally occurred on the same day? "Mason, what happened? How was he killed? Why?" All of these questions flew out at once. Ansley didn't want to believe this. It was beyond reason. Mason had suffered through both his mother and biological father being killed? She just couldn't fathom it. Personally, she'd known people who'd died from natural causes and even a friend in high school who died in a car accident, but she'd never known anyone who'd been killed.

"He was shot," Mason divulged, answering the first and second questions in a single statement. "Why?" he uttered. "Because he was at the wrong place at the wrong time."

What did that mean? "Where?"

"He showed up here," Mason acknowledged, glancing all around him. "At our house."

"Why?"

Mason didn't want to relive this scene again, but he knew he needed to. He needed to share this with another human being, and in the past seventeen years, he hadn't felt as close to any person as he felt right now with Ansley. Maybe because he believed he was beginning to fall in love with her, as absurd as that sounded every time he admitted it to himself or perhaps because she reminded him of the one person in his life that he'd been closest with until she was taken away from him. Ansley Stone reminded him so much of his mother. The way she looked. The way she talked. The way she laughed. The way she cared. It was like Ansley was a reincarnation of his mother, just younger and attractive. Not that his mother wasn't attractive, but she was his mother, so of course he didn't see her that way even though he knew she was a beautiful woman inside and out. He was almost certain that these were the reasons behind why his dad had pushed Ansley to come here, and he had to admit to himself that he hated and loved him for it at the same time.

With tears in his eyes, Mason began to tell the story.

I was in my bedroom playing a new video game my parents gave me for my birthday when I heard an unfamiliar voice in the living room—a man's voice.

"Where's my boy?" the man called out.

At first, I froze. His voice was loud and intimidating, then I heard my mother's voice, and I knew I needed to intervene.

"Get out of here," I heard my mother yell.

I was hustling down the hallway when I heard the man say, "Today's my boy's eighteenth birthday, and I'm here to see him."

When I walked around the corner and saw just inside the front door who stood there staggering and slurring his words, I felt more confused than I ever had.

"Leave," my mother screamed. "Now!"

Then, he saw me. "Mason," he said, lowering his voice as if to show affection for me. "Happy birthday, son."

My mother stepped toward him with forceful intention, and that was the first time I'd ever seen her lay her hands on anyone. She slapped him across his red face so hard that it echoed throughout the room. Then she took a step back and turned to me. "Mason, go back to your bedroom," she demanded.

But, I was eighteen now. I no longer had to do what she or anyone else told me to do. I would have, of course, under normal circumstances. I would have done anything my mother told me to do, but I felt like both she and I were in danger. Mr. Hatcher had just called me his son. He was drunk, I could tell that, but it's not every day that an intoxicated man shows up at your house and claims that you are his son. When my mother slapped him, I knew there was something to the story he'd come here to tell.

"Why did you call me your son?" I demanded to know. I was kind of surprised that Mr. Hatcher hadn't tried to retaliate when my mother slapped him, but I think he had other intentions on his mind. Plus if he had touched her, I would have been all over him before he knew what was happening.

"Because you are," he said simply.

"How?" I inquired. In hindsight, it was a question I wished I hadn't asked.

"Because your mother and I had sex," he spelled out, snickering beneath his breath as he spoke the words that have been etched in my mind ever since.

By this time, I had worked my way between the two of them, and I was close enough that I could smell the vodka on his breath.

"What?" I clamored. I glared at him then turned to my mom just in time to catch her attempt to lunge at him again.

He laughed as I caught her in my arms.

"Happy birthday," he said again. "I knew your mamma wouldn't tell you, and out of respect for her and your daddy, I waited until you turned eighteen to let you know that you're my boy," he said as if he now had entitlement over me.

"You're not my father," I said to him, but at that moment I suddenly realized I looked more like him than I looked like the father who'd raised me. Out of all the times I'd stared into mirrors before that day, I'd never once thought that even when Mr. Hatcher had lived in the other cabin on our property. He'd stayed there until my daddy abruptly fired him. As that thought entered my mind, another light bulb flickered on in my head. There was the explanation for why my dad had let him go.

"I am," he assured me. "If you don't believe me, you can do one of those DNA test things."

I shook my head.

"Mom, is this true?" I investigated. I wanted to know, but I didn't want it to be true.

"Tell him, Violet," he insisted.

I could tell she didn't want to answer me. Why would she? She was acting on a plethora of emotions. Anger. Embarrassment. Guilt.

Before I could even think about what to say or do next, my daddy came barging in the front door like the FBI raiding the house of one of the most wanted men in America. I later realized that he must have recognized Mr. Hatcher's truck parked out front because it was apparent that my dad was on a mission different from the one he'd left for earlier. Before leaving, he had told me that he was going to pick up my other eighteenth birthday present, but it wasn't in his hands. Instead, he was gripping the high-powered rifle that he kept in his truck for deer hunting. Actually, at that point, he was aiming it at Mr. Hatcher's forehead.

"I told you never to come back here," my daddy roared.

Mr. Hatcher had turned to face my dad when the door had flung open, instantly creating a hole the size of the doorknob in the wall. "Cleve, I'm not here to cause any harm," he slurred. "I just brought my boy a present for his eighteenth birthday," he said, holding up a small box that must have been hidden beneath his jacket.

Behind me, my mother was crying, but the sound of her tears soon faded as she scampered off into the kitchen.

"Leave," my daddy demanded with rage in his voice like I'd never heard before. "Or I'll shoot you dead."

I wanted Mr. Hatcher to leave, too, but I also wanted to know if he was my real father. The look in my daddy's eyes was telling me to move so that he could shoot this man . . . a man that might be my biological father. I didn't want that to happen. I wanted to know what had taken place eighteen years ago, but then what my daddy said next caused me to understand why my mother had run off.

"I told you if you ever came back here, I'd kill you," he confirmed, and I could tell he meant it. My gut told me that my mother had been there the first time he'd said it.

I knew I had to do something. I didn't want my daddy to go to prison, so I quickly maneuvered myself around Mr. Hatcher and began to reach for the gun in my daddy's hands. I figured if I could keep him from shooting Mr. Hatcher, I could learn the truth and save him from spending the rest of his life in prison. Before I realized what had happened, my ears began to ring from hearing the loudest sound I ever remember hearing in my life.

A moment later, I remember watching Mr. Hatcher crumble to the ground like a slinky, holding the hole in his chest from where blood began to spew, instantly staining his brown jacket and running onto the floor.

At almost the same time, I heard the gun crash to the floor, and a moment later, Mr. Hatcher was just as still as the rifle laying at my daddy's feet.

A few seconds later, my daddy fell to his knees.

A complete and eerie silence took over the entire house, and I stood overtop the rifle, my daddy, and Mr. Hatcher. It was as if the whole world was standing still. I expected my mother to come rushing out of the kitchen, but she didn't. I expected to wake up from this bad dream, but I didn't. I expected something to happen next, but nothing happened, not for a long while anyway.

Everyone and everything seemed to be suspended at that moment. Then, I happened to glance toward the kitchen, wondering why I could no longer hear my mother's cries.

That's when I spotted something that I haven't been able to force myself to quit looking at since my eighteenth birthday. There was a perfectly round hole in the wall that led into the kitchen.

20

Dr. Roman ambled around Cleve's bed then sat down in the chair where Ansley always sat when listening to The Date Night Jar stories. As usual, Cleve's eyes were locked shut, and he hadn't moved a muscle since the doorknob twisted. Now, the door was closed, and Dr. Roman was in here alone with a man who wasn't fond of her. As she stared at the eyelids beneath his stringy gray hair, which looked like it could use a wash, she couldn't help but wonder how he always knew when she was the one entering the room.

"What is going on with you and Ansley?" Dr. Roman demanded to know.

Cleve didn't budge.

She glanced at his vitals, then turning her attention back to him, shook her head. "Cleve, if you want me to give you the message from Mason, I need you to tell me why Ansley comes in here to visit you so often."

A moment later, Cleve's nostrils flared, and his eyes sputtered to life. "Why are you trying to blackmail me?"

On the inside, Dr. Roman smiled. *Step one, complete*, she thought to herself. She couldn't remember the last time she'd seen this man's brown eyes.

"I'm just trying to find out what's going on in my hospital."

"This isn't your hospital," he argued. "And what Dr. Stone and I talk about is none of your business," he huffed. "Haven't you heard of patient-doctor confidentiality?"

Dr. Roman smirked arrogantly. "Cut the crap, old man. You're not a patient, you're a prisoner," she whispered after leaning toward his bedside but making sure to stay out of reach. "And why don't you just call her Ansley like you do when no one else is listening? It's obvious to everyone around here that you two are on a first name basis."

"Why do you care what I call her?"

"Everyone is going to be calling her Ansley when she loses the fancy initials that come at the end of her name," she offered with a snicker.

"What is that supposed to mean?"

"She's gotten herself into some hot water," Dr. Roman explained. "But you know that, right?"

Cleve had been worried sick about both Ansley and Mason ever since he'd received the phone call from Ansley. So much so that Betty had to give him muscle relaxers to keep him calm. Otherwise, he doubted he would have gotten any rest. Now, Dr. Roman wasn't helping him keep his blood pressure down.

"Dr. Stone is a smart gal," Cleve said. "She knows how to take care of herself."

"You're right about that, she is a brilliant person," Dr. Roman agreed. "But she's dealing with a criminal who's pretty wise himself, and if you're as smart as I think you are, you'll tell me why Ansley is in Oriental with your son Mason."

Mason. Cleve didn't like the way that Dr. Roman said his son's name because he knew she was up to no good.

"Just tell me what Mason said," he demanded, yanking harshly at the cuffs holding his wrists to the metal-framed bed.

Startled by the sudden movement, Dr. Roman bounced

backward. "Don't make me report you for harassment," she demanded.

"That's a bunch of bull," Cleve yammered. "If you're afraid of me, why don't you just call the guard in here to have this conversation with us?"

"Do you want him to know what Mason said?"

"I don't care," he clamored. "*I* just want to know what Mason said." He wanted to know if there was trouble. If Mason was okay. If Ansley was okay. Was she really in hot water? Or was that just a ploy being put on by Dr. Roman?

"Mason wants to talk to you so that no one gets into trouble because of this situation that's happening," she told Cleve.

Was that the truth? Cleve wondered. He felt like he couldn't trust a word this lady said. "What trouble?"

"You think you're clever, Mr. Fields," Dr. Roman spewed. "Ansley is in trouble because she's in Oriental with your son. So, you need to tell me why she's there, or I'm going to release to the authorities some photos I snapped with my phone."

Cleve tried his best to keep a straight face. "What are you talking about?"

"Cleve," she uttered, whispering again. "I saw that phone that you were hiding under your wrinkly old face," she revealed. "I made sure to snap a photo with the phone that was in my hand. Of course, you didn't notice that because you were pretending to be asleep, as always."

Cleve wasn't sure how to respond. Dr. Roman had to be telling the truth about spotting the phone, right? The only people who knew it was in here that night were him and Betty, and of course, Ansley. But neither of them would have opened their mouths. He knew that for certain. Ansley and Betty realized their jobs were on the line, and they were also close friends. Whether or not Dr. Roman had taken a photo, he had no way of knowing. "I don't know what you're talking about," he finally combatted. "If you

have some picture of me sleeping with a phone, show it to me?"
he encouraged.

"Not going to happen, old timer," she answered. "You're not
going to manipulate me like you've manipulated Ansley and
Betty."

Suddenly, something else popped into Cleve's mind. He'd
been in prison long enough that he'd learned a thing or two about
criminals and evidence. "If you have a picture of me with a phone,
you would have already turned it over to the authorities," he
uttered.

"I'm a little smarter than that," she revealed with pride lining
her voice. "If I had turned over the image to the authorities, then
I would no longer be able to use it for my own blackmail
purposes," she announced with pleasure. "Now, tell me why
Ansley is with your son, and I'll show you the picture, and I'll even
delete it if I believe you."

Cleve was staring at the phone in Dr. Roman's hand. He'd
noticed that she'd been glancing down at it often, and he could
tell that she was up to something. Most likely recording this
conversation, he determined. "If I give you the information you
want, you'll delete the photo and tell me what Mason said, right?"

"Sure," she agreed with a forced smile.

Cleve lifted his head from the pillow and spoke with grit in his
voice. "Record this," he demanded. "Dr. Roman, you are either
a liar or an idiot. Because if you have said pictures and you didn't
turn them in to the authorities the moment you walked out of this
room, you are withholding evidence that will cause you to lose
your own job," he declared, dropping his head and closing his
eyes the moment he spoke the last word.

Dr. Roman didn't physically sink down in the chair beneath
her, but mentally she felt herself falling right out of it and onto
the cold floor. Cleve Fields had just outsmarted a physician, she
realized.

A moment later, she pushed her body up from the chair and began to stomp out of the room, but then, she suddenly realized she had more ammunition. Cleve hadn't denied that Ansley was in Oriental with Mason. "Oh, one last thing," she began, approaching the opposite side of the bed where his back was turned to her. "The moment I walk out of this room, I'm calling the authorities and having them send the police to Mason's address," she informed him, and after touching a few more buttons on her phone, she spewed out the address she'd searched for and found last night.

Tears had been streaming down Ansley's face the entire time that Mason had been telling the story about the worst day of his life. Never in her life had she heard anything like this, and she imagined that flashes of this story would pop into her mind for as long as she lived. She couldn't even begin to imagine what these memories looked like to Mason. He'd been there when this happened in real life. To him, it wasn't just a story, it was a reality.

Then there was the hole in the wall, the one she had noticed, but only because she'd recognized that every time Mason walked by it during the past few days, he touched it. She wondered if he even realized he did that, or if it was one of those habits that he did without even thinking about it.

When Mason went on to tell her that on that awful day he'd walked slowly toward the opening that led into the kitchen, and upon peeking around the corner, his worst nightmare had come true, she lost it.

This is what he had been talking about when he said he lost all of his parents that day. His biological father had been shot, and the bullet that had erupted out of the high-powered rifle had traveled right through the wall and also taken the life of his mother. As for Cleve—well, she now knew exactly why Cleve had ended up in prison and, ultimately, in her hospital.

Ansley wasn't sure what to say, but she felt like she needed to say something. As Mason had told the saddest story she had ever heard, Callie had maneuvered herself to his side and now had her head rested on his lap. She'd let out a whimper when he'd spoken the final words about finding his mother.

"It was an accident, Mason," Ansley uttered.

"It was murder," Mason disagreed. "The police, the judge, and my daddy all said it was murder."

Ansley furrowed her brow. "Cleve said that?"

"Yes," Mason revealed.

"But why?" Ansley asked.

"Because he didn't want a trial. He said he didn't want me to have to sit in front of a judge and a jury and relive that horrific scene."

"That was mighty brave of him," Ansley declared.

"Yeah, I guess so," Mason admitted.

"So how come you don't go see him?" she asked.

"He told me to never ever talk to anyone about what happened that day. Not to the police. Not to reporters. Not even to him," Mason explained, then he paused as he recollected his father's words. "He told me not to ever come to see him at the prison because seeing him there would remind me of why he was there, and he didn't want me to see him like that."

"I'm so sorry, Mason." All along Ansley had figured that it was Mason's choice not to visit his father.

"I lost them all that day," he cried. "All three of my parents."

Ansley scooted over to Mason and held him as tightly as possible, and he held her back as tightly as possible without breaking her bones.

"I have one question," Ansley uttered. "If your father told you to never talk to anyone about what happened that day, and you've granted that wish for eighteen years, what made you decide to tell me?"

"Because you remind me of my mother," he revealed.

21

nsley spent the rest of the night in Mason's arms. Neither of them spoke another word, and they didn't finish their game of Battleship. The pizza box didn't get taken to the kitchen nor did Ansley's or Mason's emptied beverages. Everything in the room just seemed to remain suspended in time. At least until Callie moved to the foot of the bed where she slept soundly until the following morning.

When Ansley and Mason awoke, they each brushed their teeth, changed clothes, and later met on the front porch for another round of coffee in the dark as they waited for the sunrise. Today, the view would be a bit different because raindrops were trickling off the roof. As Callie followed Mason out, her four paws stepped a bit slower than normal.

"This is so much better than meeting a woman at a bar for beers," Mason said out of left field, wearing a smile that circled his face.

Ansley nearly spewed her coffee all over him. "You're a hoot," she responded with her own full-faced grin.

The word hoot came to mind because last night she'd begun to drift off to the gentle sounds of an owl hooting outside the cracked window until the rain started to tap dance on the roof, and she loved each sound as much as the other. Here in Oriental, Ansley Stone felt free in a way she had never felt before. It didn't matter that she no longer had a phone to keep up with her life beyond this place, and she had somehow completely let go of anything that might come of Dr. Roman prying into her business at work. If she lost her job, then so be it. She had come here in an attempt to reunite Mason with his father, and even though she had yet to accomplish that goal, she now felt like it was a possibility.

Something else had happened here, too. Something Cleve had asked her to come here to remind Mason of, and although she hadn't seen this coming and would have never predicted it, she knew she was falling in love with Mason Fields. Convincing him that The Date Night Jar could bring him love had seemed like an impossible feat the night she showed up on this front porch. But, this morning, as she watched him sip his coffee with a seemingly renewed zest for life, she had a hunch that he was falling in love with her, too.

Although he was quite possibly one of the oddest people she had ever come across, he was without a doubt one of the most genuine human beings she'd ever met. Last night, as he shared the story about losing his parents, she felt as though he had given her a piece of himself that could only ever be given to one person. He had chosen her. In those intimate moments, he'd broken her heart and somehow mended it at the same time, and she prayed that his heart now felt less heavy and more secure, too.

"When I go home on Saturday, will you go back with me to visit your dad?" Ansley asked.

Mason didn't want to think about Ansley leaving. Over the past few days, he'd felt something he'd never felt before, and he was pretty sure that it was love. He wished that she could stay, and he also wished that he could go see his father, but the chance of either of those things happening was slim to none. "I can't do that," he uttered without explanation.

Somehow, Ansley now felt a connection with Mason that she had never felt with any other human being, and something deep within her soul told her not to say another word for the time being.

As the rain picked up, beating steadily on the ground beyond the porch railing, Mason unexpectedly stood and reached for Ansley's hand. Not sure where he was taking her, she followed anyway. A few moments later, they were running through raindrops in the middle of one of the strawberry fields. Their dry clothes quickly became splotchy, then completely soaked. The two of them ran up and down and in and out of the rows together before Mason finally pulled Ansley in close and kissed her more passionately than he'd ever kissed anyone.

Their lips moved to a rhythm that their bodies began to mimic, slow dancing under the hidden morning moon as it began to give way to the light of the sun rising behind the cloud-covered sky. Mason's and Ansley's unified movements eventually led them to the soil that had held this farm together for generations, and it was there between countless rows of ripened strawberries that he fully gave himself away. He let go of the entrapment in which he'd brought upon himself and shared his purest form of raw emotion with the only person he'd given love to in the past seventeen years of his life.

As the two of them moved in unison, Ansley realized that she had no idea where she and Mason would end up, but right now she couldn't imagine being anywhere with anyone else doing anything else. She loved the feel of Mason hovering above her with their bodies intertwined, his lips on her lips as the rain slapped against them while they shared this intense passion for one another.

Callie never left the porch, and when Mason and Ansley came trotting back up the steps like two teenagers experiencing love for the very first time, she peered up at them as her snout rested gracefully on the floorboards.

The two of them had lain in the field for almost two hours, enjoying one another and eventually feeding each other strawberries. Ansley forgot all about whether or not the fruit was organic, and it hadn't taken Mason long to realize that he wasn't going to get any work done today. With the forecast calling for steady precipitation, he'd known it would be a slow day anyway, and he'd actually sent out a message first thing this morning letting his workers know not to show up for picking. So, when he and Ansley had ended up in the middle of the strawberry plants, he had realized that they would have the fields all to themselves.

After brushing off as best they could outdoors, Mason and Ansley headed for the bathroom where they ended up in the tub beneath a mountain of foamy bubbles.

"I'm not sure if I'm comfortable enough with my body to sit in a bathtub naked with you," Ansley had revealed honestly when Mason brought up the idea. She was somewhat surprised by her own reaction since just last night she was thinking about how him being in the tub with her would have been perfect.

"How about a bubble bath?" he suggested. "Bubbles cover up everything."

Ansley grinned. How could she turn down a bubble bath? "I find it hard to imagine that you have a bottle of bubble bath sitting around the house."

Mason held up a finger. "Have you already forgotten my secret?"

"That you love to take baths?" she recalled with a tainted smile.

"Yes, that one," he acknowledged.

"Nope, haven't forgotten," she clarified. "But I still don't think you have bubble bath."

"You're right," he admitted, "but I do have water, soap, honey, and an egg."

Ansley lifted an eyebrow. "O—k." She paused. "What does that mean?"

"Those are the ingredients for a homemade bubble bath."

"Really?"

"Never underestimate a man who grew up on a farm in the country," Mason shared. "Dad taught me how to build a fire with nature's ingredients, and Mom taught me how to make a bubble bath from scratch."

Ansley laughed, and a few moments later, she couldn't believe how high the mountain of bubbles reached. After working his magic, Mason, being a gentleman, left the room to let her climb in first, then joined her after a few minutes passed. He left the door open so Callie could wander in and out, and she did just that as Ansley and Mason relaxed. Ansley had given her a checkup this morning, and Mason felt relieved when the doctor-in-the-house said his dog was recovering just fine. It would only take a little time for her to find her way back to normal, Ansley explained.

Mason and Ansley talked and laughed over the bubbles, and shared stories from their childhood. Ansley told Mason about the time she and Wanda had gone to the state fair, and she even admitted to that being her one and only fishing experience.

"Then we have to go fishing while you're here," Mason exclaimed. "You'll love it," he promised.

Ansley wasn't so sure about that, but she decided that she would try anything with him once. Plus, Mason went on to promise to take her shopping in the village—there was that name for the town again, which this time he explained had been derived from the sailing steamer Oriental—if she would fish with him. While on the subject of fishing, they decided that they would head out to the waterfront this evening to pick up fresh catch for dinner.

"They'll be out fishing in the rain today?" Ansley inquired.

"Definitely," Mason acknowledged. "Some of the best fishing happens when it's raining."

THE DATE NIGHT JAR

Ansley laughed. "That's where I draw the line, though. I'll fish with you sometime, but not in the rain."

Regardless, Mason knew he was already hooked. Beneath the bubbles, his legs were caught up in Ansley's legs, and he wanted to spend the whole day with her in this bathtub. Eventually, the water became cool, and the two of them got hungry. All the talk about having fish for dinner hadn't helped.

They spent the rest of the morning eating more fruit, finishing their game of Battleship, and enjoying one another's company. In the afternoon, they ate baked potatoes for lunch and lounged on the couch afterward. The TV was on in the background, but they spent most of the time learning more about each other. Mason was shocked when Ansley informed him that while in college she often played cornhole and she was excited when he told her that he'd just finished building two custom boards.

"I might beat you," she teased poking him in the ribs with her pointer finger.

"I might let you," he replied, grabbing ahold of her hand then her torso.

They began to kiss and soon fell into the couch where they spent the next thirty minutes locked in one another's embrace.

In all the years Mason had been playing cornhole, he had never played with or against another person. Sometimes, in the evenings after work, he would simply wander out into the backyard and throw the bags until he decided to do something else. Usually, he'd carry a beverage out there with him, and sometimes he'd turn on some music. Most of the time, he just enjoyed being outdoors and taking in the magic that surrounded him.

He liked the idea of sharing moments like that with Ansley. He could imagine her standing on the other side of the board with a beverage in her hand, maybe a glass of wine. They'd make a great team, he thought.

When evening rolled around, Mason mentioned heading into

town. The rain had slacked off, and they'd be able to walk around the waterfront without getting wet.

"You know what we forgot to do?" Ansley said as they lifted their bodies from the couch.

"What?"

"Pull another scroll from The Date Night Jar."

Mason shrugged his shoulders. "Technically, I guess our last date isn't over."

Ansley giggled. "True," she agreed, "but we should pick another one. Maybe it will be something we can do while we're in the village," she said, mimicking the local word.

Mason noticed her word choice and laughed. A few moments later, they were sitting at the kitchen table overlooking the old jar that was filled with more stories than it was slivers of paper.

"It's your turn to pick," Mason reminded Ansley.

Of course, she hadn't forgotten that.

She dug her hand in, all the way to the bottom this time and slowly pulled out the paper between her fingers. With her eyes closed just like last time, she held it in front of her face before opening them.

"You have it turned the wrong way," Mason laughed, and then he watched her rearrange the position of the paper with her fingers, and it looked as if she was trying to solve a Rubik's Cube with her eyes closed.

"Is that better?" she asked without looking.

"Flip it over," he instructed.

She flipped it the right way then read the words aloud: "*Explore A New Place Together.*"

Mason's eyes lifted. "That's perfect," he said. "I can show you all kinds of places in the village." He had one specific place in mind, but for now he was going to keep that a secret.

"But those places won't be new to you," Ansley rebutted.

"One of them will," he shared.

"It will?"

"Yes," he confirmed. "Just trust me on this one."

The moment Ansley had read from the paper, Mason remembered his mother telling him the story about her and his dad going on this particular date. It was perfect because he could take Ansley to the same place where they had ended up.

Your father always had a way of surprising me. When we selected a date from the jar, and it told us to: Explore A New Place Together, *I had no idea where we would end up. Surprisingly, our parents agreed to let us have an evening in town together for the very first time, but we'd both grown up in Oriental and I couldn't imagine him taking me to any place where I hadn't already been.*

I remember wishing we could go out of town to New Bern, which was just a county over and a bridge apart from where we lived or maybe to a place in Washington, North Carolina, which was the first town named after George Washington, and because of that, the locals claimed it as the original Washington. There was rumored to be a field of fireflies there—a somewhat secret and magical place where the game of baseball was once played. In my wildest dreams, we would end up in England, but as poor as I was at geography, there was a better chance of me losing London on a map than ever actually visiting the place.

Your daddy showed up on my doorstep looking more put together than I'd ever seen him. I guess because this was our first official public date. He wasn't wearing a suit, but he had on a dark-colored flannel shirt with a matching tie, and his shirttail was tucked into a pair of jeans real proper like. He even wore a belt and a pair of shoes that didn't have a hole in them.

I figured he was probably as uncomfortable as a fish out of the water. As for me, I was wearing a purple cotton dress that Mamma and I handmade just for this occasion. We'd spent every evening that week working on it and just did tie the last thread before

Saturday evening rolled around.

Your daddy's face told me exactly how beautiful my dress was that night. He lit up like a candle in a dark room when he saw me standing there. Father had even let me be the one to open the door. He teased me about standing behind me with a shotgun, and I remember turning around to make sure he wasn't serious. Thankfully, he wasn't there—he was in the den watching television when my handsome farmer showed up.

A few moments later, your daddy was in there with him, and he was getting the talk about how my father wanted his daughter to be treated in public. I later found out that he'd said, "Make sure you open every door for her, let her be the first one to sit down at the restaurant, protect her against anybody or anything that might bring her harm, and keep your hands to yourself." He'd also said, "Bring her home as beautiful as she is right now and don't do anything to make her cry or break her heart."

I'm sure your daddy didn't tell me everything because there were probably some threats in there that included the shotgun. Father was really protective over me, but your daddy was growing on him like a weed on a fence post. Our game night seemed to be the most significant turning point, but I also knew that Mother had been saying nice things to Father about your daddy. She liked him a lot, and I imagine when she and Father lay in bed at night, she made sure to highlight his positive traits.

When your daddy and I walked out to the car, he made sure to open my door just as he had when we walked out of the house. Then, he drove us carefully into the village. I wondered if he always drove so slowly or if he was being extra cautious because of the talk my father had just had with him. Either way, it was fine with me. I just enjoyed being with him.

When we made it into town, he opened the door that led into Brantley's Village Restaurant, and we sat in the corner booth—the same one we've sat at on every visit since then. If it's occupied when we get there, we wait for it to become available. It became one of those traditions that was really special to both of us since that's where we sat on our first public date. That night, we ate seafood amongst the locals and had a hunch that the people all around us were talking about us being out in town together. I knew some of them would probably report back to my parents and his parents, so I reminded him that we needed to keep our hands to ourselves. Oh, my, was that difficult because your daddy was a handsome fellow, but I might have already told you that.

That night, we ate shrimp and grits and had a good ole' time. We laughed a little, reminisced about stories from the schoolyard while I took mental snapshots of our first real date. Of course, back then, neither of us owned a camera, so memories were all we had which made them even more special if you ask me.

At the end of our dinner, your daddy paid the bill with cash that he'd earned from working on the farm. I'm sure Father reminded him that such was his responsibility, but I don't think your daddy needed that reminder. He was a gentleman in every way, shape, and form. As we'd partaken of our meal, he'd told me how jubilant he was about having his own money in his wallet. Ever since he'd turned eighteen, his father had begun to pay him a small wage for his labor. Before that, he was paid just like the rest of us kids with food on the table, clothes on his back, a bed in a bedroom, and a modest gift or two for his birthday and Christmas. We didn't have allowances or get paid to do chores. Helping out was never an option. You either did it or else.

When we left the restaurant, we walked along the waterfront. We eventually came upon a little path that led into a small patch of woods, and your daddy led me through it. As soon as we were out of eyesight, he grabbed ahold of my hand. I had no idea where he was taking me, but I was glad I was with him. Eventually, the trail opened up to a small sandy shore, and we could see the water nestled in a cove.

"This is the special place I was telling you about," he acknowledged.

We walked just a little way down the shoreline before we came across a live oak tree that you couldn't miss, but that I'd never seen in my entire life. It wasn't visible from the roadside where we'd been just minutes ago. From where we were standing, the roots, however, were visible from where the tide had washed the sand out from beneath the tree. I guess enough of the tree and root system was connected to solid ground to keep it stable when the storms came through.

"The cove protects this tree from the fiercest winds," your daddy explained to me when I asked him about the exposed roots.

It was the most gorgeous tree I'd ever laid my eyes on, and as you well know, Oriental is filled with beautiful trees.

We sat on one of the larger roots that protruded outward as if it had been stretching toward the waterline for hundreds of years. It was the perfect little bench for a couple of teenagers who were falling in love. It was just long enough for the two of us to fit on it together and just short enough that we had to squeeze in real tight.

A few moments later, your daddy kissed me. I remember hoping that no one would catch us. We kissed longer than we ever had, and he wrapped his arms around me, and I recall feeling safe in his embrace.

When our lips fell apart, I told him for the very first time that I loved him. I hadn't said it the night that he'd first spoken those three magical words to me, but only because I wanted to be absolutely sure that what I was feeling was love, and it was. Our love was as deep as the roots of the tree on which we were sitting.

Eventually, your daddy pointed to a small hole near the base of that tree. The roots in that spot were perfectly rounded as if they'd been created to hold something. It almost looked like a bird's nest but formed by the root structure rather than made from straw and twigs and whatever else a bird can find to entwine its home. It had always amazed me how God's creatures knew how to take care of themselves from instinct.

"Why do you think the roots are formed like that in that spot?" I asked.

"I know exactly why," he said.

"You do?"

"Yes, and that's the main reason I brought you here."

I remember being somewhat surprised. Don't get me wrong, the bird's nest-like root area was a really neat feature of this live oak tree, but the tree itself was magnificent, and its surroundings were breathtaking. The two of us were somewhat in the middle of the village but completely hidden.

I waited for him to explain.

"Sometime in the 1800s, one of my ancestors discovered . . ."

22

D r. Roman called Betty into the office.

"Shut the door behind you," she instructed. "And have a seat, please."

Betty wasn't sure what was going on, but this wasn't standard procedure. Of course, she didn't normally answer to Dr. Roman because she was technically Dr. Stone's nurse, but for now, Dr. Roman was still in charge, and she knew she had to put up with whatever shenanigans this woman was up to at the moment. Most likely, it had something to do with either Ansley or Cleve.

"Am I in trouble?" Betty asked in a sweet yet slightly sarcastic voice.

Dr. Roman ignored the question. "There is an important safety issue that I need to discuss with you," she explained. "I need you to tell me everything you know about Ansley being in Oriental with Mason Fields."

"Child, what is you talkin' about?"

Dr. Roman wore a pretend smile. It was apparent to her that Betty was going to play dumb just like Cleve had. If that's the way she wanted to be, then they could play hardball.

"I have photos of the phone that was underneath Cleve Fields' head," she revealed, then she went through the same spill that she had used on Cleve, only cleaning it up a bit this time even though she didn't think Betty was intelligent enough to catch on like Cleve had. "The photos have been turned over to the authorities, and an investigation is underway," she revealed.

Betty wasn't sure what to say, if anything. She knew her job was on the line, and so was Ansley's. She definitely didn't want to get fired with retirement on the horizon.

"How did he get a phone?" Betty asked, stalling for time.

"Betty, I think you and I both know the answer to that question," she said slyly.

"I don't," Betty uttered, but she knew exactly which way Dr. Roman was pointing—directly at her even though her fingers were tapping on the desk between the two of them.

"Betty, you were the one in the room when I walked in with security and took over. No one else came in or out of that room."

Betty grimaced. She had thought the phone was hidden well enough beneath Cleve's head that Dr. Roman wouldn't have spotted it. Maybe he had moved, she contemplated. How else would Dr. Roman have known there was a phone there? Only she, Ansley, and Cleve knew that.

"Betty, I know that Ansley put you up to letting her talk to Cleve," she pretended to know. After a little thought, that had been the only sensible answer. "So, here's how this can play out. I can either tell the authorities that I have no idea where the cell phone came from, and Ansley can lose her job. Or, I can tell them that you were the last person in that room and that I believe it was your cell phone, and both of you can lose your jobs," she threatened with a smile on her face.

Betty wasn't born yesterday, and she had grown up in a neighborhood full of criminals which made working here easier on her than it was on most of her coworkers. These people didn't scare her one bit. "Child, if you tell them that you don't know whose phone it was, how they gonna tie Ansley to the call?" Betty asked. If Dr. Roman had actually seen the phone, taken photos of it, and turned them into authorities, then it would do her no good if no one knew where the phone had come from which would ruin Dr. Roman's plan of getting Ansley fired. Betty knew that's what she was aiming for with all of this. Eventually, she was bound to have to tell them whose phone it was so that they could search the call records. Apparently, she was telling the truth by saying that she hadn't yet told them; otherwise, Betty knew that she'd be having this conversation with a person with a badge rather than Dr. Roman.

Dr. Roman closed her eyes briefly before staring down at her desk. She hadn't considered that part of the equation. "Betty, just tell me what's going on with Ansley and Cleve's son Mason. Why is she in Oriental with him? Is she in danger?"

Based on Dr. Roman's response, Betty began to wonder if the pictures even existed. The part about her seeing the phone must be true, she figured, so all of them weren't completely out of hot water.

"Ansley is in Myrtle Beach," Betty lied.

"There aren't tractors in Myrtle Beach," Dr. Roman mentioned.

"What?"

"Ansley is in Oriental shacking up with Mason," she said. "I can feel it in my gut."

Betty laughed out loud. "Ansley, shackin' up with a farmer. Now that's funny," she snorted. "That girl is high-class, and you know that."

Dr. Roman's eyes danced up and down. Betty was right about that. A farmer wouldn't fit very neatly into Ansley's world, but she wasn't going to agree with Betty and let her win. "Maybe she's desperate, she's always talking about those cheesy dating sites," Dr. Roman mentioned.

Betty laughed. Partially because that was funny and somewhat true, but mainly because she had just come up with a way to detour Dr. Roman's thoughts. "Ansley is dating a lawyer," she mentioned.

"No, she's not," Dr. Roman spat back.

"Sure is."

"Prove it," she demanded.

"They have a date this Saturday night, in fact." Price Wayne Johnson, III was the perfect alibi for Ansley. Ansley had told Betty all about how her mother had set her up with this man who turned out to be a hunk. Betty figured that she could let Dr. Roman in on their plans, and she knew that as nosy as the woman was, she'd spy on them to make sure it was true.

"If you're telling me the truth, I want to know his name right now, and I want to see a photo of him so that Ansley can't hire some escort to be her date."

Betty shared his name and even encouraged Dr. Roman to look up his firm's website which was sure to have a picture of him posted.

"He's a hottie," Dr. Roman exclaimed when she found his biography online within a matter of moments, then she turned back to Betty. "You can go back to work now," she instructed. "And I'm going to have my eye on you."

"Well, then, child, I hope you like big butts," she said as she turned and waddled out of the office, grinning the whole way.

Mason steered the truck into a space facing the Oriental waterfront. Beyond the parking curb, there was a walkway, a short wooden rail that doubled as a bench, and a large assortment of enormous boulders that protected the seawall. Right next to where the truck sat, there was a small grassy park dotted with picnic tables, climbing trees, and multi-colored Adirondack chairs that overlooked the picturesque view of the massive Neuse River and Intracoastal Waterway.

Excited about the scene surrounding her, Ansley was the first to step out of the pickup, and she took in the smell of the sea as the steady breeze whisked through her blonde hair. As if on cue with the wind itself, she turned to let it blow her hair away from her face then pulled it into a ponytail.

Mason led Callie to the bed of the truck, and with a little nudge from his hand, she hopped onto the open tailgate. Once it was shut, she wandered around aimlessly, obviously enjoying the wind cutting into her thick coat of fur.

Out of habit, Mason pulled out a water jug and filled a bowl that he kept in the truck bed for times like this. He also opened a small container of food and left it there for her to munch on in case she became hungry.

"We'll be back in a little while," he told Callie.

Mason had no clue how long Ansley would want to walk around, and he wasn't sure Callie would be up for the exercise quite yet, especially since, on the ride over, Ansley had advised that Callie didn't need to overdo it today.

Once Mason assured Ansley that Callie would be just as happy sitting in the pickup truck watching people walk by and playing in the wind, she didn't feel so bad about the idea of leaving her there all alone. The rain had stopped entirely; otherwise, they would have had to come up with another plan.

As they began to walk, Callie barked but only once. Up above, seagulls were swarming in the air, squawking, and balancing on pylons and any other place where they could land their two webbed feet.

"There are so many of them," Ansley pointed out. "And they're so cute," she added. In Raleigh, she would come across seagulls once in a while, usually when near water, but she'd never seen this many in one place.

"They're annoying," Mason said with a serious face.

"And you're mean," Ansley spouted, pushing his left shoulder.

"Are you sure Callie will be fine?" she double checked just like she had at the restaurant on her first night in town.

"Yep," Mason assured her. "When she barked, she was just telling you not to spend too much money," he said, humoring himself.

Ansley nudged him with her right hip, then when he bounced back into her, she wrapped her arm around his as they followed a sidewalk that led through a couple of blocks of cottage-style homes. They crossed over the road and took a right turn to enter the area where the village shops and restaurants were nestled.

There, the road began to snake, and on the left Mason pointed out the Oriental Marina and Inn—a favorite of tourists and also one of the places he'd considered mentioning for Ansley to stay when she first arrived. Of course, he knew better than to bring that up at this point, and now he was so glad he hadn't sent her down here that night. After these past few days, he couldn't imagine having not spent this time with Ansley.

Mason knew that the water followed this road even though it wasn't visible for a short stretch where the wind died down a bit. Out of the blue, he grabbed Ansley's hand and led her across the inn's gravel parking lot and through a small outdoor hallway-like opening to the backside of the inn. There, beyond the swimming pool and tiki bar, lay an amazing view reserved for guests and people like him and Ansley who snuck back there.

Docked amidst a quaint harbor in Raccoon Creek, dozens of large fishing boats were scattered about, the masts reaching toward the clouds, and the nets climbing up to the top of some of the vessels. Ansley found herself wishing that her phone hadn't drowned just so that she could snap a photo and enjoy this view anytime she pleased.

For a short while, she stood there in awe, absorbing the beauty of her surroundings as Mason pointed out details that he thought she might find interesting. When they ventured back out to the sidewalk, the first shop they came to was Marsha's Cottage, and there Ansley zigzagged through a handful of rooms filled with clothing, handbags, and other accessories that she knew her mother would absolutely adore. If her mother were here, Ansley knew she would walk out with multiple shopping bags lining her arms.

Even Ansley couldn't resist picking out an outfit for herself, and the woman managing the shop was quite helpful during the process. When Ansley mentioned the views of the water, she even provided a complimentary map of Oriental and went on to explain how all the rivers, creeks, and other waterways were settled around the town.

Until now, Mason had never had any reason to step foot into the shop, so he figured the lady assumed that he was a tourist, too. Based on the touristy questions Ansley had been spitting out ever since they'd stepped foot through the door, it was quite obvious that she wasn't a local. So, Mason just played along.

The Village Gallery was the next place they ventured into, and before stepping inside, Ansley noticed that most of the shops in the village looked more like houses and each one seemed to have a front porch where patrons could sit and relax.

While perusing pieces by local artists, Ansley shared with Mason the story about her mother purchasing the painting to adorn her mantle. His eyes widened when she mentioned the price tag.

On the left side of the art gallery, the walls of an open room were lined with paintings, and in the center of the area, a variety of other art mediums were decadently arranged for display. Mason had to admit that he felt a little out of place here, and just like the last shop they'd visited, this was his first time inside these walls.

On the opposite side of the gallery, the floor was constructed of cobblestone, which reminded Ansley of trips her family had taken to Savannah and Charleston over the years. She liked the way the stone felt on her feet, and a smile grew on her face when she noticed Mason balancing on one of the rounded bulges. Upon realizing he'd been caught, he gave away a shy grin.

The small exhibit room where they were browsing led into a narrow hallway where quaint stall-like areas housed the collections of individual artists. One of the spaces toward the back was even set up as a studio where a partially painted canvas was being supported by a wooden easel, and a table next to it held a variety of brushes and a fancy paint tray.

When they wandered out of the art gallery, the harbor and all of the boats were in full view, and Ansley couldn't help but stop on the porch for a moment and take in this town's charm. Before, she hadn't noticed the boathouse on the opposite side of the harbor— her eyes hadn't made it through all of the boats, she guessed.

Now, she was beginning to think this place looked more like a movie set than a real town. Here they were walking through paradise, and she could feel herself falling in love at first sight with the village.

"We can have a cup of coffee next door and take in the scenery for a while longer if you'd like," Mason suggested. The view was somewhat normal to him, but he still appreciated it very much.

It didn't take any convincing for Ansley to end up docked on the front porch of The Bean. She and Mason sat there for quite some time, chatting about everything from the names on the boats to the taste of their beverages. When they finished, they held hands and walked across the road to where the water met the boardwalk which kind of looked like a little bridge. On the side of the street they'd just come from, there was a small body of water surrounded by tall marsh grass, and Ansley wasn't sure whether it was fed by the water from the harbor running under the road or if it was a creek or something else altogether. She just knew that she loved all of this—the water, the shops, and the good time she was having with Mason Fields.

"Are there always this many fishing boats here?" Ansley asked.

"There are more today than normal because a lot of the crews leave out on Sundays and come back on Thursdays," he explained, "which is why I mentioned coming down here to pick up fresh fish today." He paused. "This is about as fresh as you can get them unless you catch them yourself."

"Where do we buy the fish?" Ansley wondered aloud. She could see the fishermen wandering about on a mission on the boats and the docks. Some still wore their waterproof gear, which for some reason caused her to imagine them out in the middle of the ocean fishing for their lives. She'd always heard that commercial fishing was a dangerous job, and she could envision them holding on as the waves sprayed across the boat while they worked together to pull in a sizeable catch.

In response to Ansley's question, Mason pointed across the street to a tiny, tattered wooden building on the opposite side of the marsh as the coffee shop. "We get the fish right there at the fish market," he revealed.

Beyond the market surrounding the marsh were a variety of homes, some belonging to residents and others being used as vacation rentals. During the summer months, this place was hopping with tourists.

The faint smell of fish was distinctive, and Ansley pointed it out as she peered across the road to take in a new perspective. "You know, I kind of like that smell," she admitted as if it was an odd thing like the teacher she'd had in high school who'd sworn she craved the odor of laundry detergent while pregnant.

"That's good because we kick people out of our village who don't like the smell of seafood—cooked or uncooked," Mason disclosed chuckling. "It's one of those things that people should appreciate, like the sound of a fighter jet if you live near a military base." He paused for a moment and a frown overtook his face. "Similar to farming, local commercial fishing is a dying breed, and it's unfortunate if you think about."

Ansley nodded in agreement. "Well, we'll definitely support the local fishing industry today," she reminded him as she thought about the dinner they had planned. "Should we go ahead and pick up the fish now?"

"Let's wait until we're finished walking around," he suggested. "It might not be a good idea to carry the fish around out of ice or for them to sit in the truck longer than they have to."

"Oh, yeah, that makes sense."

"However, we'll probably need to venture back to the fish market before we wander off to the new place we're planning to explore, just in case they're closed by the time we could make it back."

"Okay," she agreed without hesitation.

"Want to check out this store?" Mason asked pointing to a good-size metal building attached to the boathouse. "It's kind of like a general store," he explained. "They have everything from fresh produce to clothing to fishing gear, and they sell the best strawberries in the world," he added proudly.

"Oh, they do, huh?" Ansley responded with a smile. "Then we *must* check it out."

As they climbed the steps, Ansley spotted a row of kayaks next to the building.

"They rent and sell those, too," Mason revealed.

"That's awesome. I love this place already."

Ansley had always enjoyed kayaking, and if Mason had a kayak at his pond rather than that bulky canoe, she probably would have been out there paddling around this week.

When they walked through the front door, the lady at the counter greeted them. "Hello, Mason," she hailed.

"Hey, Teresa, how are you?"

The three of them exchanged pleasantries, and then Ansley and Mason wandered around the store where they spent way more time browsing than he would have ever imagined. Ansley seemed interested in examining every item, and they had thousands of those. Magnets. Books. Watches. Oriental t-shirts. And knick-knacks galore. However, she didn't seem as interested in the fishing aisles where Mason would have preferred to spend most of his time. He did manage to wander into that section a couple of times, but he also made the best of his time spent with Ansley picking up random items that he'd never even noticed before. Each one seemed to spark a new conversation, which made things more interesting. Any other time he'd visited this store, he'd simply walked in, picked up exactly what he needed, and walked back out to his truck with a bag or two.

While Mason was studying fishing lures, Ansley all of a sudden came bouncing up to him. "Look, they have insulated coolers," she showed him, carrying one in her hands. "I'm going to get one so that we can put some ice and the fish in here," she said grinning.

Mason almost replied, *That won't be necessary.* He felt like buying something he already had at home would be a waste of money. However, he hadn't thought to bring a cooler, and he could tell that Ansley was excited about the idea. Plus, it would definitely keep the fish cold while they spent more time in the area.

Once they checked out, Mason took Ansley down the street next to the general store and showed her another portion of the waterfront area where the docks were filled with sailboats, and on the horizon a bridge crossed over the waterway. He made sure to point out M&M's Café, and he promised her that they served the best onion rings in the world.

"That means you're going to have to take me there sometime," Ansley suggested.

"How about tomorrow night?" Mason asked on a whim. It would be her last night in town, and it would be nice to do something special to celebrate, he thought.

Ansley smiled. "Yes, that sounds lovely," she answered.

Eventually, they wandered back around to the fish market, and Ansley had to admit that she'd never seen anything like it in all her life. To enter, they had to push through a heavy plastic freezer-strip door that gave the feel of walking through a set of vertical blinds, just the material was much heavier and clear. Well, maybe *cloudy clear* would be a better way to describe it, Ansley thought to herself.

Inside, there was only enough space for a few people to stand and there was an assortment of coolers set out on steel-framed tables. Each cooler was labeled with a specific type of fish. They also sold shrimp, scallops, oysters, and crab meat.

The gentleman running the market wore a cap, glasses, and a gray beard. It was apparent that this wasn't his first rodeo, Ansley quickly realized, as he told her all about the history of the market. There were lines drawn on the wall showing how high the water had come up during Hurricane's Irene and Florence, and surrounding those marks were photos of all kinds of things from people holding fish to river otters that had climbed onto the docks across the street. He mentioned how prior to the most recent hurricane—that had risen five feet and six inches up that wall—he and his partners had to remove all the refrigerators so they wouldn't be damaged. He also told Ansley the same thing Mason had mentioned earlier about the fishermen's schedules, and he recommended the flounder.

"We need to buy ice, too," Ansley mentioned. "Do you have any for sale?"

"For sale?" he murmured. "No ma'am, but I'll give you some."

Ansley smiled. All of the people she had crossed paths with in the village were so kind. She could see why the Fields's family had chosen to live in Oriental, although she didn't understand why Mason didn't get out and enjoy this place more. He seemed to be a homebody, and she guessed that was okay if that's where he liked to spend his time. She also figured if he had someone to enjoy the village with that maybe he would want to spend more time roaming around like they had today.

"Thanks," Mason and Ansley said at the same time, then the man poured a few scoops of ice into their cooler.

Before they walked back through the freezer-strip door, the fellow, who was about as nice of a person as you could ask for, even offered them a piece of candy. "And Mason," he called out just as they reached the flaps. "Here's a treat for that dog of yours," he offered, tossing it through the air.

Then Ansley and Mason walked back in the direction of the truck prior to heading to the place he wanted to show her. Callie was excited to scarf down the treat, and Mason wedged the cooler into the toolbox where she couldn't get to it. He doubted she would be interested in messing with the fish, but he decided not to take that chance. Plus, the seagulls were still cruising around, and they'd be way more interested than Callie, and they'd probably drive her crazy if they started landing on the truck.

"You mean you don't like the smell of fish enough to leave the cooler in your truck?" Ansley teased.

Mason couldn't help but chuckle, and a few moments later they were walking again. Hand-in-hand, they passed by a park, and the first thing Ansley pointed out was the tennis court.

"You didn't tell me there's a tennis court down here," she said excitedly. There were also swings, slides, seesaws, and other playground equipment for children.

"Do you play tennis?" he checked, although assuming that she must.

"Yes, I grew up playing, and I still play from time to time," she explained. "I have racquets and balls in the trunk of my car."

"So you're a pretty serious player?" he observed.

"I'm decent," she responded before sharing the next thought

that came to mind. "How about we make a deal?"

Mason hesitated. "What kind of deal?"

"I'll go fishing with you tomorrow if you'll come here and play tennis with me."

As their legs continued to move, Mason contemplated the idea. "Technically, you already said you'd go fishing with me with no strings attached," he said laughing at the pun.

Ansley nearly bent over with laughter. "No strings attached," she repeated. "That's a good fishing line," she uttered, amusing herself with a pun of her own.

Mason couldn't help but join her in laughter. "Nice one," he congratulated.

"About fishing . . . technically, I didn't say I'd go tomorrow," she clarified.

"True," he uttered, feeling defeated but being okay with it. "If we play tennis, go fishing, and eat dinner in the village, when am I going to work?" he probed.

"Tomorrow is Friday," she responded nonchalantly. "Take the day off."

With a smile on his lips, Mason shook his head. "I already took off today."

"You got rained out," she clarified. "There's a difference," she mentioned with a smirk.

As the park disappeared behind them, it didn't take much arm twisting for Mason to agree to take the day off tomorrow to spend with Ansley even though he added to the deal that she had to promise to help him with a few necessary tasks around the farm.

Mason himself didn't know the exact location where he was taking Ansley, but from the story his mother had shared, he had a good idea of the general area where they would find the trail that led to the hideaway. Once he saw a thicket and a cluster of trees between two familiar landmarks, he was confident that they had stumbled upon the entrance to the path.

Mason glanced around to see if anyone was watching as if they were trespassing on private property. There was a chance they were, he considered, but he didn't see a posted sign. Not that such a warning would have put a halt to the plan, but even so, he made sure the coast was clear then led Ansley down the same trail that his daddy had led his mother down many years ago.

Moments later, they stepped out of the small thicket and into a tiny piece of paradise. "This is it," Mason confirmed as he began to survey the area.

Ansley, just as she had when she stepped out of the pickup truck at the waterfront and when they'd entered the village holding hands, breathed in the beauty of her surroundings. But, this time was different. This time, she could see that Mason was taking it all in along with her. They were experiencing this place together for the very first time, just like The Date Night Jar sliver of paper had proposed.

Somehow, after just being in the village amongst people and shops and life going on all around them, it now felt as though they were alone on a remote island in the middle of nowhere. On the horizon, the sun was sinking down in the sky, shining on the water that was slapping timidly near their feet. The cove seemed to have a calming effect on the entire area surrounding them.

Soon, both Mason's and Ansley's eyes were drawn to the live oak tree where the roots were exposed—probably even more now than when his parents had first visited—but it was still standing strong and sturdy, seemingly unhindered by the winds and the water and the years between then and now.

Mason led Ansley to the place where his parents had sat side-by-side, and he couldn't help but think about them at that moment, about how they must have felt when they first explored this place together. They were young and innocent and falling in love. For himself, he felt like life couldn't get any better. Almost like this was a dream and at any moment he was going to wake up, and reality was going to punch him in the gut. But, it was real, and he was reminded of that in the best way when Ansley leaned in and kissed his lips without notice, the sensation feeling as natural as the sand at their feet.

As they'd made their way here, he'd wondered if in this moment they would share a kiss that they'd one day tell stories about just like his parents had. Upon nestling in on the root that made a bench meant for two, he hadn't even had a chance to think about whether to lean in toward Ansley. She'd made the move, and Mason found himself wanting to embrace her longer, but he also wanted to show her the natural burrow at the base of the tree where the magic had first begun.

"You see that spot right there," he said pointing behind where they were sitting a moment after their lips fell apart. Then, he watched Ansley's blue eyes travel to the bird's nest-like feature naturally woven into the tree. "That's where one of my ancestors discovered The Date Night Jar."

23

The moment Mason pointed out the exact spot where The Date Night Jar had been found, Ansley realized she had traveled here before. Like a flood, the memory all came rushing back at once, and she closed her eyes to let it sink in again.

She remembered being led into the brush, down the windy trail and then standing in amazement when she noticed the serenity of the cove that surrounded her. After taking in the first glimpse, she'd walked this sandy shore toward the tree with spider-like roots reaching for the calm water near her feet. She'd sat on this nature-made bench and glanced into the burrow where The Date Night Jar had come to rest all those years ago.

When she opened her eyes and saw Mason sitting next to her, reality crept in again, but in a good way. Physically, she hadn't traveled here, but mentally she had lived in this scene as Cleve shared the story about his ancestor stumbling across The Date Night Jar which would eventually become a tradition to pass down from generation to generation.

"Sometime in the 1800s, one of my ancestors discovered an empty glass jar nestled in this very tree," I explained to Violet. Her eyes opened wide, and she was loving every moment of being here

in this place, especially now that she was learning the history of The Date Night Jar. All the same, I was enjoying telling her this story that had become so special to my family, and I knew she would appreciate the added value it placed on the jar. "He was sailing through the area when a storm snuck up on him, and he nearly lost his life trying to steer the boat out of harm's way. Thank God, he found reprieve in the mouth of this cove. Then, when he stumbled across the jar, he knew it was fate that had brought him to this exact spot. You see, he was en route to share a very important message with someone whom he had grown very fond of, and until finding the sea-stained glass jar, he wasn't sure how to share what needed to be said." *Holding Violet's gaze and complete attention, I smiled as she hung onto my every word.* "Then, he climbed up to the top of this tree," *I pointed out, glancing up at branches that couldn't have been placed much more perfectly if they had been man-made stairs.* "And guess what he saw?"

"The village," *Violet exclaimed, imagining what it would look like from overhead.*

"He saw the future," *I said with a twinkle in my eye.* "It was the 1800s, and this land had yet to be settled. There was no village. There was only bountiful timber, fresh soil, plentiful hunting, and vast bodies of water for fishing."

"So, your ancestors discovered Oriental?" *Violet inquired with excitement about the idea.*

"It depends on whom you ask," *I answered honestly.* "The Native Americans were the first known people to inhabit this land. So, technically, they have the right to that piece of history," *I acknowledged.* "In the 1870s, there was also a man who went by the name of Uncle Lou who properly founded the village. Like my ancestor, he was sailing through this area when he was forced to seek refuge from a storm in a similar cove," *I explained.* "Over the years, many sailors have sought refuge in the coves that surround Oriental. Back then, once the storm died down, it was* *routine to climb the tallest tree one could find and peer out over the land to determine if it was inhabited. The sailor would often sit on the highest branch and watch for any impending dangers."*

"That's so neat, I've never heard any of this," Violet admitted.

"Legend has it that Blackbeard himself climbed this very tree," I shared. "There are also rumors that some of his treasure is buried along the shores of Oriental."

"That's very interesting, Cleve. I'm so impressed that you know all of this history," she acknowledged. "Of course, I've heard stories about Blackbeard, and I knew that he once lived in Bath, North Carolina."

"He sure did," I confirmed. When I was a young lad, I had been fascinated with pirates, and I knew all kinds of stories about Edward Teach, who was known to most as Blackbeard. "Who knows, maybe The Date Night Jar once belonged to Blackbeard," I suggested. Of course, I'd heard those exact words from Father more than a dozen times, and I'm sure he'd heard the same from his father.

Over the next thirty minutes, Violet and I chatted about the history of Oriental, the legends of Blackbeard, and the discovery of The Date Night Jar. Then, we realized that I better be getting her back home before her father sent out a search party. Prior to leaving the cove, our lips met again, and I knew the taste of Violet Horne would never become old.

Ansley let Mason tell the same story that Cleve had shared with her not so long ago. She listened intently as he spoke with excitement lining his voice, and as he described his ancestor finding the jar, climbing the tree, and falling in love with the land, she felt as if she was hearing the adventure for the first time all over again—probably because Mason's perspective was utterly unique. The overall story was basically the same, but he told it differently. He used distinctive wording and even climbed up in the tree as he told the part about his ancestor viewing the land for the first time. Of course, Cleve hadn't been able to do that because he'd been lying in a hospital bed. The fact that she was here for this round of the story, physically hearing the sounds of the river sloshing gently on the bank and seeing with her very own eyes the beauty in this quaint little hideaway, made the experience surreal.

Unlike Cleve and Violet, Mason and Ansley didn't have parents to report to nor did they have to be anywhere at any particular time. They'd made plans to grill the fish but maybe they would eat at a reasonable time or perhaps they would eat late. It didn't really matter. Callie would be fine. She was probably playing with one of the dog toys in the bed of the truck or maybe even sleeping by now. Dogs seemed to find contentment in almost any circumstance, and Mason knew that Callie always made the most of her environment.

Letting go of all the noise inside his mind, Mason slid his arms around Ansley's waist and slowly maneuvered the two of them to the sand beneath their feet. It was damp but soft and soothing as they fell into it gingerly. Ansley felt nearly weightless as Mason had taken her into his arms, and once again she was surprised by his strength even though she'd previously experienced surges of his masculinity. His fingers began to travel on her skin following her veins as the tenderness of his touch sunk into them and found its way into her inner confines. At the moment, when Mason kissed her tenderly, she felt her stomach quiver as she locked her arms around his neck pulling him even closer into her body.

As the water slowly crept toward them, and the sun—which had barely been peeking between the clouds—fell entirely below the tree line, they gave way to the nature all around them. This moment, Mason believed, had been many years in the making, and he was so happy he had never brought any other woman here. He was even glad that he had waited for his first visit to this spot to be with Ansley Stone. He had a hunch that this memory would last for all of eternity and hoped it would be part of a larger story passed down from generation to generation.

A little later, when darkness began to take over, Ansley and Mason brushed the sand from each other's bodies.

"What's the deal with us always ending up on the ground?" Mason asked rhetorically.

He smiled when Ansley said, "Well, it has been said, and basically scientifically proven, that we are made of dust."

After dusting off, they worked their way back through the cluster of trees, sticking close together, this time moving even slower than before. Using their eyes and hands to watch and feel carefully for stray limbs and uninvited vines, they eventually came to the edge of the road. Once there, they began walking beneath the streetlights toward the pickup truck where Callie was eagerly awaiting their arrival.

Mason reached his hand into the truck bed to pet his dog, and Ansley followed suit. "You've been a good girl," she complimented as Mason dropped down the tailgate.

During the ride home, Callie sat between Mason and Ansley just as she had for the ride into the village. On the way back, though, Mason stretched his arm across his dog's body and let his palm linger on Ansley's thigh. She covered his hand with hers and held a smile on her face as she decided to embrace his slow driving. They passed by Brantley's Village Restaurant and the Piggly Wiggly, and then a few miles down the road, they cruised past the stop sign where the two of them had laughed hysterically about the name of the grocery store. At each landmark, Mason and Ansley glanced in one another's direction and grinned. *Fun times*, Mason recollected. *Great memories*, Ansley thought.

This place and Mason were growing on her, Ansley realized. She wasn't sure if she could live in a town this small long-term, but if she enjoyed life as much as she'd enjoyed it with Mason these past few days, she couldn't imagine being happier anywhere else. It had all happened so fast, but at the same time it had seemed like a slow fade into a new chapter of her life.

⁕

Eleanor Stone was worried sick about her daughter. It wasn't like Ansley to disappear like this even though she'd finally found the decency to let her know that she was out of town and safe. In the past, Eleanor had always known exactly where her daughter was, especially if she went out of town, as well as who she was with and what she was doing. She didn't like the unknown, particularly when it came to her child.

She also wasn't buying this story about Ansley's cell phone being lost. It just didn't add up. How did the phone get into the water? It was too cold to go swimming unless her daughter was at an indoor pool or had traveled to a warmer climate. Plus Ansley was a careful person. Eleanor couldn't imagine a sensible individual jumping into water with a phone in her hand or pocket. Ansley was smarter than that. She also doubted that she'd dropped it in the toilet or off a bridge or something random like that.

If her phone truly had been damaged or lost, why hadn't she just taken a trip to the local cell phone store wherever she was and asked them to fix it? Or buy a new one? It wasn't like she couldn't afford it.

The conclusion that Eleanor had come to was that Ansley was hiding something from her. Her phone was probably working just fine. She probably hadn't really had to call from someone else's phone. She'd most likely just done that little trick that technology savvy people knew how to perform where they could block their number from caller ID. If she had called from another person's phone, then whose phone had it been? When she'd asked as much, Ansley wouldn't share that bit of information, which told her that she was most likely with someone whom she was embarrassed to be with, like that farmer that Dr. Roman had mentioned when she gave her a call yesterday to check on Ansley because she, too, was worried.

Since arriving at the hospital for her shift this evening, Betty had been avoiding Dr. Roman as much as possible. She had taken note of the fact that her temporary boss had been in and out of Cleve's room more than normal. Betty assumed that she was trying to twist his arm for information the same way she'd attempted with her. She wished she could ask Cleve herself what Dr. Roman was up to, but the woman had all but forbidden her to enter his room.

"There are other nurses on staff who can adequately handle the care of Mr. Fields," she'd said when she spouted out the order.

"I disagree," Betty rebutted. "Mr. Fields has been my patient for quite some time, and I know his health history better than anyone in this hospital."

"Even better than Dr. Stone?" she asked out of pure spite.

Betty knew exactly what Dr. Roman was fishing for, but she wasn't about to bite the hook. "Yes, even better than Dr. Stone," she responded, surprising the doctor. "I spend more time with my patients than anyone in this hospital," she explained. "However, Dr. Stone and I are a team, and she relies on me to report back to her on all our patients. She understands the complex nature of Mr. Fields' case better than I do because of her expertise as a physician, but as for daily care, it's my job to know every patient as well as I know myself."

"That's one of yours and Dr. Stone's problems," she argued although she was surprised at how sophisticated Betty could sound when she wanted to. "You know your patients too well, and it interferes with your medical judgment."

The conversation might as well have ended there because nothing was going to be accomplished. Betty knew she wouldn't be able to convince Dr. Roman to let her into Cleve's room until Dr. Stone came back and going above Dr. Roman's head would only complicate the situation. She'd bring up the cell phone incident to the higher powers and who knows what would happen. They'd probably all be looking for new jobs.

The fish were on the grill, and Ansley was helping Mason make homemade hushpuppies from scratch. The family recipe they were following was in a handmade cookbook that had been handed down through generations. Each generation had added recipes, and it was one of the neatest things she'd ever laid eyes on. The pages were worn from being thumbed through many times over the years and browned due to age. The book was held together by twine rather than glue or some other type of binding, and as it sat on the counter in front of them, it was open to the page where Mason's mother had left her hushpuppy recipe.

Two pots were sitting on the stovetop burners, each filled with near-boiling grease. One was waiting on the hushpuppy batter and the other for a batch of freshly cut potatoes that Ansley had sliced up earlier while Mason was lighting the charcoal and waiting for the temperature of the coals to reach the point where he could slap the fish on the rack. As they prepared the meal together, Ansley and Mason joked about how the fish would be the healthy part of their dinner, and the French fries and hushpuppies would be the not-so-healthy portion.

"Now it's a balanced meal," Mason pointed out when they decided to add a side of green beans.

Once they sat down to eat, both Mason and Ansley recognized right away that all of the items on their plates were delicious, regardless of their nutritional value. Ansley had been a bit hesitant about the hushpuppies since the recipe had called for onions. Generally speaking, she wasn't a fan of onions, but Mason had diced them up into tiny pieces and promised that they'd only add flavor and not texture. After the first bite, she fell in love, and the seasoning he'd added to the fries was also a perfect touch.

As normal, Mason washed his food down with a cold Mt. Dew as Ansley sipped on a glass of sweet tea. One new thing that she discovered was that he liked to put his soda can in the freezer for about ten minutes before drinking it to get the contents extra cold. Different, Ansley thought, but why not.

As they ate at the table, Callie nibbled on a bowl of her own food, and Mason even tossed her a few fries and a piece of his fish. He'd never been one of those people who forbid feeding human food to his dog, but at the same time, he'd taught her early on not to sit at the edge of the table and beg. Ansley had noticed this the first night they'd had dinner together at this table, and although Mason hadn't attempted to toss Callie a fork full of spaghetti, he had given her half of the piece of his garlic bread.

Ansley knew her mother would have a problem with this. She didn't even think that dogs should be kept indoors. "Dogs are animals," she said on many occasions. "Animals that were created to live outdoors with all of the other animals." Growing up, Ansley heard this quite often when she would ask for a pet. Maybe this was one of the reasons she'd chosen not to have a pet as an adult, but then also she'd known friends who'd done the opposite. If their parents had been against indoor pets, they ended up with a house full of them as an adult. *To each his own* was her way of viewing this debate.

After dinner, Mason and Ansley decided to take it easy. They made their way to the couch and watched two different movies back-to-back. One was a romantic comedy and the other a thriller. Ansley leaned into Mason's left shoulder, and the two of them cuddled up real close in their comfy clothes. There were moments when they couldn't keep their hands to themselves and then during other parts of the evening they were content with just lounging together with no other agenda in mind.

Before going to bed, they remembered that they needed to draw another date from The Date Night Jar.

"Should we even do this since we already have our whole day planned out tomorrow?" Mason inquired as Ansley skipped back to the couch holding the jar firmly with two hands.

"Of course," she replied without hesitation. "Whatever it is, we'll find some way to work it in."

"Why not," Mason agreed, sliding his hand into the jar as she peered over the shoulder she'd been leaning on earlier.

A moment later, they were reading the ink on the yellowed paper.

"This one is different," Ansley noticed, as she digested the words: *Give One Another Something Special.*

24

The final full day of Ansley's stay in Oriental flew by even faster than the ones that had come before. The morning began like every other morning she'd spent here, at least for the most part. The first seemingly minor difference was that Mason was the first to sit down on the front porch, and he purposefully left the rocking chair to his left empty, which was a major change for him.

"You're letting me sit in your chair?" she asked openly shocked by the gesture.

"Yes," he said as Callie lay between the two chairs enjoying the steady breeze drifting across the porch. "I'm giving you something that is very special to me," he said genuinely. "Plus, now I'll be able to hear you better."

Although very appreciative of the gift, Ansley couldn't help but furrow her brow. "What do you mean?" she probed.

Even though Mason knew she could probably barely see the gesture from her vantage point, he pointed to his right ear. "I'm deaf in my right ear," he revealed.

At first, Ansley was completely surprised by this bit of information. She'd spent the entire week with this man, yet she hadn't even noticed this. As a trained physician, she was supposed to pick up on social cues, she reminded herself. But the more she thought about it, the more it made sense. She had in fact subconsciously taken note of him almost always standing or sitting on her right when they were side by side, but she'd chopped that up to him being cognizant that she was left-handed.

"Were you born deaf in that ear?" she asked, finding this fact interesting from both a personal and professional perspective.

"No," Mason answered, then he dropped the bomb, and she immediately knew why he hadn't brought it up until now. "The gunshot inside the house caused me to lose hearing in that ear."

It made perfect sense, Ansley realized, and she couldn't help but wonder if that was one of the reasons that Mason wasn't more social. When people encountered traumatic changes later in life, they seemed to let them control their social situations more than others who wore born a certain way. That wasn't a topic she wanted to dive into with Mason on her last day with him, but at some point, she'd be interested to learn more about how he dealt with being deaf in one ear.

"I completely understand how such an echo would disrupt the ear's ability to function properly," she relayed. She made sure not to say *I'm sorry* or *that's unfortunate* or any other common sympathetic response to such a comment. His being deaf in one ear didn't change the way she viewed him as a person. It didn't change anything, really. "Does this make you my right-hand man?" she teased, wanting him to feel her acceptance of the news he'd chosen to share with her.

Mason chuckled along with her for a moment then said, "Of course." He couldn't help but wonder what Ansley would think about him being deaf in his right ear. He'd always figured that people would think it was weird, but he didn't know for sure because he had never told anyone. He'd just made adjustments as the years went by. He'd learned to stand on the right side of a conversation, or if he was around a group of people, which was rare, he would turn his body just enough so that his good ear could pick up audible communication from as many angles as possible.

Regardless of the reasons why he'd given her his rocker, Ansley decided that she felt honored, maybe even more so because he'd said he wanted to be able to hear her better, which meant that he cared about what she had to say and even to the point that he was willing to give up his favorite spot. Based on the date night slip they'd pulled last night, she was almost certain that he wasn't just letting her sit there today, but that he was giving her the chair anytime she ended up on this front porch with him.

From there, the conversation traveled in many directions, and after each of them took their final sip of coffee, Ansley followed Mason rather than continuing to relax on the porch. In the backyard, she climbed onto the padded four-wheeler seat behind him and wrapped her arms around him just above his midsection.

"You're going to get dirty," he'd said when they'd walked into the house and set their coffee mugs in the sink. Then he'd ventured off into the back of the house and returned with a pair of overalls. "You might want to wear these," he suggested.

"I doubt your overalls will fit me," Ansley said, hoping he wouldn't take offense to the comment.

"These were my mom's," he revealed. "You're about the same size," he added with a shrug of his shoulders.

Ansley wasn't sure how she felt about wearing clothes worn by someone else. It wasn't something she'd done at any point during her life. Growing up, her mother took her shopping for a new wardrobe every semester when she was in school. If she'd had a big sister, she doubted very seriously that she would have ever worn hand-me-downs. Her family had often donated barely worn clothes to the less fortunate. But . . . this was different. Mason was offering to let her wear his mother's overalls. Like his rocking chair, she was sure this was a big step for him. Plus, the more she looked at them as they hung from his hand, the cuter she realized they might look on her.

As Mason pressed the gas, the tires on the four-wheeler spun mud into the air and Ansley could feel it spraying against her back. Beneath the overalls, she had on a black shirt, and Mason had fetched her a pair of his mother's work boots that were a size too small but still fit, although snugly. On the days earlier in the week when Ansley had ventured to the pond, she'd worn either her tennis shoes or her own boots, but even then she'd gotten them dirtier than she'd anticipated. Of course, her tennis shoes were ruined after the unexpected swim in the pond. Once she made it back to Raleigh, she'd definitely buy new ones and probably a replacement pair of boots as well.

Mason introduced Ansley to his morning routine of unlocking the market and making sure everything was ready for the customers. As she strolled around the bins of fruit, vegetables, and many other items that she hadn't expected to discover, Ansley found herself wishing that she'd made it here earlier in the week. Everything looked delicious, and there was more variety than she would have ever imagined.

Once the pickers began to arrive, Mason introduced Ansley to each one, and he could tell that most of them were very curious about her presence. None of them knew him well enough to ask questions, but some were familiar with his patterns and realized that this was the first woman he'd ever brought to the market and, more noticeably, first thing in the morning.

When talking, Mason got straight to the point with his workers, Ansley noticed, and it kind of reminded her of the beginning of the shift meetings she had with her staff. He emphasized to the pickers that they'd lost production time yesterday and that they needed to try to make up for that as best as possible. He also shared with them that he wouldn't be as accessible today because he had some personal matters to take care of, which Ansley was pretty sure everyone understood since she was standing next to him. She tried not to smirk as she noticed many of the eyes in the market wandering around, and she was pretty sure she'd spotted a few grins.

As soon as the group dispersed, Mason helped Ansley climb onto the tractor with him and Callie. They rode around to check each field on the farm. Mason said that he was particularly interested in the water levels since he hadn't surveyed the fields at all yesterday. Well, on second thought, he remembered that he'd actually run through and lain in one of them with Ansley, but at that point, his mind had been elsewhere.

"I thought the rain was a good thing for crops," Ansley mentioned.

"For the most part, it is," Mason confirmed. "But when there is too much rain, the ground becomes oversaturated, and oxygen to the roots of the crops is cut off."

Ansley nodded her head, displaying that she'd definitely learned something new today. "But, it didn't rain that much, did it?" she asked.

"It rained quite a bit overnight although we didn't get enough where I'd be concerned about entire fields, but some areas are prone to collect more water than others," he explained. "Those are the ones I have to keep a close eye on at times like this."

"I see," she responded.

"We've had a lot of rain in the past month or so, so the ground isn't absorbing water like it would if it were dry."

"So farmers don't want the ground too dry, but they don't want it too wet either," she acknowledged.

"Exactly," he confirmed.

As they drove from field to field, Mason taught Ansley how to operate the tractor, and although it was similar to driving a vehicle, it was different. The steering wheel was bigger, and in a way, it took more effort to turn. The wheels were also much larger, and there was a wider gap between the ones in the back than the front tires, which just made things feel odd. She was pretty sure she'd squished a couple of crops, but Mason didn't seem upset. He just laughed it off and explained how to avoid that mistake the next time. It didn't take her long to get the hang of it, and she had to admit that she liked being so high up off the ground.

They came across a couple of spots where they had to hop down from the tractor and use a shovel to clear trenches so that water could escape flooded areas. Ansley found herself ankle-deep in muck several times, and there were splashes of mud up to her waistline. Callie, for the most part, watched from the tractor.

Ansley had known there was a lot of farmland surrounding the log cabin, but Mason took her to places that she had yet to discover, and she was surprised at how many fields were on the property. Most of them had some sort of tree line between them, and ditches ran all over the place. Mason was well versed at explaining how the drainage system worked, and she had to admit that she'd never realized how extensive that part of farming could be.

When they finished work, they swung back by the house to pick up the fishing equipment from the barn. From there, they drove the four-wheeler to the pond where Mason taught Ansley how to cast a line. It took her a while to figure out which way to flip what she called *the clicker*. Mason informed her of the technical name, but he couldn't help but laugh as she continued to call it the clicker. He made sure to watch closely as she snapped her rod and let the line fly. The first few times it ended up in some odd spots, like behind them, which was kind of the equivalent to trying to throw a football and it somehow ending up flying backward. Mason had to remind himself that teaching Ansley how to fish was like teaching a toddler how to throw a football. She'd never done this before, except at the fair, which he made sure to tease her about a time or two. "You do know that doesn't count as fishing, right?" he laughed, and she, rather than debating the subject, cackled along with him.

Once she got the hang of casting her line, they loaded the poles and tackle box into the canoe. Callie hopped in just as easily as she did onto the back of the pickup truck. Mason paddled them from one location to another on the pond, and surprisingly, Ansley was the first to hook a fish. At first, she joked that she hoped it was her phone. Unfortunately, the fish took off with her bait before she could reel in what she called *the big one*, which aggravated her, but it was a step in the right direction, Mason explained. Soon thereafter, he caught a good sized bass, let her see it up close, then he threw it back.

Ansley ended up catching two decent sized fish before Mason rowed them back to the shore where she asked, "Can you fish from a kayak?"

"Definitely," Mason assured her. "I've thought about getting one but just never have been able to justify the expense when I already have a canoe."

An hour later, they were eating peanut butter and jelly sandwiches at the kitchen table.

"I think I've eaten more of these this week than I have in the past year," Ansley announced.

After lunch, they ended up at the tennis court. The park inside which it was situated was surrounded by a community of homes where they'd walked through yesterday. Today, Ansley had driven because the tennis racquets and balls were in her vehicle, and she'd said it didn't make any sense to transfer them to his truck, plus it was her turn to drive.

"Our parents would be proud of us," Mason said.

Ansley wasn't sure what he meant. "Why is that?" she questioned.

"Because we are good at taking turns," he pointed out, chuckling. "We took turns driving, we took turns rowing the canoe, and we took turns picking from The Date Night Jar."

Ansley snickered at the thought. "I guess that means we're good at sharing," she mentioned. With the idea of sharing and The

Date Night Jar on her mind, she was reminded again that she needed to decide what she wanted to give Mason. Something special, the jar had specified. She had something in mind, she just didn't quite know how to make it happen.

They spent the next hour playing tennis on a blue court. Well, from Ansley's perspective, she was playing tennis. As for Mason, he was hitting the yellow balls that she'd pulled out of her bag. She'd been trying to show him how to position his racquet and how to turn over his wrist so that the ball wouldn't either fly over the fence or into the net every time he hit it. But, kind of like her with fishing, it was taking him some time to figure out the technique. The basics of tennis, however, were probably a bit more complicated to catch on to than casting a line. In fairness, mastering either sport was probably equally difficult, she imagined.

Eventually, Mason began to volley with her some even though she had to ease up on her shots from what she would if she were playing with an experienced player. She'd taught lessons in the past, so she was used to varying her level of play, and that allowed her to be able to enjoy the game with him regardless of his skill set. He had more raw power than her, so every now and then he'd surprise her and land a shot that she didn't expect. Most often, she could still return it, but it was more difficult than normal because she wasn't prepared for it as she would have been if playing an equal opponent.

After working up a good sweat, they took a water break on a bench next to the court where they found a plastic bin filled with pickleball equipment.

"Have you ever played this game?" Ansley asked.

"Nope," Mason said. "Never heard of it."

Ansley hadn't played pickleball either, but she knew it had similarities to other net sports such as tennis, ping-pong, and badminton. From what she'd heard, it was simple to learn and play for people of all ages regardless of their skill levels at other racquet and paddle sports.

Curious, Mason reached into the bin and immediately noticed that some of the paddles were made of wood and others of a more high-tech material. Looking along with him, Ansley saw that almost all of them were relatively worn, which she figured was good because that meant they'd been getting used. It sure was courteous of the park to leave them out here for others to enjoy, she thought.

The balls were similar to wiffle balls which Mason noticed when he picked one up, but they seemed a bit smaller. Ansley picked up another one and tossed it to Mason. "Let's try playing," she suggested.

"Okay, sounds fun," he agreed, and they each took one more swig of water before stepping back onto the court.

As they began to volley, Mason quickly realized he had a much better chance of competing with Ansley at this game. Her skill at maneuvering her feet and positioning herself for any shot on the court would still benefit her tremendously, but the fact that the wiffle ball traveled much slower helped him make up some ground. It was also to his benefit when Ansley explained that the ball had to bounce once on each side of the court before volleying could begin which meant it couldn't be served as hard.

While playing tennis, Mason had learned that she was in much better shape than he was which was made evident by the sweat on his shirt compared to hers. As they continued to play pickleball, he noticed that she was beginning to exert much more energy at this sport. He appreciated her for trying this game with him because he was smart enough to realize she could have beaten his socks off at tennis. It was kind of comparable to playing a professional baseball player at baseball then playing him at wiffle ball. The professional might still have the edge at wiffle ball, but the game would undoubtedly be a lot more equal than baseball.

All of that didn't really matter. Mason was having fun on this blue court with Ansley regardless of which game they were playing. And now, he wasn't launching the ball over the tall black fence. As they volleyed back and forth for the next hour or so, neither of them kept score. They just poured sweat and had fun playing a new sport together.

When they packed up their gear and put it in the car, Ansley found herself wishing she had let Mason drive his truck. Their sweaty bodies were going to give her car an unwanted smell. Before leaving the house, she hadn't thought about how when she played tennis at the country club she always went directly into the clubhouse to shower. She didn't want to make a big deal of them being sweaty in her vehicle, but then she came up with a good idea that wouldn't make her sound like her mother.

"You want to swing at the playground for a little while?" It sounded a bit childish, but it also sounded fun.

"Sure," Mason responded.

It ended up being a great time. From their vantage point at the swing set, they could see glimpses of the river through the trees. The higher they would swing, the better the view, they quickly realized, and soon it became a competition to see who could soar the highest which caused them to sweat a little more, but nothing like when they'd been playing on the tennis court. It also helped when they gave up on being acrobats, and spent their time in the swings slowly rocking back and forth while talking about the week they'd spent together.

"What has been your favorite thing that we've done this week?" Ansley asked, gripping the chains while looking at Mason.

"That's a tough question," he admitted, taking a moment to think about how much they'd packed into her one-week vacation as he kicked the woodchips beneath his feet. "I might not ever live this one down," he started, "but probably pulling activities from The Date Night Jar has been my favorite," he disclosed with all honesty.

Ansley smiled real wide. "Me too," she shared before giving Mason a chance to ask her the same question. "When I asked you the question, I was trying to decide if that would be a legit answer since we've technically pulled a handful of dates out this week."

"I think it is," he responded.

"I do, too," she agreed. "The Date Night Jar is kind of its own activity, completely separate of the dates that follow."

They spent the rest of the afternoon reliving many of the special memories they'd made together this week: Beginning with their first awkward night from the moment they met on the front porch to eating at Brantley's Village Restaurant to each of them falling asleep with a stranger down the hall. Then Ansley surprising Mason with spaghetti for dinner. The trip to Piggly Wiggly. The campfire and ending up on the ground next to it. An unexpected swim in the pond. Ansley saving Callie's life. Ordering pizza and playing Battleship. Running in the rain. Making out in the mud. Exploring the village and visiting the spot where The Date Night Jar had been found. Last night on the couch. Working this morning, fishing, and playing on the court behind them. Everything had been amazing.

"I'm falling in love with you," Mason admitted as their hands dangled together loosely between the swings, the chains above moving as slowly as the wind.

25

Dr. Tanya Roman was so glad about deciding to give Eleanor Stone a call. It was a bit risky, but it turned out that the woman was like a busted water pipe when it came to spilling out information. In less than ten minutes, Tanya discovered that Ansley's phone had apparently been destroyed in some sort of water incident, but Eleanor admitted that she wasn't buying the story. She also mentioned the farmer guy again, which Tanya just knew had to be Cleve's son Mason even though Ansley's mother had said that the suspicion was nothing more than a hunch based off hearing a tractor in the background. Then when Eleanor added the bit about thinking that Ansley was embarrassed about their relationship because of the difference in social classes, that sparked a little something more in Tanya's mind.

The best part of the conversation happened next when she informed Ansley's mother that there might be another reason Ansley would want to conceal a relationship with the farmer—because she had a hunch that he was the son of an inmate named Cleve Fields, she revealed.

Tanya had to admit that she felt a little guilty about increasing a mother's worry. Who wouldn't be terrified if they thought their daughter was secretly spending time with a man who might possibly be a criminal like his dad? Tanya hadn't needed to suggest that; it's just where people's minds went when piecing together such a puzzle. Like father, like son.

Honestly, Tanya didn't know anything about Mason Fields, other than the fact that he'd recently tried to reach out to his father.

She still hadn't been able to wrap her mind around the whole thing. Why would Ansley have wanted to meet Mason Fields in the first place whether that had happened for the first time earlier this week or if there had been a previous encounter? On the flip side, why would Cleve want Ansley to meet his son? Ansley wasn't the type of person whom she could see helping plan a prison break. Such a trail of thought quickly led to a dead end because in all honesty the man's days were numbered. His health had even shown a noticeable decline this week.

After leaving the park, Mason and Ansley went back to the log cabin to take a shower. Ninety minutes later, they were walking up to M&M's Café near the Oriental waterfront. The parking lot was packed, which was to be expected for a Friday night. Through the wrap around screened-in porch, a dull roar of voices flowed out into the open air along with the occasional sounds of clanking beer bottles and serving dishes being tossed around.

Mason mentioned that the restaurant had been converted from an old house, which was evident in its layout, as the hostess led Ansley and Mason out of the bar area which Ansley assumed had once been a living room. The next room was a bit smaller with tables lining either side of the walkway and a bricked fireplace built into the wall on the right-hand side. The area where the young woman sat them also led to another room in the back that appeared to be more of a banquet-style area.

Mason and Ansley ended up at the far corner table with window views into the wrap around porch. If the windows were open, they'd be able to reach out and touch the people dining on the other side. Beyond those patrons and through the porch's screen, they could also see a glimpse of the water at the end of the road as well as into the parking lot where Callie was sitting in the back of the truck on her hind legs, apparently watching the commotion.

When Ansley flipped open the menu, she discovered the type of food she expected although she found humor in the titles of the two main pages: From The Land and From The Sea. Mason ordered a burger and onion rings because he said he'd had enough seafood this week. Ansley had eaten seafood twice, but because she was rarely ever able to find seafood as fresh and delicious as what she'd enjoyed on this trip, she ordered the salmon sandwich and opted for the onion rings because of how good Mason promised they were. They also added a basket of hushpuppies as an appetizer.

"They're not as good as my mother's recipe," Mason revealed, "but they're still pretty good."

Much of their dinner conversation centered on their surroundings: The atmosphere. The people. The village outside the aqua-colored walls featuring white trim. Ansley liked the taste of the hushpuppies but agreed with Mason that his mother's recipe was even better. Her sandwich was quite scrumptious, and as Mason had guaranteed, the onion rings were to die for. In fact, they were so good that she could see herself driving to Oriental on the weekend, even if Mason didn't live here, just to eat a plate full of them.

After finishing their meals, Mason paid the check, and Ansley demanded she leave the tip. Then they walked around the village in the dark; this time, with Callie in tow. Her energy level seemed to be up quite a bit today, and Ansley mentioned that it helped that she'd been drinking plenty of liquids. She'd also eaten what little leftovers Ansley and Mason brought out of the restaurant.

On the sidewalk in front of the place, Ansley had discovered the cutest tiny pine cones she'd ever seen in her life.

"We don't have these in Raleigh," she announced. "At least not that I've ever seen."

"They're rare here, too," Mason divulged, "but you can find them here and there."

Ansley took a handful of them back to the truck and said she was going to use them for decorations at her townhouse.

"What if they have bugs in them?" Mason teased.

"They'll climb off in your truck," Ansley laughed.

The village at nighttime looked different yet the same. The glow of the moon on the water made their walk more romantic, and for the longest time they even sat at the end of the dock and watched the fishing boats sway in the water. That's where Ansley fell onto Mason's shoulder and whispered, "You know what, Mason Fields; I believe I'm falling in love with you, too."

When he'd spoken the same phrase earlier, she'd hopped out of her swing and climbed onto him, wrapping her legs around his waist and sitting on his lap facing him. She pulled in close, holding him as he held the chains, and she kissed him passionately but said nothing; then they swung in that position until it became uncomfortable.

This time, Mason leaned in and kissed her, and he found himself wishing they were in the cabin on one of the boats floating out in the creek rather than sitting on a public dock with their shoes dangling above the water.

A steady stream of people were walking by and Callie was resting behind them without a care in the world. Mason had taken note all week that his best friend didn't seem to be jealous of him spending time with Ansley. It probably helped that Ansley loved on her nearly as much as he did, and Mason was glad that she had been okay with his dog being around so much. Of course, if she hadn't been, he still would have brought Callie along, and she'd have had to deal with it or leave. He'd had those conversations with previous women, and they didn't always end well, so it was nice for it not to be an issue with Ansley.

After a while, they waltzed around the sidewalks amongst the shops and the houses and all the other scenery that made up the village. Ansley knew that she was going to miss this place even though she hadn't spent that much time down here. She was going to miss Mason, too, which is why she eventually asked him if he wanted to go back to the log cabin and enjoy the rest of the evening alone.

There, with beverages in their hands, they ended up in the backyard playing cornhole. Each of them threw four bags at the board on the opposite end of the one from which they were standing. Then they walked hand-in-hand to that board to tally up the points before throwing toward the board at which they'd begun. This went on over and over as they played to twenty-one each game. When Mason had won two and Ansley had won two, they decided to end the night tied rather than feeling the need to declare a winner.

Inside, they both felt like losers when they talked about life going back to normal tomorrow. Mason would still be here in Oriental, and Ansley would be back in Raleigh. No matter what anyone said that was reality, and neither of them knew what to expect after that happened. Even though the thought of being pulled away by time and space dulled the mood for a little while, all it took was Mason running his fingers through Ansley's hair to rejuvenate the fire between them. A few touches later, the two of them found themselves wrapped up in sheets and each other in Mason's bed, ending the night on a positive note.

The following morning came way too soon, but it felt good to both Ansley and Mason to wake up holding one another just the way they'd fallen asleep. They stepped onto the porch with coffee mugs in their hands, and for a moment everything felt the same as it had all week. But, as Ansley sat in the chair Mason had given her, she realized that everything was different.

One last time, they watched the sunrise and the animals frolic in the fields. Then they had breakfast together, and Ansley spoke the words that neither of them wanted to hear. It was time for her to head back home. Reality hit well before her car—with the new tire that Mason had so kindly put on for her earlier in the week—rolled slowly down the dusty driveway. They'd both fought tears, and in their own way, each had succumbed to their emotions. It was physically painful to walk away, to let their embrace fall apart, and to kiss one last time not knowing what would come next.

As Ansley reached the end of the driveway and glanced at the market, she wished that leaving was easier. Honestly, she wished that she could just stay. She wished she could turn the car around and run back into the log cabin and be there with Mason forever. But, she had a life in another city. She had family and friends there and a career. At least, she hoped that she still had a job when she returned. Through her tears, she looked forward to taking care of her patients, and she couldn't wait to open the door that led into Cleve Fields' room and tell him that she'd fallen head over heels in love with his son, and that The Date Night Jar had made magic happen all over again. Now, when he would tell her date night jar stories, she would have her own date night jar stories to share with him. She might leave out the more intimate moments, but he would know what happened. He was wise, and he'd be content knowing that his son had fallen in love. But . . .

26

r. Roman picked up the phone to call Mason Fields. She hated doing this, but there was no other way.

"Hello, is this Mason Fields, son of Mr. Cleve Fields?" she asked. It sounded so official, but it needed to, it had to—there was no other way to relay this message. Mason needed to know that this was serious or else he might not come.

"Yes, it is," Mason responded as he finished screwing in a new bulb for the front porch light that had been burned out for far too long.

"This is Dr. Tanya Roman," she introduced herself. "I am one of the physicians who is responsible for the care of your father."

Mason felt his throat drop into his stomach. He recognized the name Dr. Roman from the conversations he'd had with Ansley, but he couldn't be sure if the voice on the other end of the line now was the same one he'd heard the night he'd tried to reach his dad, but that wasn't what concerned him. The tone of her voice scared him to death.

"Yes," he uttered weakly.

"Your father has taken a turn for the worse," she reported. "He's asking for you," she shared, closing her eyes. "If you want to have one last conversation with him, I'd suggest that you head to Raleigh as soon as we hang up."

With tears flowing down his face, Mason sprinted to his truck. He hadn't had to tell Callie to follow along she'd done so out of habit, but probably more so because she knew he needed her by his side right now.

As the wheels beneath the pickup kicked dirt through the air, Mason found himself wishing he could talk to Ansley, but, of course, she didn't have a cell phone at the moment. Before leaving, she'd keyed her number into his phone so that he'd have it once she was able to get a replacement. That didn't help him now, and even if she was to get a new phone at some point today, he had no idea of knowing when that might happen.

He glanced at the clock below his dashboard and realized Ansley had left his house about four hours ago. She'd never said exactly what time her shift would start tonight, but he was sure she'd want to go home and sleep a while before heading into work for the overnight shift she'd mentioned.

As he sped down backroads, he dialed Ansley's number just in case he was wrong. After a handful of rings, he heard what he thought he would hear—her sweet voice asking callers to leave a voicemail. She probably had an inbox full of messages, he imagined.

Before Mason had met Ansley this week, he'd always figured he would never see his dad again, never even have another conversation with the man who had raised him. But, something changed the night she showed up on his doorstep. When she'd held up that jar, and he thought it meant his father had died, reality, or at least what seemed like reality at that moment, hit him like a ton of bricks. All of a sudden, the thought of never seeing his dad scared him to death. He hadn't admitted that to her, not that night and not even when he'd begun to share details about why he didn't see his father.

This week, while with Ansley, he had pretended that he didn't want to visit the man whom she'd become such good friends with.

However, when he listened to her stories about him, it made his dad real again. Before, it was almost as if Mason had thought of him as already gone.

So when he received the call from Dr. Roman today, he knew he had to go. He should have already gone years ago, but if this was his last chance, he wasn't going to miss it. He wasn't going to live the rest of his life saying *what if.*

These thoughts circled in his mind for nearly three hours as he drove toward Raleigh. Several times along the way, he reached for his phone—resting on the vinyl seat next to Callie—and made attempts to call Ansley again just in case. But, he'd had no luck.

He also found himself hoping that someone at the hospital would reach out to Ansley and let her know about his dad's sudden change in condition. The only reason he hadn't asked Dr. Roman if Ansley knew was because he still wasn't certain of the doctor's motives. Maybe if Ansley's friend Betty was working, she would notify her. But . . . was she in the same boat as he with no way to contact Ansley? If she was even at work with the knowledge that his dad had taken a turn for the worse, would she have time to search for Ansley? Probably not. She'd probably be taking care of his dad. At least, he hoped she would be. Ansley had talked so highly of Betty even saying that she trusted her more than any other doctor or nurse that she'd ever worked with.

Mason was almost certain that if Ansley had heard the news about his dad, the first thing she would have done was call him. Then, he knew, she would head to the hospital. If she'd found out as he'd driven through all the towns between Oriental and Raleigh, he figured he'd hear from her, but he hadn't. His phone hadn't rung a single time.

As he approached the address that Dr. Roman had provided, he dialed the number she'd given him. It must have been her personal phone because she answered rather than a receptionist or a nurse.

"I'll be waiting for you outside the front gate," she informed him.
Gate?

With his left turn signal on, he peered out the window and couldn't help but notice two rows of barbed wire fence that surrounded what appeared to be the prison. He'd assumed he was coming to the hospital, not the prison. But, what did he know, he'd never been here before. In fact, he'd never even been to Raleigh. Ansley had always called the place where she worked a hospital, but as he thought about that, he remembered that she also referred to the people she cared for as patients rather than prisoners.

As Mason pulled into the lot, he looked up at the tall lookout tower where a guard with a high-powered rifle was stationed, and it gave him the chills. Not because he was holding a gun, but because the thought of the father who'd raised him all those years walking around inside the parameter of these confines all of a sudden became real.

When the tires on the truck came to a screeching halt, he prayed he would find Ansley standing there with Dr. Roman, but she wasn't. There was only some lady wearing a white lab coat standing near the guard gate.

Leaving Callie in the cab of the truck this time, he hurried toward her. "Are you Dr. Roman?" he called out before he even made it within normal talking distance. As he spoke, he was still taking in the surroundings: The bricked buildings. The inmates wandering around the yard.

The lady stepped toward him. "Yes, and you're Mason, I assume?"

He wanted to skip the pleasantries and make it to his dad's bedside as soon as possible. "Yes."

"Your father has been moved to an undisclosed location—a hospital—and we'll have to drive there from here," the doctor informed him.

Mason's brow furrowed. "It was my understanding that he'd been in the hospital for a while," he contested.

"That's correct, sir. We have an onsite hospital here on the prison grounds, which is where your dad has been housed up until his condition worsened," she explained. "Due to security restrictions, I was not able to provide that information over the phone."

Mason assumed that made sense. "Okay."

"I will drive us there," she offered, pointing to the closest car in the lot. "My car is right there."

None of this made sense, but Mason hurried to the passenger side door anyway, but then, as he sunk into the seat, something hit him. "My dog is in my truck," he remembered out loud.

"What?" Dr. Roman quizzed.

"My dog," Mason confirmed. "She's here with me."

Dr. Roman looked at Mason with her head cocked then glanced toward his truck. "Sir, what are you asking?"

"My dog goes everywhere with me."

She furrowed her brow. "Even into the hospital?" she asked then quickly added, "Is he a support dog?"

"*She's* my support dog," he answered.

"If the animal doesn't have proper identification, security will not allow her to enter the hospital facility," Dr. Roman explained.

"I really need her right now," Mason combatted. "I definitely don't want to leave her here alone without knowing when I'll make it back to my truck."

Dr. Roman wasn't sure how to respond. She hadn't expected anything like this to stand in the way of the plan she'd devised. But, she decided it was only a minor hiccup. "Well, go get your dog then, and we'll deal with it when we get to the hospital."

A moment later, Callie climbed into the backseat, and the three of them were headed . . . to some hospital.

When Ansley arrived home earlier, she had crashed onto her mattress and stayed there until the alarm clock sounded. Normally, she would have set the one on her cell phone, but since she didn't currently have one of those, she'd set the alarm on her nightstand which made a God-awful noise that she wasn't accustomed to hearing and nearly caused her to have a heart attack.

After rolling out of bed earlier than she would have liked to, she'd rummaged through her luggage to find the items she needed to shower and get ready for the evening. As she'd dragged the bags into the townhouse, she'd found herself wishing that Mason or that big strong guy who'd been selling produce on the roadside in Kinston had been here to carry her bags. Earlier in the week, she'd mentioned to Mason that she wanted to take that gentleman a gift on her way back through that area. So, this morning, she and Mason walked through one of the fields and hand-selected several quarts of strawberries for the man. When Ansley spotted his truck parked in the same spot on the side of the road, she couldn't help but smile. Of course, she hadn't had any way of knowing whether he'd be there today. He remembered her as soon as he saw her, and when she handed him the berries, he said thank you and then told her those were some of the finest-looking strawberries he'd ever laid eyes on. She bragged a little on Mason and the strawberry farm then pointed out her new tire. "I think this man is a keepa'," the gentleman said before she went on her way.

Upon showering, applying makeup, and getting dressed, Ansley had made sure to gather a few items she needed for work and thrown them into a shoulder-bag that she always carried to the hospital. Since she had some free time before her shift would begin, she had decided that she was going to be a good daughter. She was going to show up at her mother's house unannounced and invite her out for dinner. But then, her plans changed when instead of being the one knocking on a door to surprise someone, a knock had come on her door.

At first, she laughed under her breath as she approached the door, having a gut feeling that it might be her mother. When she twisted the knob and laid eyes on the person on the other side, she quickly realized that it wasn't at all who she thought.

"You made it here quickly," Dr. Roman said, trying to make small talk as she drove with a stranger in her passenger seat.

"I was speeding," Mason admitted.

"Don't worry," she mentioned. "I work at a prison, but I don't carry a gun or a badge, and I can't give you a ticket," she laughed. Then she felt kind of dumb because she realized that a prison guard couldn't give him a ticket for saying he sped. In fact, a prison guard couldn't give anyone a ticket. "I'm just a doctor. They don't give us much authority," she added.

Dr. Roman continued making meaningless small talk before breaking some news to which she had absolutely no idea how this man would react. "We have to make one stop before we get to the hospital."

Ansley opened the door and found someone very unexpected standing on the other side. She recognized him immediately, but couldn't believe that he was here. More so, she couldn't believe what she had forgotten.

As the plans that Ansley had allowed her mother to make for her earlier in the week all came rushing back in at the sight of this man in a fancy suit, she watched him reach out his hand. "Hi, I am Price Wayne Johnson the third," he said with confidence.

She just stood there. Speechless. How had she completely forgotten about this date? She'd been so caught up with Mason this week that this hadn't even registered in her mind during the past few days.

After waiting a little longer than normal for a response, Price wrinkled his brow. "I assume you are Ansley Stone," he verified.

Ansley cleared her throat. "Yes," she uttered. "I am." But, she wasn't sure what to say to him next. She knew what she wanted to say, but here she was standing in front of him in a black dress and high heels, looking like she was ready to go on a date with him. In fact, she was supposed to go on a date with him, but she wanted to say, *I'm in love with someone else.* That, however, would make both her and her mother look like complete idiots, and she knew without a doubt that she would never hear the end of it and she'd probably be banned from the country club. She might even be banned from the Stone family.

So, she made the decision which in the spur of the moment felt like the best way to handle this conundrum. She reached for the coat hanger, pulled off a light jacket, and walked out the door with Price.

On the ride to the restaurant where her mother had told her that he'd made reservations, she felt beyond embarrassed. Not only because after this first date was said and done, she knew there wouldn't be a second one, and she'd somehow have to break that to him, but also because she'd eventually have to explain this to Mason.

When Dr. Roman had mentioned making the stop, Mason had simply said, "Okay. I hope it's quick because I really want to see my dad before it's too late."

"It shouldn't take long at all," she assured him. "We're actually making the stop on your dad's behalf."

"We are?" he inquired, all of a sudden interested.

"Yes, he has been eating prison food all these years, so due to the circumstances, I'm going to make an exception and pick him up a nice dinner," she informed him.

It seemed a little odd, but Mason guessed it made sense. If he'd been eating prison food, he was sure he'd want something else, too. Then that made him wonder if Dr. Roman thought that this might be his dad's last meal. It added up that way, especially when he took note of the fancy restaurant they pulled up to.

As Dr. Roman eased into a parking space, she wasn't sure how this was going to play out with Mason's dog being in the car. Initially, she had just planned to ask him to come in with her to carry the food. But, now, was he going to want to stay with his dog? Or, based on what he'd said earlier, was he going to want his dog to come inside the restaurant with them? That wouldn't go over well. Not here.

Then, something unexpected happened, and Dr. Roman immediately realized that she couldn't have planned it out any better if she'd been writing a movie script. Less than thirty yards in front of them, Ansley Stone stepped out of a limousine parked in the valet line. The man who Dr. Roman assumed was Price Johnson appeared behind her and placed his hand on the small of her back.

Dr. Roman turned her attention to Mason, wondering if he would even notice what was happening right in front of them. She knew he had a lot on his mind, and to be honest, she didn't have any concrete evidence that he even knew Ansley. When she realized that he was staring straight out the front windshield, the look on his face answered most of the questions she'd been contemplating the entire week.

Mason felt his body heating up. He was almost one hundred percent sure that the woman he was staring at, with blonde hair flowing over a black dress, was Ansley. But, who was that man? And, why did he have his hand on her?

"What's going on here?" Mason said to Dr. Roman, keeping his focus on Ansley.

"What do you mean?" she inquired, acting innocent and

surprised. "Do you know Dr. Stone?" she asked. The color of red covering Mason's unshaven face answered the question. It answered a lot of questions, actually. "Maybe we should leave," she mentioned, reaching for the gear shift, but knowing the wheels on this car wouldn't be rolling quite yet.

"Absolutely not," Mason screeched, opening his door and making a beeline for the restaurant as Ansley and the man who she was with disappeared beyond the entrance.

Dr. Roman hopped out of her car and closed the driver's side door. She didn't want to take the time to walk around to shut the door that Mason had left wide open, but she didn't want his dog to jump out and end up getting run over on the busy road in front of the parking lot. However, by the time she made it around the car, she watched the collie pounce out of the vehicle and run into the restaurant behind Mason.

❧

"Right this way, Mr. and Mrs. Johnson," the host said to Price and Ansley in a very proper tone of voice.

The young man with the menus in his hands was dressed nearly as elegantly as everyone else in the restaurant. The atmosphere was calm, and a pianist was playing softly in the corner.

Ansley began to speak up, "We're not—"

But, then Price spoke over her. "We're not expecting special treatment just because we arrived in the family limousine," he declared. He leaned toward Ansley's ear and whispered. "Just go with it," he suggested. "The host will be embarrassed if he realizes he's misspoken."

Ansley furrowed her brow, but at the same time, she found the gesture made by Price on behalf of the host to be kind. The comment about the limo, however, was a little over the top. In his defense, he'd had to think quickly.

Once seated, the server began a spill about the wine selection.

Ansley appreciated a fine dining establishment like this one, but she suddenly found herself wishing she was back in Oriental with Mason at one of the more low key restaurants.

As that thought drifted through her mind, she began to recognize that the dull roar of conversation was growing a notch louder. Then, she swore she heard a dog bark. A moment later, she heard a woman's voice call out from somewhere behind her, "Oh, heaven's Jerry, there's an animal in the restaurant."

Ansley turned her head as the commotion began to rise. That's when she spotted Callie trotting between the row of tables where she and Price were, heading in her direction. As the dog approached, Ansley reached out, but she was pretty sure that Callie had found her and not the other way around. But what . . . what was going on, she wondered, as she caught a glimpse of Mason out of her left eye. He was moving hastily in the direction of the table where she and . . . *oh my*.

"What is going on here?" Mason asked in the calmest voice he could muster although all eyes in the restaurant were on him, Callie, Ansley, and the man sitting across from her.

Ansley sat up straight. "I can explain," she uttered.

"Sir, is that your dog?" the host interrupted, pointing at Callie with the expensive pen in his hand.

Mason ignored the host's question. "Go ahead, Mrs. Johnson," he requested sarcastically. He'd made it through the front door just in time to overhear what the man now standing next to him had called Ansley and the man whom she was with. Her husband, he assumed.

By this time, Dr. Roman had wiggled her way as close to the table as possible, but she was trying to stay hidden as she shot video of the scene with her phone. A few others began to do the same, but they probably wanted to share this moment with friends who couldn't be here to witness it live or post the video online somewhere for the humor value. A dog and a man come storming into one of the finest restaurants in Raleigh, North Carolina, and then there is a confrontation between a man and a woman who is dining with another man—this was sure to go viral.

Ansley didn't know where to start.

"Has that dog had his rabies shots?" the host suddenly quizzed.

Hastily, another patron shouted what he thought he'd heard, "The dog has rabies."

At that point, the restaurant erupted into a new level of chaos. People were jumping onto tables, spouting out phrases like *rabid dog*, and running frantically out the nearest door.

Mason spoke up again. "Actually, Ansley, I'd rather you not say another word," he called out, then he turned to the man at the table. Mason knew that some men in his shoes would want to punch that man in the face but not him. Honestly, he was kind of surprised that the man hadn't attempted to aggress him yet, come to think of it, but he hadn't. He'd just sat there wide-eyed like half the other people in the restaurant—the half that wasn't acting like they were now at a circus. "Mr. Johnson, your wife has been at my house for the past week," Mason revealed. "Of course, she didn't explain to me that she was married," he stated. "And we were romantic," he shared. "For that, I apologize to you, sir. If I had known that she was your wife, I would have never allowed her into my home," he assured the man.

Ansley's face was as red as the wine the host had offered, and Price's face was a close match. All he could think of at the moment was when he'd told Ansley to "just go with it."

Mason continued. "By the way, I didn't come here to check up on you," he made sure to clarify. "We came here to pick up my dad's last meal because he is in the hospital about to die at any moment," he stammered, then he flew out the front door much quicker than he'd scampered through it on the way into the restaurant.

Laughing hysterically, Dr. Roman followed suit wanting to get out of there before Ansley, whose head was currently buried in her hands, spotted her.

When she made it to the car, Mason was in the front seat fuming. His dog was sitting in the floorboard with his head in the man's lap.

"Please, let's just go," Mason requested.

27

few minutes after the scene at the restaurant, Dr. Roman steered her vehicle onto the highway.

Mason was feeling completely overwhelmed by emotions, and he didn't really want to talk, but he had questions circling his mind. "Why did you do that?" he finally asked. "And is my dad really in bad condition or was that just your way of getting me here for what just happened?"

"Yes, your dad's health has taken a turn for the worse," she confirmed. She didn't mind Mason thinking that she was a conniving person, but she didn't want him to think she was cruel. "In response to your other question, I was pretty sure that Ansley had been in Oriental with you this week, and I didn't think that was right for so many reasons," she explained being careful to tiptoe around the facts.

"So why didn't you just tell me that she was married instead of putting me in that situation?"

Dr. Roman thought her way through the best response before saying anything. "Mason, you don't know me, and Ansley doesn't like me, so I doubted you would believe anything that came out of my mouth."

Nodding his head slowly, Mason pursed his lips. "I can't believe this," he finally uttered as he rubbed Callie's fur.

He wanted to ask Dr. Roman a hundred other questions, but he really didn't want to talk right now. To anyone! Definitely not Ansley Stone, he considered. He didn't even want to think about her, actually. Not after what she'd done to him, but he could still see the look in her pitiful eyes as he'd walked away, and for some reason, he could even smell that restaurant.

Suddenly, Mason found himself wishing he was at home alone with Callie. That wasn't possible, he reminded himself, and soon they would be at the hospital where he would be reunited with a man that he actually did want to talk to—he guessed.

In silence, Dr. Roman continued to drive. She was relieved that Mason hadn't kept asking questions. In sticky situations, she'd found that the less a person said, the better. So, she didn't mind riding the rest of the way to the hospital without talking.

Once they pulled into the area of the parking lot where the doctor's parked, Dr. Roman spoke again. "Mason, you can bring your dog in with you if you'd like; I think we can get him through security." She wanted Mason to realize that she was trying to help him, and she was almost certain her credentials would get the dog in without question. "By the way, you can call me Tanya," she suggested as she grabbed a bag from the backseat.

"Okay," he replied. "Thanks, Tanya."

A moment later, they were entering the hospital through a somewhat hidden back door, and when they walked past the gatekeeper inside the hallway, Dr. Roman flashed her ID and addressed the man with authority. "This gentleman, his service animal, and I are headed up to visit Mr. Cleve Fields. He was admitted earlier today," she clarified, adding the room number.

"Thank you, doctor," was all the man said in response.

They rounded a corner, stepped onto an elevator, and then walked through a small maze of hallways before coming to a closed door where a guard was sitting. He stood as the two of them and the dog approached, and once again, Dr. Roman flashed her badge. "This is Mason Fields, the son of Mr. Cleve Fields," she explained. "And this is his service animal."

The guard asked Mason to pull out any items in his pockets and instructed him to remove his belt. Then he waved a wand over both sides of his body before patting him down.

A moment later, Mason laid eyes on his father's face for the first time in seventeen years. He noticed that his eyelids were closed and his body was motionless. Age hadn't treated him well, Mason recognized, but in many ways, he still looked like the same man. The most noticeable change was the long gray hair that he recalled being black and shorter.

As Mason stepped closer to the bed, he noticed the wrinkles and the dark spots on his dad's face. His hands and feet were cuffed to the bed, and he was attached to all sorts of monitors. Mason would have asked Dr. Roman what the machines were doing, but she'd remained in the hallway to give him privacy with his father. Mason appreciated the gesture, and he'd felt relief having Callie trot in beside him, and his companion was now sitting on her hind legs at the bedside. Claiming her as his emotional support dog wasn't far from the truth.

"Dad," Mason finally whispered, feeling as though he might burst into tears at any moment.

It took a few seconds, but eventually, Cleve's eyelids fluttered open at the sound of a strange voice. He blinked them several times, trying to figure out who was standing above him, but he didn't say anything until the man spoke again.

"Hey, Dad," Mason said in a normal tone this time.

"Mason," he uttered with a gasp, his lips trying to stick together as he spoke. He used what little muscle strength he had left to raise his head just a bit, allowing for a closer look at his son whom he'd wondered if he'd ever see again.

"Hey," Mason said a second time, not sure what else to say.

After not seeing his dad for all these years, he realized he should have plenty of conversations stored away for this moment. But, he didn't.

"I'm so glad you're here," his dad said next.

"Me too," Mason agreed.

"How are you?"

With his hands in his pockets, Mason shrugged his shoulders. "I'm fine," he lied. There was no way he was going to unload his problems on his dad while he was on his death bed. "How are you feeling?"

"Tired," Cleve admitted, then he flinched when he spotted the dog.

"I can imagine."

Cleve continued to stare at the dog. "Is that the same dog?" he finally asked.

The skin between Mason's brow appeared to form a question mark. "What same dog?" he inquired. When his dad was around, they'd never had a dog, but it wasn't because Mason hadn't asked for one over and over and over.

"For your eighteenth birthday, your mother and I got you a puppy, a collie, because when you were a little boy, you watched every episode of Lassie at least a dozen times," he reminded Mason, smiling as he recollected the moments sitting on the couch with his son and his wife watching that television show. "You even called yourself Timmy sometimes and you'd often make believe that Lassie was by your side."

Mason's mind began to rewind to when he'd found Callie. It had been the evening of his eighteenth birthday, not long after his world was completely shattered. All this time, he'd thought Callie, that little bitty puppy he'd found on the side of the road, had been a gift from God. "Callie was the present you'd left the house to get?" he probed.

"Yes, she was in the front seat of my pickup truck when I arrived back at the house that day," he explained to Mason. "But, then I forgot all about her . . . with everything that happened, you know."

Mason felt a whirlwind of emotions swirling all the way from the pit of his stomach up to his throat. "But I found her on the road—"

"I must have left the truck's door open when I jumped out with the rifle," he realized out loud. He'd actually thought about this often while in prison. Early on, there were many times when he'd wanted to contact Mason to ask if he'd found the puppy, but he had wanted Mason to move on without any contact with him, so he didn't. He just prayed for the best, but he'd always wondered what had happened to the dog. In his mind, he'd imagined that Mason found the puppy in the truck and raised it. This thought had actually given him comfort while living inside a barbed wire fence with no contact with his son or the outside world. "She must have run away when she heard the gunshot," he mentioned, shaking his head.

As if on cue, Callie stepped closer to the bed and nestled her snout on the mattress. Cleve leaned in and let her lick his face, then he rested his head against her as she remained there as if she'd come here to love on him. Mason knew that Callie could sense that something was wrong with his dad.

During the ride here as Mason had wondered what he and his father would talk about, he knew he hadn't wanted to bring up that day. Although he did want to know more about his biological father, and he realized that this was his last chance to search for answers. For some reason, the thought of Mr. Hatcher prompted a response that Mason hadn't seen coming. "I burned down the guest cabin," he admitted. He hadn't come here to get that off his chest, but he knew his dad had helped build that cabin, and he deserved to know that it was gone.

"On purpose?" he inquired, squinting his eyes as he spoke.

With his lips closed, Mason nodded his head north to south.

"Good for you," his dad gritted.

"You're not mad?"

"Mad? Why would I be mad?"

"You helped your dad build it," Mason reminded him.

"I should have burned it down myself," he admitted. "That man destroyed any good memory I ever had about that cabin."

Upon hearing the words *that man*, Mason knew his dad meant Mr. Hatcher.

"Why didn't you and mom ever tell me that he was my real father?" Mason decided to ask before there was any chance for the subject to change.

Cleve flinched. The words stung like a bee pricking through the skin covering his heart. "That man wasn't your real father," he declared with gravel in his voice.

Mason furrowed his brow. "That day, on my eighteenth birthday, before you came into the house with the gun, Mr. Hatcher claimed he was my biological father," Mason shared. "And Mom didn't deny it."

"Son, there's a big difference between a biological father and a real father."

The words hit Mason like a stone. "I know that," he agreed. "But, I deserved to know before I turned eighteen."

"You were a kid, Mason. You didn't need to know," he declared. "You never needed to know." He closed his eyes for a moment, remembering things he didn't want to remember. Seeing things his mind had seen while in prison—things he'd never seen in real life but knew had happened. "There are some things that no one needs to know."

"How can you say that?" he contested. "How can you say that I didn't deserve to know my biological father?"

"Because you deserved better."

"And *you* were better?" Mason combatted.

"I've never compared myself to another man," Cleve declared. "But I can tell you this, I gave you my absolute best."

"From what I remember, Mr. Hatcher was always nice to me."

Cleve sighed. "Mr. Hatcher could be a very nice man," he admitted. "He was my best worker, and for years, your mother and I argued about whether he should continue to work on the farm." He paused for a moment to let that sink in one more time, remembering how his wife had hidden the truth from him for years out of fear and embarrassment. "But, once I found out what happened, I knew he had to go, and both your mother and I agreed that he didn't deserve a relationship with you, Mason. Please believe me and leave it at that. Please," he demanded.

"I wish you had let me make that decision."

"One day you'll understand."

"You say that like I'm still a child."

"Mason, let it go," he cried. "Just let it go."

"Give me one good reason why I should let it go," he argued. "Because you're dying?" he questioned. "Because if I don't find out today, I'll never know?"

"Don't do this to me, son."

"I know this is all my fault," Mason said. "If I had never been born none of this would have ever happened. Mom wouldn't be dead. Mr. Hatcher wouldn't be dead, and you wouldn't have spent the past seventeen years in prison."

"None of this is your fault," Cleve said sharply. "It's all his fault." He paused and stared into Mason's eyes. "I've spent the past seventeen years in prison because I wanted to be here," he admitted. "I wanted that man dead."

"Why?" Mason asked. "What happened between that man and Mom was her choice. You could have left her if it bothered you that bad. You didn't have to stay and raise another man's son."

"What happened to your mother wasn't a choice," Cleve revealed, going against his wife's wishes that Mason never know the truth about what had happened to her. As he lay here on his death bed, he prayed that she would forgive him. Begged God that when he made it to heaven, she would still talk to him and love him just the same as he had on earth. "Sex is a choice, Mason." His eyes became as cold as ice as he spoke the exact words he'd spoken just moments ago. "What happened to your mother wasn't a choice."

Mason's voice fell silent. "What are you saying?" he forced himself to utter.

"I'm saying I should have shot that man the day I found out what he did to your mother," he declared. "Then maybe you would have at least had a mother all these years."

At that moment, the flood of emotions broke through, and Mason's knees hit the floor next to Callie's hind legs. He reached for his dad's embrace. "I'm so sorry, Dad," he proclaimed, realizing how naïve he'd been. Never once had he imagined this could have been the case.

"Don't be sorry," Cleve instructed with tears streaming down his wrinkled face. "One day, many years from now, you'll be lying on your death bed, and you'll have the opportunity to get something off your shoulders that you should probably die with," he said to his son. "Today, I'm going to die knowing that you know the truth and that when your day comes, you won't be cuffed to a bed."

Mason continued to sob into his dad's chest as they held each other like they had when Mason was a little boy. "Most days I wish I was the one in here instead of you," Mason uttered into his dad's thin gown, letting the tears soak right through it.

"You deserve better," his dad said. "But enough about our messy lives . . . what do you think about Ansley?" he asked, abruptly changing the subject.

Mason breathed in deeply then sighed. "That's a big mess, too," he admitted.

"How come?"

"Well, she randomly showed up at the farm with The Date Night Jar, which was a big surprise," he shared.

Cleve smiled, then a thought suddenly hit him. When Mason mentioned burning down the guest cabin, he hadn't even thought about Ansley showing up there expecting to stay in the cabin. "Oh, no, I'd told her she could use the guest cabin," he shared. "Where did she end up staying?"

Mason wanted to ask him why he thought it was okay to send her out of the blue like that expecting she could stay in the cabin that no longer existed, but at this point that didn't matter. "Well, to make a long story short, she ended up spending the whole week at the main farmhouse with me," he divulged. "She took up quarters in my old bedroom."

"That's wonderful," Cleve said hoping to hear that the two of them had hit it off. "She's a great woman, Mason. She really is," he exclaimed.

"That's what I thought, too," Mason admitted.

Cleve cocked his head slightly. "What do you mean?"

"She's married, Dad."

Cleve shook his head while he spoke. "She ain't married," he chirped.

Mason furrowed his brow. "She's not?"

"No, she's as single as a dollar bill."

Any other time, Mason would have laughed at that comment. "Then who is Mr. Johnson?"

Cleve looked at him like he was crazy. "Who?"

"At the restaurant, the host called Ansley Mrs. Johnson and the man she was with Mr. Johnson."

All of a sudden, Cleve was lost. "At what restaurant?" he inquired.

"I don't know the name of the place, but Ansley and the man were at the restaurant where Tanya and I went to pick up your special meal."

"Dr. Roman?" he exclaimed with a question mark on his face.

"And what special meal?" he probed, but instead of waiting for answers, he asked another question and followed it with a statement. "How in the world did you end up at a restaurant with Dr. Roman?" he questioned. "That woman is crazy."

"It's a long story, but ultimately, Ansley was there with some man."

"I'm sure there's a good explanation, Mason."

"Like what?"

"I don't know, did you ask Ansley?"

"Kind of," he said. "But, then I didn't really give her a chance to respond," he admitted.

"Let's rewind this story," he suggested. "Because it sounds like a setup," he pointed out. "How did you end up with Dr. Roman?"

Mason started the story from when he received the phone call from Tanya this morning then went all the way through the scene at the restaurant.

"There's more to it, Mason. I promise. Dr. Roman is just trying to stir things up. She's like that. She's jealous of Ansley. She wants her position, and ever since Betty let me talk to Ansley on her cell phone earlier this week, Dr. Roman has been trying to convince us to give her information to get Ansley fired. She swears that she has photos of that phone in my bed, but she's either lying, or she knows that she can't turn them in at this point without risking her own job."

"What does that have to do with Ansley being at a restaurant with a man who appeared to be her husband?"

"If Dr. Roman can't get Ansley fired, then she'd love nothing more than to cause conflict between you and Ansley and make me mad in the process. She doesn't like any of us," he shared.

"Tanya doesn't even know me," Mason mentioned.

"You're better off," he snorted.

"Well, I guess I'll see if I can get to the bottom of it somehow, but that's not important right now."

Something Mason mentioned earlier finally caught up with Cleve. "So, did Dr. Roman bring you here?" he checked.

"Yes."

"Where is she now?"

"In the hallway waiting, I guess," he said. "She's the one who walked me to the door."

Cleve's eyes lit up. "Please go out there and tell her that I'm awake and I want to talk to her," he pleaded.

When Mason popped his head out into the hallway, the guard stood, but Tanya wasn't anywhere to be seen. He asked the gentleman in the uniform if he knew of her whereabouts, and he informed Mason that Dr. Roman had been called back to the prison hospital, but that she left a twenty dollar bill for Mason to call a taxi. "She also said to give you this bag," he said, handing it to Mason.

As soon as Mason had disappeared from the restaurant, Ansley told Price that she needed to leave right away.

"I think that's a good idea," he agreed.

She expected that she would need to find another ride, but then Price offered to have his driver take her wherever she needed to go. In the backseat of his family's limousine, she explained the entire situation to him. She felt relief when he responded like a complete gentleman about the whole thing, especially regarding what happened at the restaurant. Chances were there were patrons amongst them that knew their families. By now, her mother had probably received a phone call.

As the limo driver headed the vehicle in the direction of the prison hospital, Ansley asked to borrow Price's phone. She wished she could call Mason, but she didn't know his number by memory. He'd written it down for her, but it had been sitting in the center console of her vehicle since this morning.

The first number she dialed was Betty's, but when the call went to voicemail, she hung up and called the prison hospital. Thankfully, Betty was the one who answered at the nurse's station. But, then her friend informed her that she'd been called in early for the shift that they were scheduled to work together tonight, only to find out that Cleve had been transferred. "Everyone been tryin' to get up with you, Ansley," she explained with worry lining her voice. "Things aren't lookin' so good," was the last thing she said.

Ten seconds later, the limousine driver made a U-turn.

Mason walked back into his dad's room, and upon opening the bag, they found a container filled with a ribeye steak, mashed potatoes, and green beans. He had no idea how Tanya had made it into and out of the restaurant with all the commotion going on and actually gotten out with the meal without him even noticing the bag in her hand. But, he had to admit that he hadn't been all that put together when she made it back to the car, plus this bag explained the smell of the restaurant lingering in his nose.

"This is your favorite meal, Dad," Mason remembered.

Cleve suddenly resembled a kid on Christmas morning. "Will you please feed me a little bit of that?" he asked Mason. "I don't have much of an appetite, but I haven't had a meal like that in a long time," he admitted.

"Sure," Mason obliged, reaching for the food.

"Knowing Dr. Roman, it might be poisoned," Cleve pointed out. "But I'm dying soon anyway," he laughed, finding humor in a grim situation.

28

Eleanor Stone had been driving around frantically looking for her daughter ever since she'd received a phone call from Betty. She had tried Ansley's townhouse first where she found her daughter's car in the parking lot, but no one answered the door. Eleanor nearly had the police come break in for her, but then her phone rang. It was Sandra from the book club who said she'd been enjoying a pleasant dinner out with her husband when chaos erupted in the restaurant. She mentioned something about a dog barking, a man who was underdressed for the establishment, and a confrontation at the table where Ansley and Price Johnson, III were sitting.

Discovering that Ansley had in fact gone on the date with Price should have been enough to make her smile. Based on her conversation with Dr. Roman and her lack of communication with Ansley, Eleanor had been worried sick that her daughter was going to cancel and make the family look foolish. But now, it sounded like Ansley had one-upped that, and as Eleanor processed the situation that Sandra was explaining, she could feel smoke puffing out of her ears. She would bet the brand new heels strapped to her feet that the out of place man in the restaurant was that farmer guy. The Mason Fields fellow whom she'd hired a private investigator friend of hers to check up on. Why a farmer or anyone for that matter would bring a dog into a restaurant, she hadn't a clue.

Unfortunately, Sandra had no idea where Ansley and Price had headed when they left the restaurant, but she did say that the two of them climbed into his limousine together. Hopefully, that was a good sign.

⌒𝒮⌒

Both Mason and Cleve turned their heads when a knock came at the door. They didn't say anything, but they watched it crawl open before Ansley Stone poked her head in through a small opening.

"May I come in?" she asked.

"No," Mason answered first.

Then Cleve chimed in. "Yes, come on in, dear," he said while looking at Mason sideways.

She stood in the opening for a moment, hoping to receive Mason's blessing to enter the room, but he didn't say anything, he just turned his head away from her. Next to him, Ansley spotted Callie at Cleve's bedside, and she saw the plate of food resting in Mason's lap. Seeing him here with his dad made her want to cry. She'd honestly thought that the two of them would never see one another again, and even if Mason shunned her for the rest of his life, now she could say that she'd fulfilled both of Cleve's wishes.

Mason rose from the chair where Ansley normally sat when she listened to The Date Night Jar stories, then he walked toward Ansley.

"Sure, come on in," he agreed. "You deserve to see my dad," he admitted, realizing how much his father meant to her and vice versa, "but I'll be waiting in the hallway until you finish."

"Mason, please—" she began, but then Cleve interrupted.

"Mason, don't be a fool," he sounded. "I want both of you in here," he demanded. "At the same time," he added.

"Why?" Mason asked.

Ansley continued to stand in the doorway.

"We have something to get to the bottom of, and I'm not dying until we do."

Ansley tried not to cry as she absorbed the words that had just come out of Cleve's mouth, but she couldn't hold back her tears, at least not the two that trickled down her left cheek.

Seeing her reaction, Mason found himself nearly swallowing his tongue. The other comments his dad had made about dying were somewhat humorous although still heart-wrenching, but this one was different.

"Actually, Mason, maybe you should go out into the hallway for a few minutes. It might give you a chance to cool down, and I can keep your dad company for a bit," Ansley suggested. "Price is waiting out there, and he wants to talk to you anyway."

Holding his palms face up at shoulder level, Mason asked, "Who is Price?"

"Price Johnson," Ansley clarified. "The man I was sitting with at the restaurant earlier."

"Absolutely not," Mason answered immediately, "because I'm not going into the hallway to have a talk with a man who probably wants to beat the snot out of me," he clarified. "Not because I'm not man enough to face my mistakes, but I won't do that while my dad is in here like this." Shaking his head, he added, "There's a guard standing right out there who will have us both in handcuffs, and I'll end up spending the night in jail rather than being with my dad."

"Mason, Price doesn't want to fight you. He wants to tell you something that you might not believe if it comes from me."

Mason glanced at his dad. He couldn't get past the fact that this sounded like a bad idea.

Cleve nodded toward the door. "Just go out there, son. Ansley wouldn't steer you wrong."

"Fine," he said, then he hugged his father and uttered the words, "I love you, Dad."

Cleve began to weep. Those words were music to any father's ears whether his son was five-years-old or thirty-five, and he cried harder when he realized this was the first time he'd ever heard his son speak those three words as an adult. "I love you, too, son," he stammered.

⤸⤷

The hallway was eerily quiet when Mason stepped out into it and stood face to face with Price Johnson. It almost felt like there should be balls of hay whirling through the air and both of them should be wearing cowboy hats and have a revolver in a holster on their hip.

But, then Price held out his hand to shake Mason's. "I'm Price Wayne Johnson the third," he said.

"I'm Mason Fields," Mason offered, feeling like he needed to state his last name, too, since Price had shared his entire name.

"Ansley told me about what happened this week," Price mentioned.

Here goes, Mason thought. *This is where things begin to turn south.*

Price continued. "I knew she was out of town, but she and I had plans to go out for dinner this evening when she arrived back in Raleigh," he explained. "But, she forgot all about our date which had been set earlier in the week before the two of you hit off. She really enjoyed being with you, and she forgot all about me," he said in a kind of sad tone.

Whether this man was Ansley's husband, boyfriend, or something else altogether, Mason was beginning to feel bad for the guy, but he continued to listen as Price explained his side of the story. Mason guessed he owed the man that much.

"She told me about her phone and said that she had no way to get up with her mother or me. Then, tonight, when I came to pick her up, she felt so bad that she had forgotten about our date that she decided to have dinner with me to avoid being rude and having her mother hate her for the foreseeable future."

Mason butted in. "Shouldn't Ansley have been more concerned about you hating her than caring what her mother thought?"

Price nodded his head. "Ansley doesn't know me," he shared. "Her mother set us up on this date, and these are the main things I wanted to tell you. Ansley and I are not married. Tonight would have been our first date, but it wasn't a real date. She was just being polite. On the ride over here, all she could talk about was how dumb she was for ruining things with you. She said she would have called you before going to dinner, but, of course, her phone is at the bottom of your pond." He paused for a moment to collect his thoughts to say the things he'd hope Mason would say if their roles were reversed. "Mason, she loves you, my friend, and I think you're a lucky guy. If for some reason you decide you don't want to be with Ansley, I'd be more than happy to take her on a second date." He paused and scrunched his face. "Technically, I guess it would be a first date since tonight didn't count." He shook his head then went on with what he was saying. "But, she doesn't want that, and based on what that woman told me in less than thirty minutes—which was quite a lot—you're a pretty good fellow, and I think you're smart enough to make the right decision."

"You did it," Cleve said to Ansley as soon as Mason had left the room.

"Did what?" she asked.

"Helped me fulfill my final two wishes," he verified.

Ansley smiled wearily and shook her head. "I'm not sure," she revealed. "I guess the jury is in the hallway."

"Well, you convinced my son to come to see me before I die," Cleve pointed out.

"Technically, Dr. Roman did that."

"That's a load of bull," Cleve declared. "If that woman had called him last week before your trip to Oriental, he wouldn't have come."

"Maybe, maybe not," Ansley responded.

"Well, he's here," Cleve said, "and the two of you fell in love."

"Did he tell you that?"

"Nope."

"Then what makes you think we fell in love, Old Timer?"

"I could see it in yours and Mason's eyes when the two of you were arguing," he claimed with a grin. "When a couple is in disagreement, that's when true love is most transparent."

"That sounds like wisdom speaking."

"I've loved a woman with every fiber of my being," Cleve admitted, "and love is the best teacher this world will ever know."

"I agree with that."

"You remind me of her, you know," Cleve said. "My Violet."

Ansley smirked. "Mason told me the same thing," she revealed. "I think it freaked him out at first."

"I'm glad he sees her in you," Cleve divulged. "I can see how that would have been a little awkward for him, initially. His mother was a good woman, the best, actually, and if a man can find a woman who will love him like his mother loved him, he'll live a happy life."

"How come you didn't tell me that I reminded you of Violet before?"

Cleve laughed, which caused him to cough, then he chuckled a little more. "Because I was afraid it would freak you out," he said.

Ansley giggled. The word *freak* sounded funny coming out of his mouth. "It probably would have," she admitted. "Especially once I arrived in Oriental and found out that Mason was my age.

The whole time I've known you I always expected that he would be older. When you asked me to take him The Date Night Jar and make sure he knew it was okay to fall in love again, it didn't even cross my mind that I could possibly be the person with whom he fell in love."

Cleve smiled. "If it was going to happen, I wanted it to happen as naturally as possible. Other than convincing you to take him The Date Night Jar, I didn't want to force anything upon either of you."

"I appreciate that," Ansley proclaimed. "My mother is always setting me up on blind dates, but they never work out," she laughed. "Tonight might have been the worst one ever, yet I think it was the best in an odd way," she shared.

"Mothers always mean best, Ansley. Fathers, too. And, in a way, I guess you could say that I set the two of you up on a blind date also."

As Ansley thought about it, she found herself realizing that he was right, and that's when the door opened.

Mason stepped around the foot of the bed, saying nothing as he walked, then wrapped his arms around Ansley hugging her as tightly as he ever had.

"I love you," he confessed.

Ansley could feel that her face was in that intermediate stage between laughing and crying. "I love you, too," she declared.

Callie let out a cute noise that made them all laugh, then she wedged and snuggled her nose between Mason's and Ansley's hug.

"I told you," Cleve mumbled, his head resting on the pillow and his eyes glazed over.

"Told who what?" Mason asked.

Ansley answered for Cleve. "He knew that we'd fallen in love."

"There's something else I want to tell you," Cleve shared. "There's one last date night jar story that you both need to hear."

A moment later, Cleve closed his eyes as he began to tell the story, and Mason and Ansley followed suit as one of the greatest love stories ever told began to trickle out of his mouth.

When our ancestor found the glass jar nestled in the tree trunk, he knew its purpose. It was to connect soulmates.

As he sat on the bank all alone, he wrote a short note to the woman waiting for him many miles away. Once the storm passed, he sailed back with her to the cove and led her to the spot where he'd left the jar. As they sat on the tree bench together, he told her all about his voyage and how he'd found the cove and the jar. Then he explained that it had a special message for her inside.

When she opened the lid and pulled out the scroll, she read the words that no other man had ever spoken to her: I Love You.

The two of them later married and literally built a life together on the land that would later become the village of Oriental. But that day, after she read those special words, they decided to take turns writing small things they wanted to do together on pieces of paper and then place them into the jar. They agreed that The Date Night Jar wouldn't just be for while they were courting, but that it would be forever. Throughout their marriage, they picked dates from the jar, and that's how The Date Night Jar tradition began.

Many years later, my parents passed down The Date Night Jar to me, and as you know from the stories you've been told, Violet and I began to go on dates that we plucked from the jar. We fell in love, and each enjoyed the pure privilege of marrying the only person we had ever loved. Believe it or not, her father and I became good friends. I helped him on his farm, and he helped me on Daddy's farm when it later became my farm. Now, it's your farm, Mason, and, hopefully, one day you'll pass it down to your children.

Which brings me to one of the most devastating days of my life. Violet and I had been trying to have kids for quite a while, but she couldn't get pregnant. We thought something was wrong with her reproductive system, but then we found out that it was me who couldn't have children. I felt terrible. I had always wanted to give her children, lots of them, but then I found out that I couldn't. I wanted to pass down the farm and The Date Night Jar, and so many other family traditions and memories, but I couldn't.

What I later realized is that when I couldn't, God could. I should have remembered that all along, but sometimes we forget, and sometimes He doesn't do things in the way that we would choose to have them done. There's beauty in that, though.

When your mother told me that she was pregnant, I thought it was a miracle. And it was. It just wasn't the miracle I would have chosen, but God allowed it, and then she chose it. She chose to have you despite the circumstances, Mason, because she believed you had a purpose on this earth. Boy, was she ever right. Not a single baby is conceived that doesn't have a purpose in this world. Your mother knew that I couldn't have children, and she chose to have you—for me . . . and for herself . . . but mostly, for you, Mason.

All because of that decision, our family will continue to leave a legacy beyond today. Our traditions, though they may be altered by choice, will live on and so will the family farm. Most importantly, The Date Night Jar brought the two of you together. I believe you're soulmates, just like your mother and I were, and just like our ancestors who started The Date Night Jar tradition.

I said all that to say that, Mason, you are the best thing that has ever happened to me. You are my real son. My love for you is stronger than any bloodline. You will carry on the Fields name, and for that, I am proud. That's why, a little over thirty-six years ago, when your mother took me to the tree where The Date Night Jar was found and sat me on the bench where we'd sat many times before, I soon became the happiest man on earth.

When I turned, I spotted The Date Night Jar in the burrow where I had once shown her that it was found. This time, it only *held a single scroll inside. Anxiously and curiously, I twisted open the top and pulled out the paper with a smile on my face because I knew it was something great. After loosening the twine, I read the most beautiful message I've ever seen:* Let's Celebrate, We're Going To Have A Baby.

29

Six months later, Mason and Ansley launched their kayaks from the village dock where they'd sat the first time Ansley visited Oriental. Since then, a lot had changed. The most recent change had begun a few weeks ago when Ansley put in her notice at work the day after Betty retired. Ansley had the gut feeling that her purpose at the hospital had been accomplished. She was thankful for her time there in large part because it was where she'd met two of her best friends in the whole world—Cleve and Betty—and had ultimately been connected to her soulmate, Mason Fields.

Dr. Tanya Roman had instantly been promoted to Ansley's former position, and somehow Ansley found it in her heart to forgive the woman for all the mess she'd stirred up. Nothing had come of it, thankfully, but that hadn't stopped Ansley from laughing silently when Betty slapped Tanya across the face in the parking lot after her retirement party. "Child, you had that comin'," Betty spewed and then walked away without speaking another word. Ansley hadn't felt the need to slap Tanya's other cheek, but it didn't mean she hadn't thought about it before climbing into the car with Betty.

Mason Fields was the reason Ansley had deleted her online

dating profile and one of the main reasons she had put her townhouse on the market and moved to Oriental this week. He'd been beyond ecstatic when she called him on her new phone, which wasn't really new anymore, and shared the announcement. All this time, the two of them had been driving back and forth to see each other as often as possible, and both felt a sense of relief about living in the same place. However, Ansley made Mason promise that they would drive to Kinston every once in a while to trade produce with the man on the roadside who'd become a friend of theirs. Each time one of them had driven through the area on the way to see the other, they'd stopped and swapped out something grown on their respective farms during that particular season. After recently finding out the man was single, Mason and Ansley had introduced him to Betty, and Ansley had her fingers crossed that the two of them would work out so that Betty would be closer to Oriental. More importantly, Betty deserved a good man especially now that she was retired and had time on her hands. For many years, she'd looked forward to spending her retirement years with her husband of forty years, but he had passed suddenly a couple years back.

Ansley had been scared to death for Mason to meet her parents, especially her mother. Ultimately, Ansley had known that she would continue to love Mason regardless of what her mother thought about him and his social differences. But, that didn't keep her from waiting over a month before setting up an opportunity for them to meet. Part of that wait, however, was her mother's doing. The first time Ansley talked to her mom following that frantic Saturday evening after she arrived back in Raleigh, she had taken the initiative to tell her mother all about Mason. As expected, her mother basically disowned her for two weeks. She was furious about the embarrassment Ansley had caused both the Stone and Price families.

Interestingly enough, the following week, Price reached out to her mother to inform her that the fiasco was partially his fault. He apologized for allowing the server to call the two of them Mr. and Mrs. Johnson, which both Ansley and Price had later found out was how Mason formed the impression that Ansley was married. Price said he could understand why Mason would have been upset, and as for the dog-in-the-restaurant incident, he defined it as hilarious. He explained that the dog hadn't wrecked the place like some of the gossipers had described, but instead, he told Mrs. Stone that the dog had merely trotted through the restaurant until she found Ansley. The people were the ones who'd acted like wild animals, he'd explained. He even ended the conversation by stating that based on his lawyerly experience with first impressions, he was confident that Mason was a good man.

Ansley's mom confessed to hiring a private investigator to dig into Mason Fields' life. This caused Ansley to become furious with her, and she even thought about taking a two-week hiatus from her mother to return the favor, but she didn't. Instead, she spent the next couple of weeks in deep conversation with her mom talking about everything from the way she'd been raised to the way her mother had been treating her as an adult. Ansley explained that she needed more space, but that she loved her mother very much and wanted a close yet healthy relationship between the two of them. While they were soul searching, Ansley even came clean to her mother about all the secret activities Wanda, her nanny, allowed her to experience when she was growing up, like washing dishes and going to the fair. It surprised Ansley when her mother smiled and claimed she already knew about all of those things. Her mother went on to share that Wanda would come clean every time she stepped out of bounds, and Ansley assumed that her parents must not have had too much of a problem with Wanda's choices or else they would have fired her before she decided to move to Virginia with relatives once Ansley turned sixteen.

Ansley was utterly baffled when she introduced Mason to her

parents, and they immediately hit it off with him. She hadn't seen that coming, for sure. She wasn't certain if it had something to do with the conversations she'd had with her mother in the previous weeks, but somehow her mother seemed to overlook Mason's differences when it came to table manners and other things that in the grand scheme of life didn't matter. Ansley had a hunch that her father may have added his two cents in as well, but she never asked. Regardless of the reason behind the anomaly, Ansley couldn't be happier with the outcome.

She felt like living in Oriental, which was only a few hours down the road from Raleigh, would be the perfect solution for a happy life. It was close enough where either she or her parents could make a day trip to see each other, but far enough away where her mother couldn't show up at her door at any given moment without warning.

Before Ansley had decided to move, she had been absolutely shocked when Mason offered to sell or lease the farm and move to Raleigh if she wanted him to. She explained that there was no way she could agree to such an idea. The family farm meant way too much to both him and Cleve, and there were so many traditions born on that property. She had already begun to imagine raising children there, and even helping Mason farm the land when he needed an extra set of hands. Of course, strawberry season had come and gone, and the crops had ended up yielding one of the most abundant harvests on record. Now, the farm was growing fall crops, and she was enjoying the brisk weather.

Ansley's primary work in Oriental would become owning and managing a quaint, private medical practice that she wanted to open for the community. Over the past months, she'd been talking with Mason about how this step in her career had always been a dream of hers, and he expressed his support to her one hundred percent. Somehow, she even talked him into becoming her first patient and having a check-up since he hadn't been to see a doctor in ages. Now, he was stuck with one, she liked to tease.

As the two of them paddled their kayaks down the river with Callie nestled in the seat with Mason and all of them wearing a life preserver, Mason reminded Ansley how much he appreciated her special gift to him. It had been sparked by The Date Night Jar selection near the end of the first week that he and Ansley had spent together. A week or so later, he'd received a call from Teresa at the general store saying that he had a package to pick up. When he told her that he hadn't ordered anything, she insisted that a large package had arrived for him and that he'd probably need to make sure the bed of his truck was empty. He was absolutely clueless until he'd shown up and found matching kayaks. One donned the inscription *Ansley's Right-Hand Man* and the other *Mason's Left-Handed Woman*.

So, as they rounded a couple of bends in the water, Mason on the right and Ansley on the left, they took in the views of Oriental from a perspective they'd grown to love over the summer months. This time, as they neared the cove where the live oak tree was nestled, something was different. They stopped at the sandy bank as usual, but when Ansley stepped out, she noticed that The Date Night Jar was snuggly tucked into the spot where it had first been found by Mason's ancestor. She turned to Mason and grinned, wondering what she would discover inside.

"What are you up to?" she asked, carrying that grin so well.

"Oh, just something special for my left-handed woman," he replied.

Hand-in-hand, they moved toward the tree as their bare toes dug into the soft sand. It was a warm October day, and the sun was shining without a cloud in the blue sky above their heads. Once they reached the tree bench, they sat down as usual while Callie frolicked around near the water's edge.

"It's your turn to pick a date," Mason gestured.

Ansley smiled then pulled The Date Night Jar from the hole.

"There's only one in here," she noticed as she peeled off the lid and slid her thin fingers through the rim.

Smiling anxiously, Mason turned his body as she closed her eyes and plucked out the neatly rolled paper before untying the twine and positioning the scroll between her fingers just like she always had.

When Ansley opened her eyes, she couldn't help but peer over the top of the thin strip of paper, realizing then that Mason had dug one of his knees into the sand.

Will You Marry Me? are the words that she mouthed as Mason, holding the most beautiful ring she'd ever seen, waited impatiently for an answer.

"Yes!" she whispered, her heart flooding with pure joy as he slid the ring onto her finger for the very first time.

Right then and there, the two of them agreed that they would do everything in their power to make sure that The Date Night Jar lived on forever, just as Cleve and Violet had done.

Both Mason and Ansley missed Cleve enormously. That night in the hospital, when the three of them had been together for the very first time, he'd slipped away from this world. His life couldn't have ended more perfectly or peacefully, Ansley had thought. Once Cleve had closed his eyes to share the most important date night jar story of his life, he'd never opened them again. It was as if fate, or The Date Night Jar, or God Himself had orchestrated the whole thing. "Most likely," Mason had said later, "it's a mixture of all three."

Sometime after Cleve had shared that final date night jar story, Ansley admitted to Mason that she didn't understand everything he'd said about Mason's birth. Based on prior conversations she'd had with Mason, she was keen enough to figure out most of it, and then Mason filled her in on what he had learned in the hospital room earlier that evening.

"I need to tell you one more thing before you officially commit to marrying me," Mason announced as he rejoined Ansley on the tree bench. His heart was pounding as he spoke, partially because he had just asked Ansley Stone to marry him but mainly because he had a secret weighing heavily on his chest.

Ansley could hear the tension in his voice. "I think I just did commit to marrying you," she confirmed. "But, you can tell me anything," she promised.

Mason was having a hard time sitting still. "The day that my mother and biological father were killed, it was an accident," he revealed.

Ansley nodded her head slowly. "I already knew that," she reminded him. She'd never really understood why his father had pleaded guilty to murder when he could have gone to trial claiming that the shooting was self-defense since the man was in his home, uninvited. The fact that the bullet had pierced through the wall and taken Violet's life, too . . . well, that was obviously unintentional. Cleve's way of handling the incident—pleading guilty and cutting ties with Mason—was something she wished she'd had the opportunity to ask Cleve about. She wanted to know why he had made that choice when he could have possibly stayed out of prison and been around for Mason, or at least let Mason visit him while he served his sentence.

"You see, my father made the ultimate sacrifice for me that day," Mason began. "When I darted around Mr. Hatcher to try to keep my dad from shooting him, I was successful. I wrestled the gun from my dad's hands, but in the process of doing so, I accidentally—" Mason paused, and as he took a deep breath, a row of tears slid down his face toward his curling lips.

"I love you, Mason," Ansley interjected. "And I am going to marry you no matter what you say," she assured him as he shivered.

With his glossy, bluish-gray eyes, Mason looked directly into Ansley's deep blue eyes. "Even when I tell you," he uttered, holding tightly onto the hand on which he'd just slid the engagement ring, knowing he didn't want to wait until the day he was lying on his death bed to confess this to the person he loved most, "I pulled the trigger."

THE END

A Note from the Author

Thank you for reading *The Date Night Jar*! I am honored that you chose to invest your time in this book. If you haven't yet read my other novels, *A Bridge Apart*, *Losing London*, and *A Field of Fireflies*, I hope you will very soon. If you enjoyed the story you just experienced, please consider helping me spread the novel to others, in the following ways:

- REVIEW the novel online at Amazon.com, goodreads.com, bn.com, bamm.com, etc.

- RECOMMEND this book to friends (social groups, workplace, book club, church, school, etc.).

- VISIT my website: www.Joey-Jones.com

- SUBSCRIBE to my Email Newsletter for insider information on upcoming novels, behind-the-scenes looks, promotions, charities, and other exciting news.

- CONNECT with me on Social Media: "Like" Facebook.com/JoeyJonesWriter (post a comment about the novel). "Follow" me at Instagram.com/JoeyJonesWriter and Twitter.com/JoeyJonesWriter (#TheDateNightJar). "Pin" on Pinterest. Write a blog post about the novel.

- GIVE a copy of the novel to someone you know who you think would enjoy the story. Books make great presents (Birthday, Christmas, Teacher's Gifts, etc.).

Sincerely,
Joey Jones

About the Author

Joey Jones' writing style has been described as a mixture of Nicholas Sparks, Richard Paul Evans, and James Patterson. The ratings and reviews of his novels A BRIDGE APART (2015), LOSING LONDON (2016), and A FIELD OF FIREFLIES (2018), reflect the comparison to New York Times bestselling authors. Prior to becoming a full-time novelist, Joey worked in the marketing field. He holds a Bachelor of Arts in Business Communications from the University of Maryland University College, where he earned a 3.8 GPA.

Jones lives in North Carolina with his family. Fun facts: He might be the only author who doesn't drink coffee. He has webbed toes (aka twin toes, duck toes, tiger toes), but says they've never seemed to help him swim better. Only one in 2,250 humans are born with syndactyly (official condition). A "joey" is another name for a baby kangaroo.

Joey Jones is currently writing his fifth novel and working on various projects pertaining to his published novels.

Book Club/Group Discussion Questions

1. Were you immediately engaged in the novel?
2. What emotions did you experience as you read the book?
3. Which character is your favorite? Why?
4. What do you like most about the story as a whole?
5. What is your favorite part/scene in the novel?
6. Are there any particular passages from the book that stand out to you?
7. As you read, what are some of the things that you thought might happen, but didn't?
8. Is there anything you would have liked to see turn out differently?
9. Is the ending satisfying? If so, why? If not, why not, and how would you change it?
10. Why might the author have chosen to tell the story the way he did?
11. If you could ask the author a question, what would you ask?
12. What author(s) would you compare to Joey Jones?
13. Have you ever read or heard a story anything like this one?
14. In what ways does this novel relate to your own life?
15. Would you reread this novel?